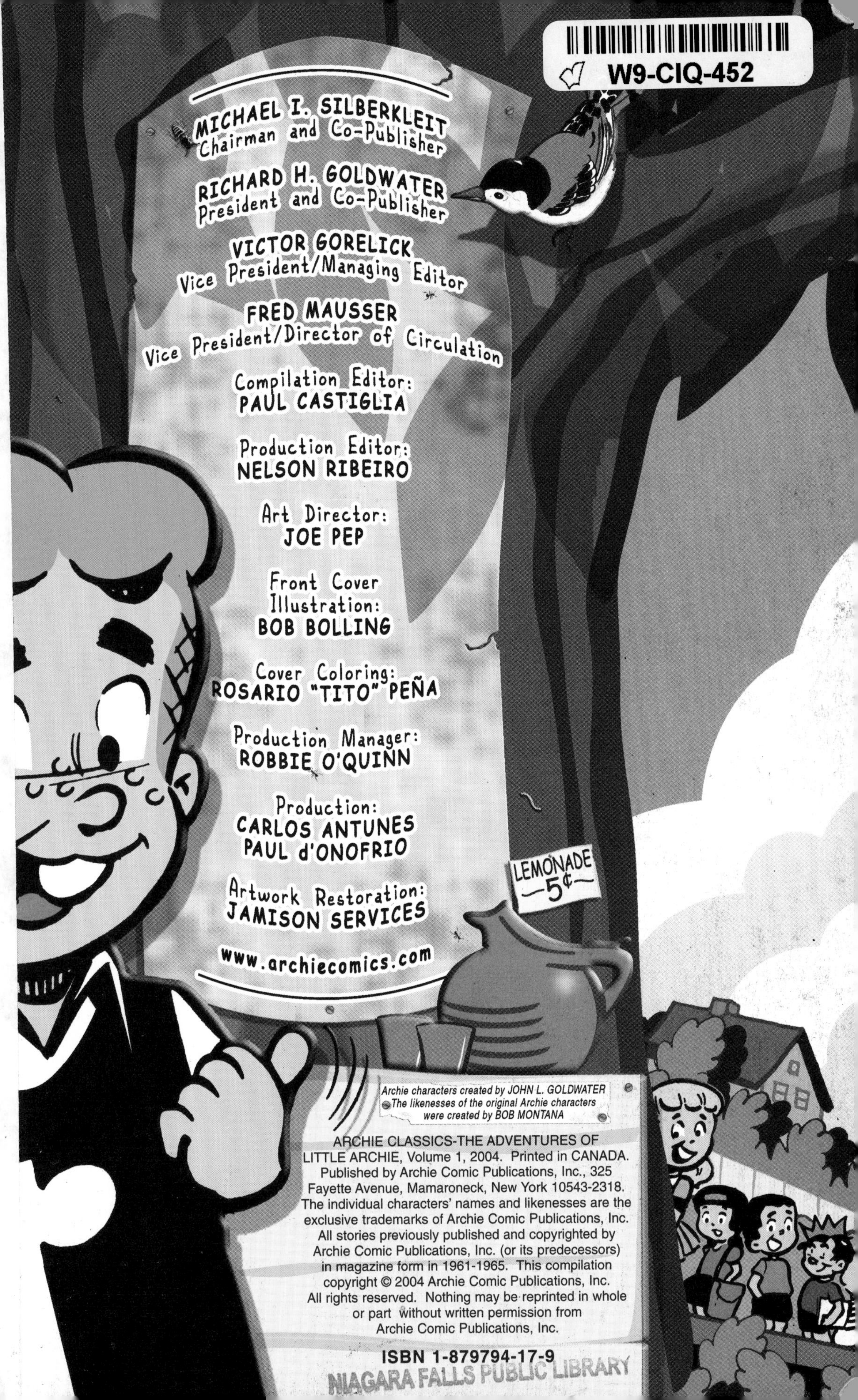
LEMONADE
—5¢—

MICHAEL I. SILBERKLEIT
Chairman and Co-Publisher

RICHARD H. GOLDWATER
President and Co-Publisher

VICTOR GORELICK
Vice President/Managing Editor

FRED MAUSSER
Vice President/Director of Circulation

Compilation Editor:
PAUL CASTIGLIA

Production Editor:
NELSON RIBEIRO

Art Director:
JOE PEP

Front Cover Illustration:
BOB BOLLING

Cover Coloring:
ROSARIO "TITO" PEÑA

Production Manager:
ROBBIE O'QUINN

Production:
CARLOS ANTUNES
PAUL d'ONOFRIO

Artwork Restoration:
JAMISON SERVICES

www.archiecomics.com

Archie characters created by JOHN L. GOLDWATER
The likenesses of the original Archie characters were created by BOB MONTANA

ARCHIE CLASSICS-THE ADVENTURES OF LITTLE ARCHIE, Volume 1, 2004. Printed in CANADA. Published by Archie Comic Publications, Inc., 325 Fayette Avenue, Mamaroneck, New York 10543-2318.

ISBN 1-879794-17-9

TABLE OF CONTENTS

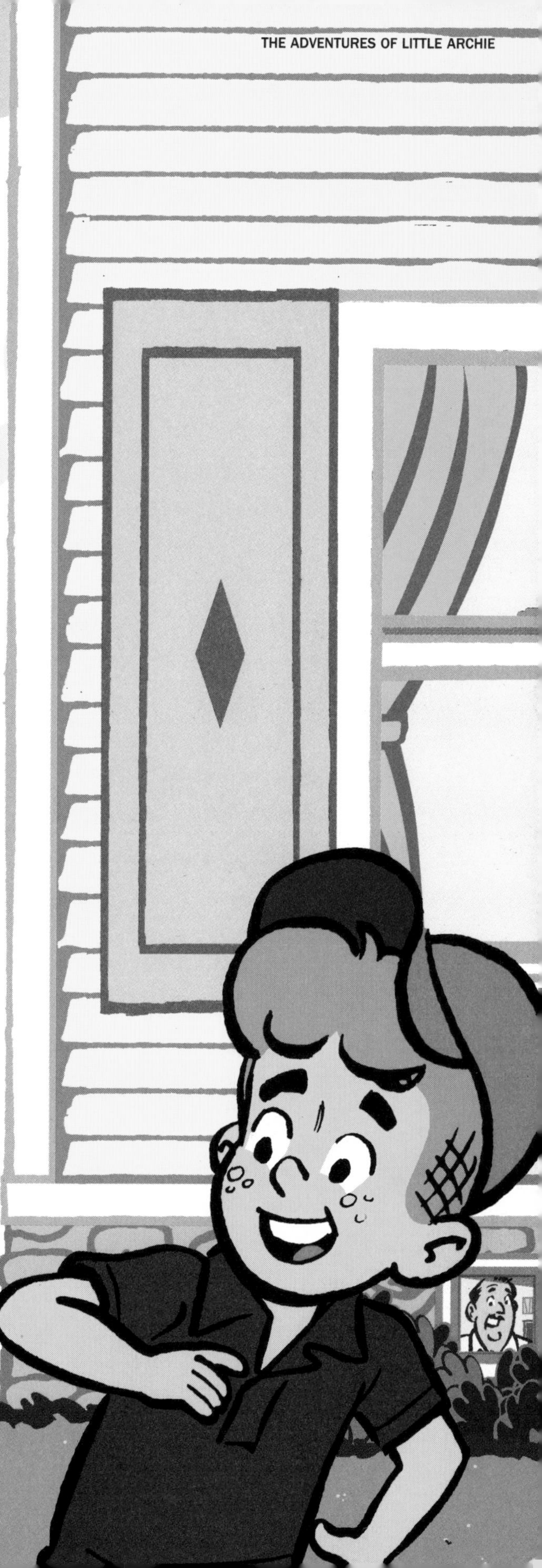

FOREWORD ☞ by Bob Bolling

After more than 15 years of reading about the hilarious life of Archie Andrews and his Riverdale friends, it was no surprise that a lot of readers wanted to know more about America's favorite teenager. What was he like as a little kid? Did he know Jughead, Reggie, Veronica and Betty in elementary school? And did Betty and Veronica battle for Archie's affections even at that young age?

In 1956, curious readers got the answers to some of their questions. Little Archie #1 hit the newsstands. The comic book cover showed the impish version of Archie, Veronica and Betty, locked in their eternal romantic triangle over a handful of flowers that should never have been picked. But, the cover also told the readers that what they held in their hands was something different and very special. In a box near the bottom, it read: "No, you're not SEEING THINGS. This is really Archie when he was a little kid." Indeed, it was just the beginning of a whole new stage of Archie's life and a continuing fascination of readers with the Riverdale gang. And the public bought it - more than 1 million copies of that first issue were purchased by children all over America.

There are several stories about how John Goldwater decided to do a younger version of Archie, but it is known that he asked then-editor, Harry Shorten, to give the concept to someone to see what would happen. I was fortunate to be that person. After I did some initial sketches of how the characters would look, John Goldwater approved them and the job of creating Little Archie's universe was given to me.

At first, many of the stories were similar to those in the other Archie comics. The characters were put in humorous situations and had to find their way out. Although those situations were more along the lines of what an 8 or 10-year-old would do, Little Archie was surrounded by the familiar cast of Little Jughead, Little Veronica, Little Betty, Little Reggie, Little Moose (if there is such a thing) and their parents.

But as I became more comfortable in my new assignment, I began adding additional supporting characters and concepts to Little Archie's world. There was Little Ambrose, the kid everyone picked on, the South Side Serpents, a gang of kids on the other side of town who were Little Archie's foes, Abercrombie and Stitch, two Martians who befriended Little Archie, schoolyard bullies like Fangs Fogarty, and of course, Mad Doctor Doom and his sidekick, Chester, whose plans to rule the world were continually foiled by Little Archie. Soon, the story possibilities for Little Archie were endless and I got to relive my own boyhood fantasies through many of these tales. Who among us didn't dream of having a neighborhood clubhouse and building rafts and cars out of scrap lumber? Or wish we could go on fantastic adventures in exotic locales like a pirate ship, a wild West ranch, or even outer space?

I'd say my favorites were the stories in which Little Archie tangled with Mad Doctor Doom. No matter where Mad Doctor Doom was, or how elaborate his plan to conquer the world was, Little Archie somehow showed up to squash those evil schemes. Sometimes Little Archie would cleverly find a way to stop Doom and Chester; other times it was by sheer luck that he would prevail.

Little Archie has always been special to me, both creatively and in my life as a professional cartoonist. I was given the chance to develop Little Archie's world as I saw it while under the guiding editorial and artistic lights at Archie Comics. It was great to know that my bosses liked what I was doing, but it was even more uplifting to learn how many readers loved Little Archie and his adventures over the years.

This first collection of The "Adventures of Little Archie" is something I'm very proud of and I hope that it brings back good memories to many readers. And, if this is your first encounter with Little Archie's world, I hope you have as much fun reading it as I did writing and drawing the stories.

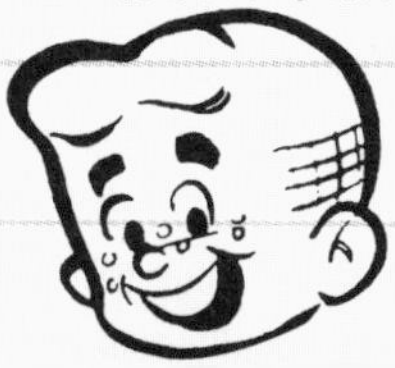

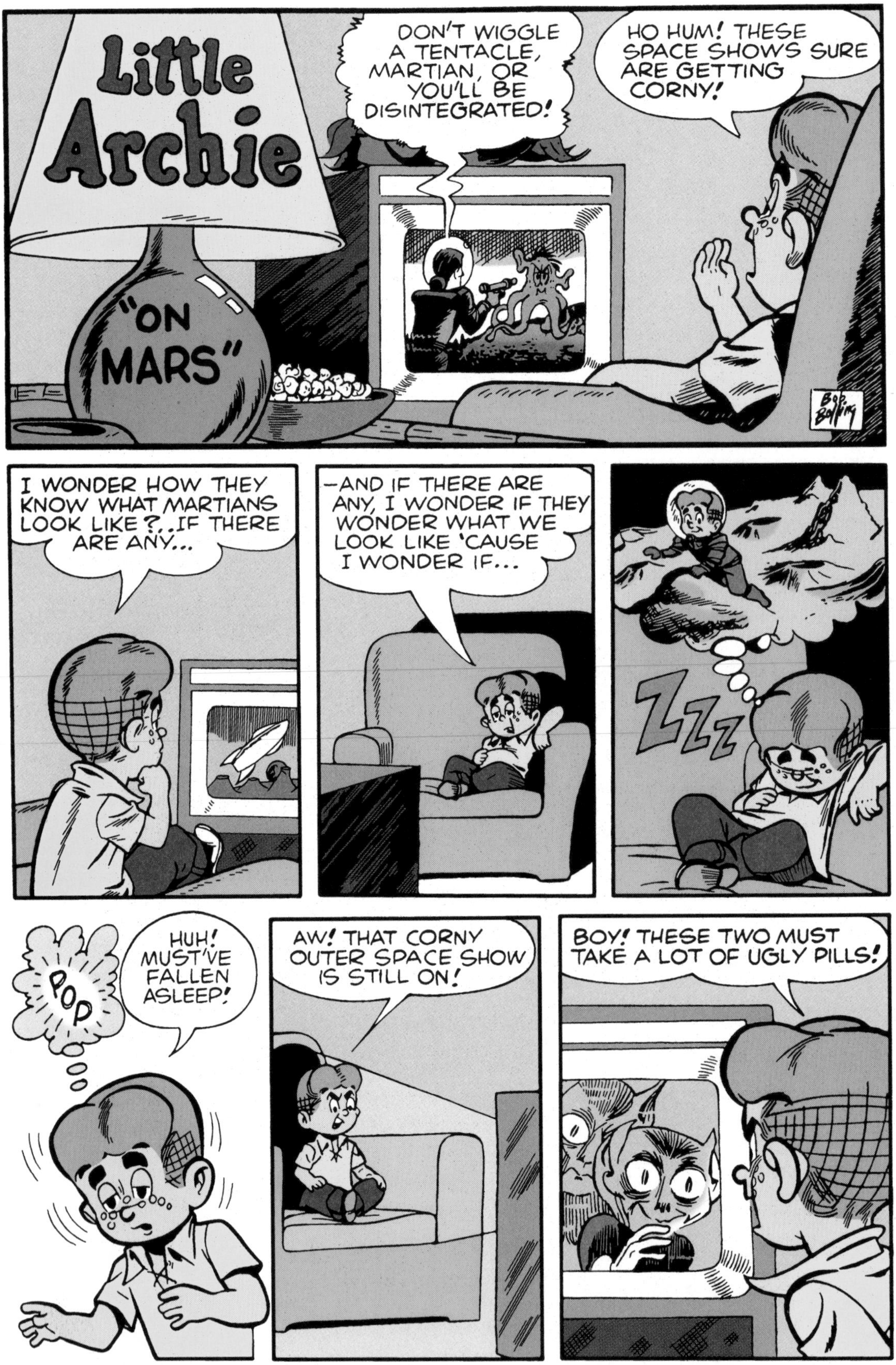
Little Archie
"ON MARS"
DON'T WIGGLE A TENTACLE, MARTIAN, OR YOU'LL BE DISINTEGRATED!
HO HUM! THESE SPACE SHOWS SURE ARE GETTING CORNY!
Bob Bolling
I WONDER HOW THEY KNOW WHAT MARTIANS LOOK LIKE?..IF THERE ARE ANY...
—AND IF THERE ARE ANY, I WONDER IF THEY WONDER WHAT WE LOOK LIKE 'CAUSE I WONDER IF...
ZZZ
POP
HUH! MUST'VE FALLEN ASLEEP!
AW! THAT CORNY OUTER SPACE SHOW IS STILL ON!
BOY! THESE TWO MUST TAKE A LOT OF UGLY PILLS!

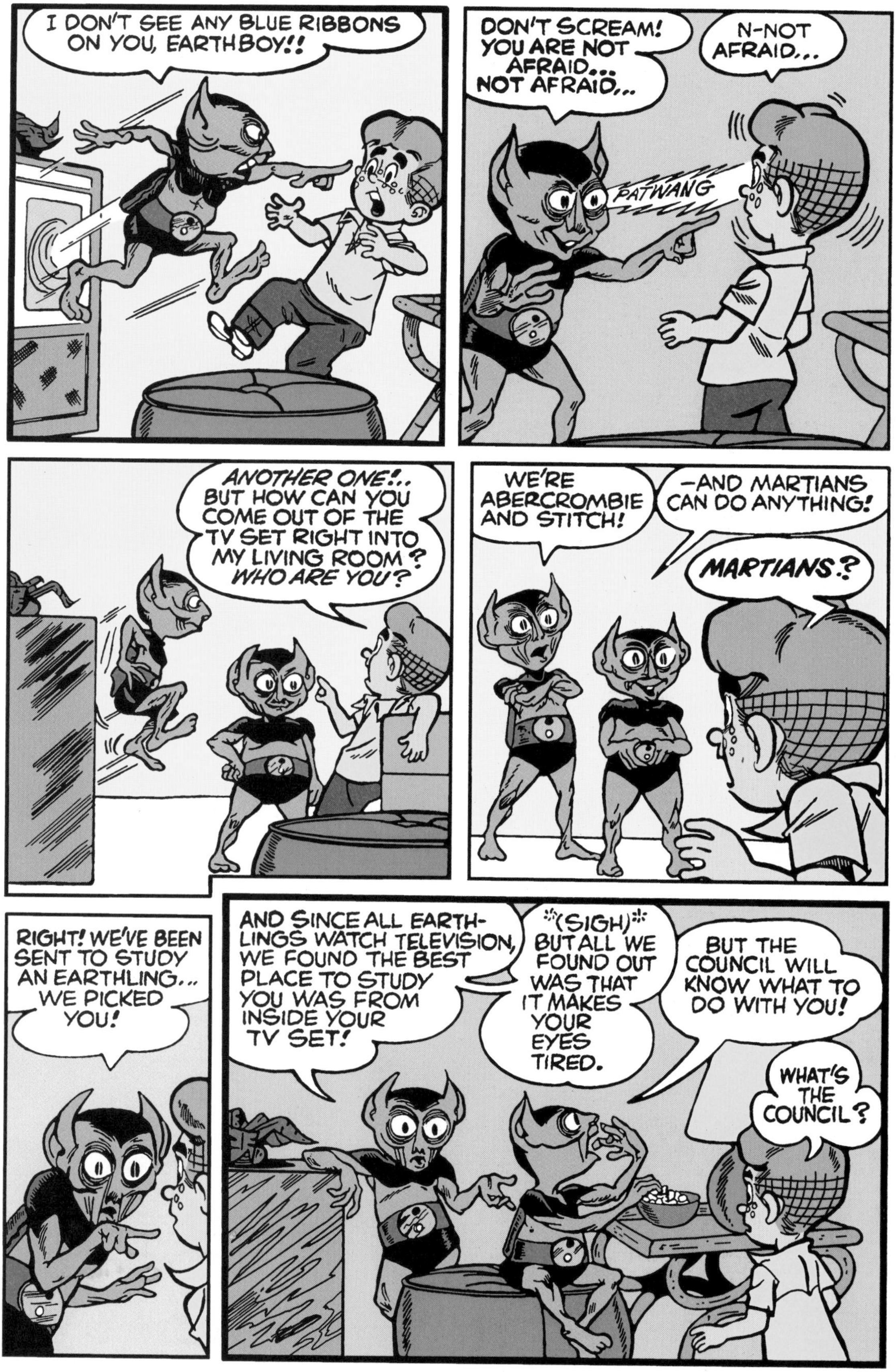
I DON'T SEE ANY BLUE RIBBONS ON YOU, EARTHBOY!!
DON'T SCREAM! YOU ARE NOT AFRAID... NOT AFRAID...
N-NOT AFRAID...
PATWANG
ANOTHER ONE!.. BUT HOW CAN YOU COME OUT OF THE TV SET RIGHT INTO MY LIVING ROOM? WHO ARE YOU?
WE'RE ABERCROMBIE AND STITCH!
—AND MARTIANS CAN DO ANYTHING!
MARTIANS?
RIGHT! WE'VE BEEN SENT TO STUDY AN EARTHLING... WE PICKED YOU!
AND SINCE ALL EARTHLINGS WATCH TELEVISION, WE FOUND THE BEST PLACE TO STUDY YOU WAS FROM INSIDE YOUR TV SET!
(SIGH) BUT ALL WE FOUND OUT WAS THAT IT MAKES YOUR EYES TIRED.
BUT THE COUNCIL WILL KNOW WHAT TO DO WITH YOU!
WHAT'S THE COUNCIL?

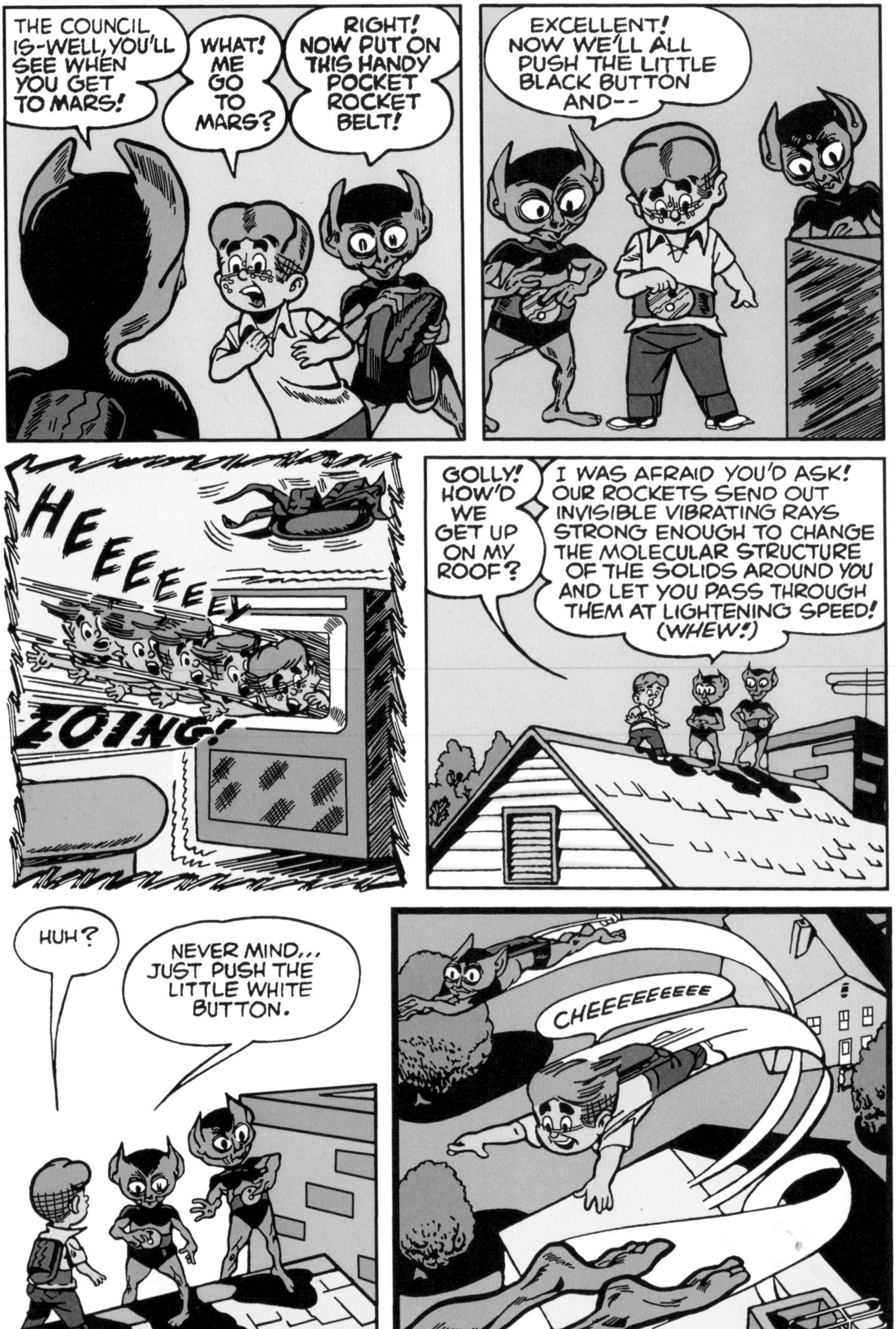
THE COUNCIL IS-WELL, YOU'LL SEE WHEN YOU GET TO MARS!
WHAT! ME GO TO MARS?
RIGHT! NOW PUT ON THIS HANDY POCKET ROCKET BELT!
EXCELLENT! NOW WE'LL ALL PUSH THE LITTLE BLACK BUTTON AND--
HEEEEEEY
ZOING!
GOLLY! HOW'D WE GET UP ON MY ROOF?
I WAS AFRAID YOU'D ASK! OUR ROCKETS SEND OUT INVISIBLE VIBRATING RAYS STRONG ENOUGH TO CHANGE THE MOLECULAR STRUCTURE OF THE SOLIDS AROUND YOU AND LET YOU PASS THROUGH THEM AT LIGHTENING SPEED! (WHEW!)
HUH?
NEVER MIND... JUST PUSH THE LITTLE WHITE BUTTON.
CHEEEEEEEEE

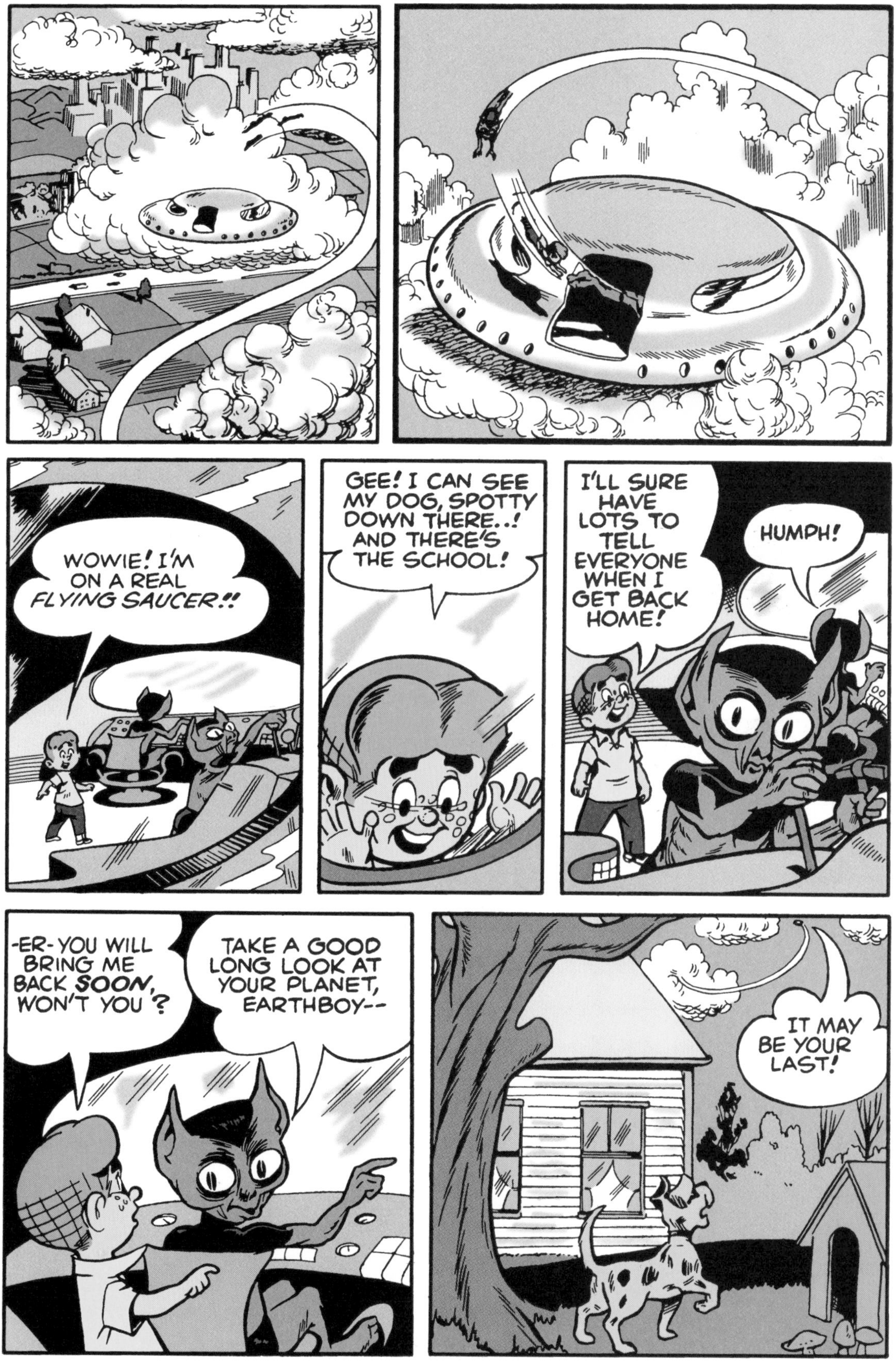
WOWIE! I'M ON A REAL FLYING SAUCER!!
GEE! I CAN SEE MY DOG, SPOTTY DOWN THERE..! AND THERE'S THE SCHOOL!
I'LL SURE HAVE LOTS TO TELL EVERYONE WHEN I GET BACK HOME!
HUMPH!
-ER- YOU WILL BRING ME BACK SOON, WON'T YOU?
TAKE A GOOD LONG LOOK AT YOUR PLANET, EARTHBOY--
IT MAY BE YOUR LAST!

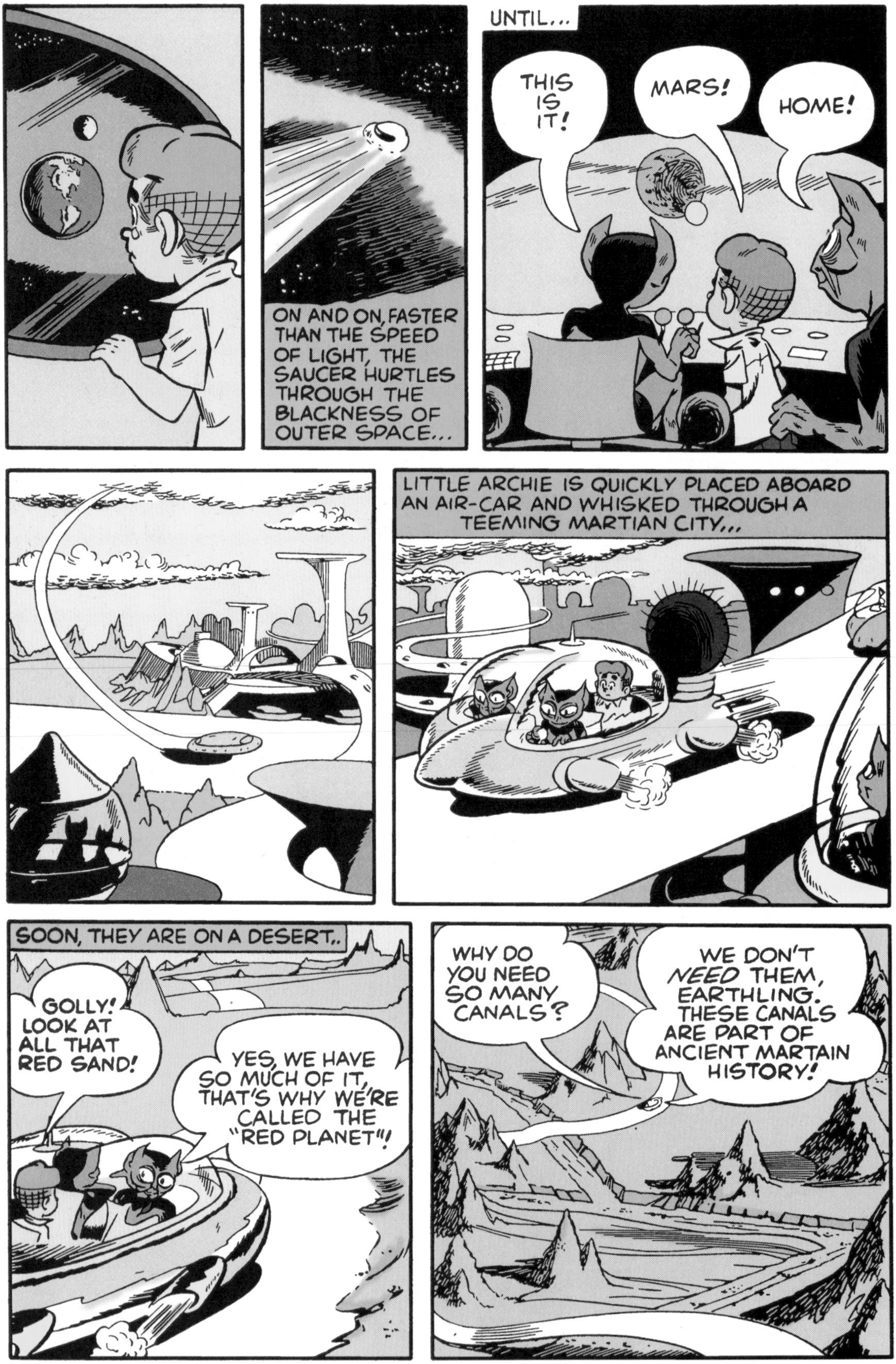
ON AND ON, FASTER THAN THE SPEED OF LIGHT, THE SAUCER HURTLES THROUGH THE BLACKNESS OF OUTER SPACE...
UNTIL...
THIS IS IT!
MARS!
HOME!
LITTLE ARCHIE IS QUICKLY PLACED ABOARD AN AIR-CAR AND WHISKED THROUGH A TEEMING MARTIAN CITY...
SOON, THEY ARE ON A DESERT..
GOLLY! LOOK AT ALL THAT RED SAND!
YES, WE HAVE SO MUCH OF IT, THAT'S WHY WE'RE CALLED THE "RED PLANET"!
WHY DO YOU NEED SO MANY CANALS?
WE DON'T *NEED* THEM, EARTHLING. THESE CANALS ARE PART OF ANCIENT MARTAIN HISTORY!

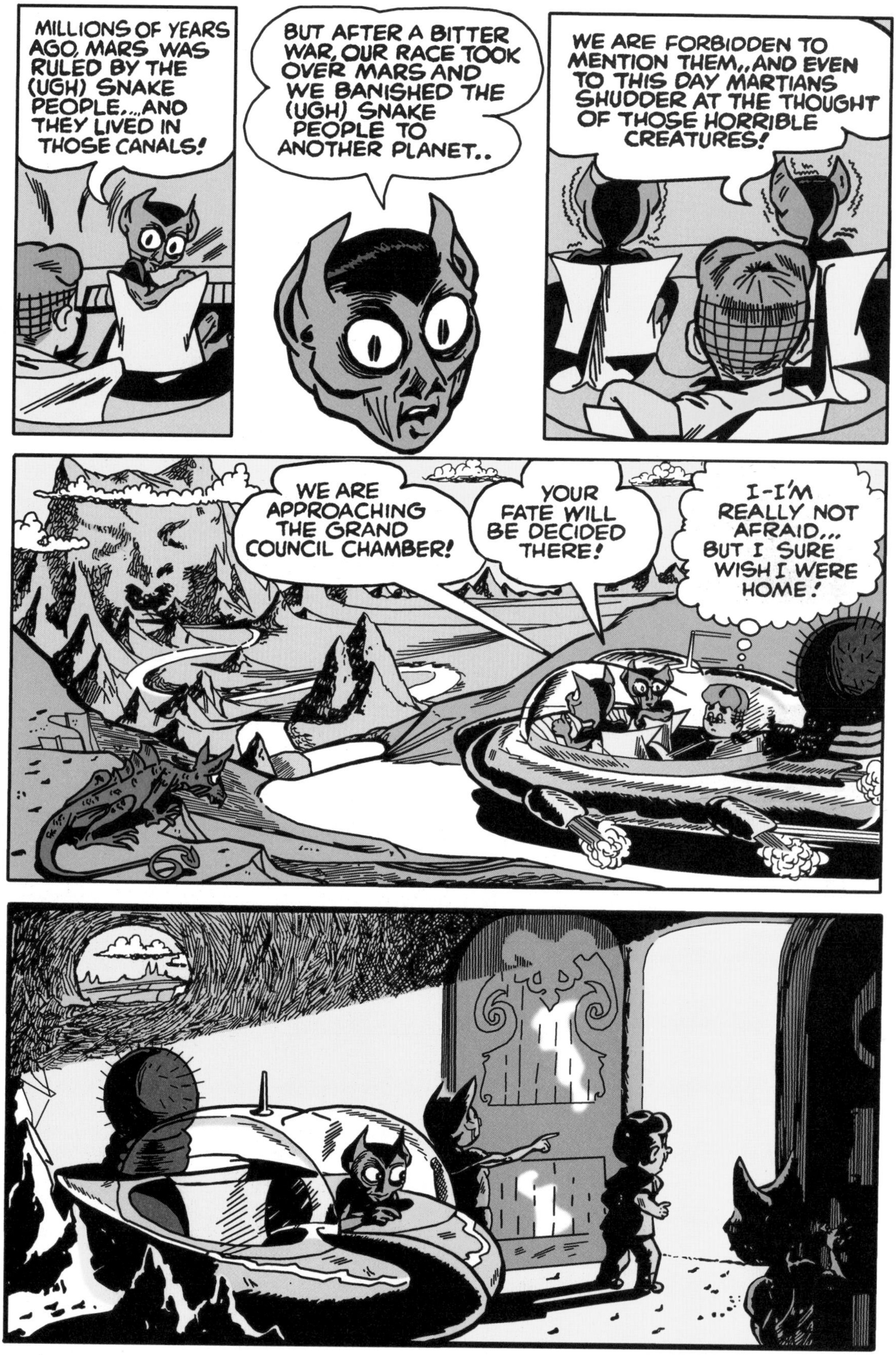
MILLIONS OF YEARS AGO, MARS WAS RULED BY THE (UGH) SNAKE PEOPLE,...AND THEY LIVED IN THOSE CANALS!
BUT AFTER A BITTER WAR, OUR RACE TOOK OVER MARS AND WE BANISHED THE (UGH) SNAKE PEOPLE TO ANOTHER PLANET..
WE ARE FORBIDDEN TO MENTION THEM,,AND EVEN TO THIS DAY MARTIANS SHUDDER AT THE THOUGHT OF THOSE HORRIBLE CREATURES!
WE ARE APPROACHING THE GRAND COUNCIL CHAMBER!
YOUR FATE WILL BE DECIDED THERE!
I-I'M REALLY NOT AFRAID,.. BUT I SURE WISH I WERE HOME!

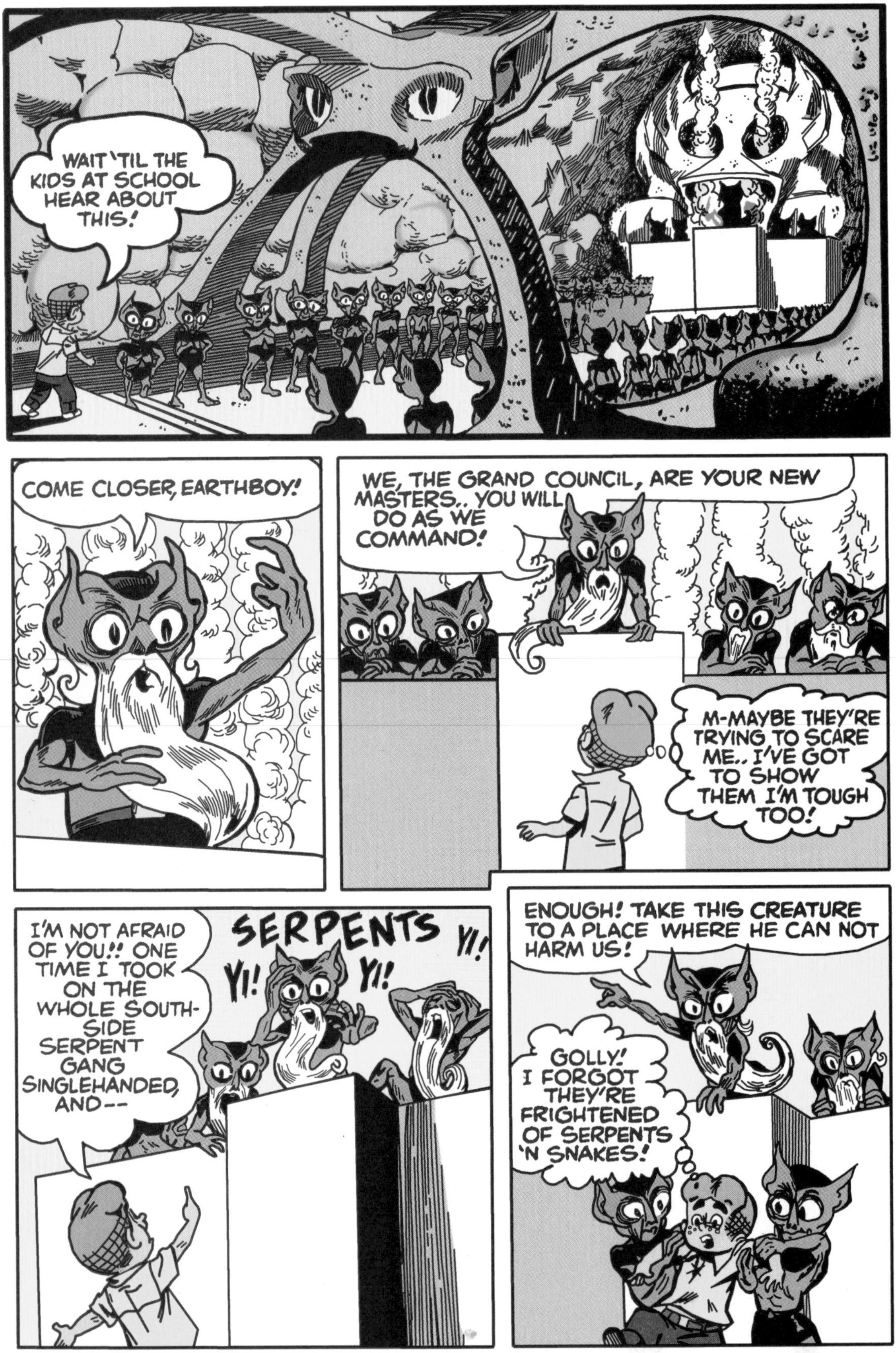
WAIT 'TIL THE KIDS AT SCHOOL HEAR ABOUT THIS!
COME CLOSER, EARTHBOY!
WE, THE GRAND COUNCIL, ARE YOUR NEW MASTERS.. YOU WILL DO AS WE COMMAND!
M-MAYBE THEY'RE TRYING TO SCARE ME.. I'VE GOT TO SHOW THEM I'M TOUGH TOO!
I'M NOT AFRAID OF YOU!! ONE TIME I TOOK ON THE WHOLE SOUTH-SIDE SERPENT GANG SINGLEHANDED, AND--
SERPENTS
YI!
YI!
YI!
ENOUGH! TAKE THIS CREATURE TO A PLACE WHERE HE CAN NOT HARM US!
GOLLY! I FORGOT THEY'RE FRIGHTENED OF SERPENTS 'N SNAKES!

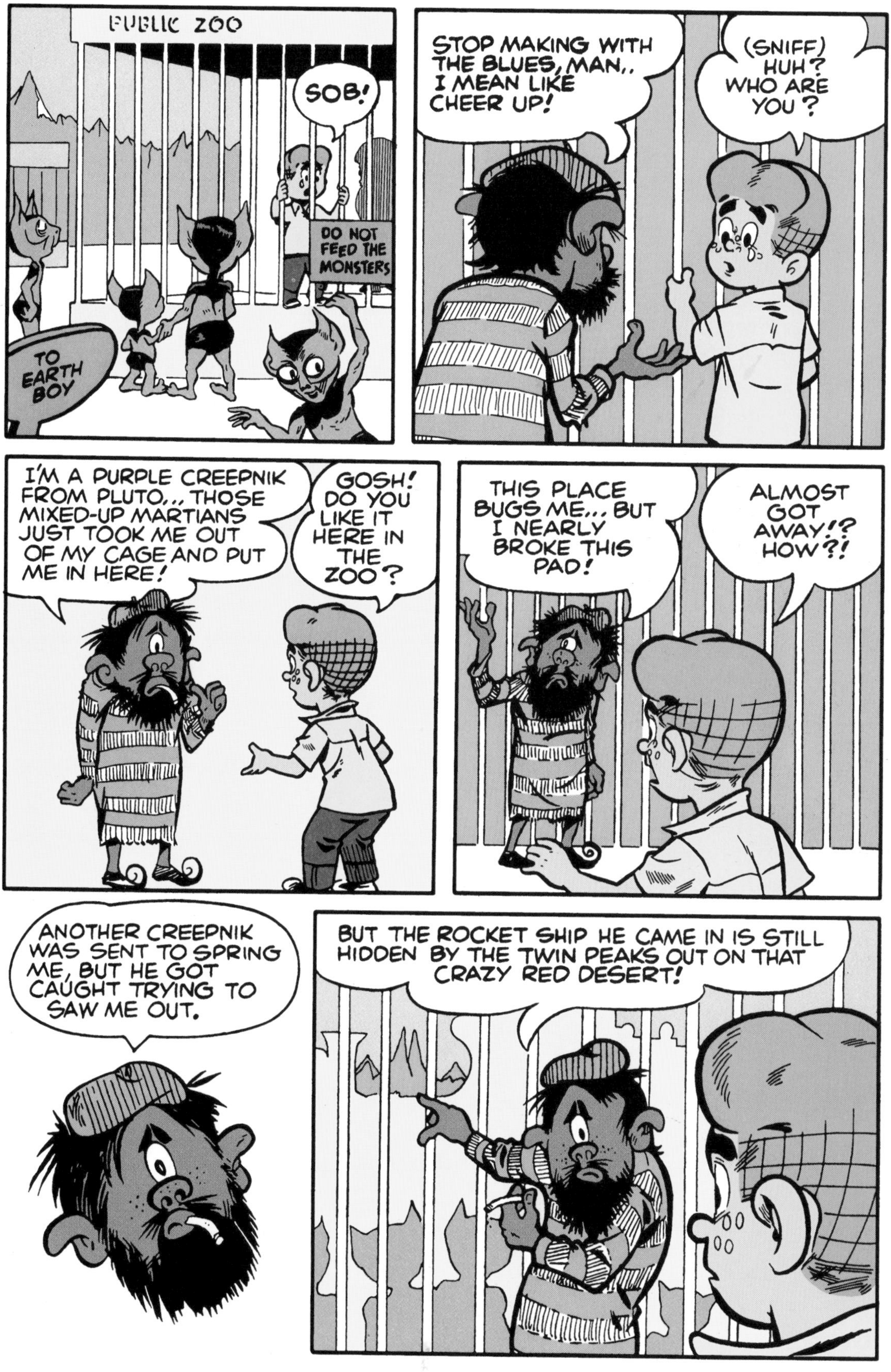
PUBLIC ZOO
SOB!
DO NOT FEED THE MONSTERS
TO EARTH BOY
STOP MAKING WITH THE BLUES, MAN,. I MEAN LIKE CHEER UP!
(SNIFF) HUH? WHO ARE YOU?
I'M A PURPLE CREEPNIK FROM PLUTO... THOSE MIXED-UP MARTIANS JUST TOOK ME OUT OF MY CAGE AND PUT ME IN HERE!
GOSH! DO YOU LIKE IT HERE IN THE ZOO?
THIS PLACE BUGS ME... BUT I NEARLY BROKE THIS PAD!
ALMOST GOT AWAY!? HOW?!
ANOTHER CREEPNIK WAS SENT TO SPRING ME, BUT HE GOT CAUGHT TRYING TO SAW ME OUT.
BUT THE ROCKET SHIP HE CAME IN IS STILL HIDDEN BY THE TWIN PEAKS OUT ON THAT CRAZY RED DESERT!

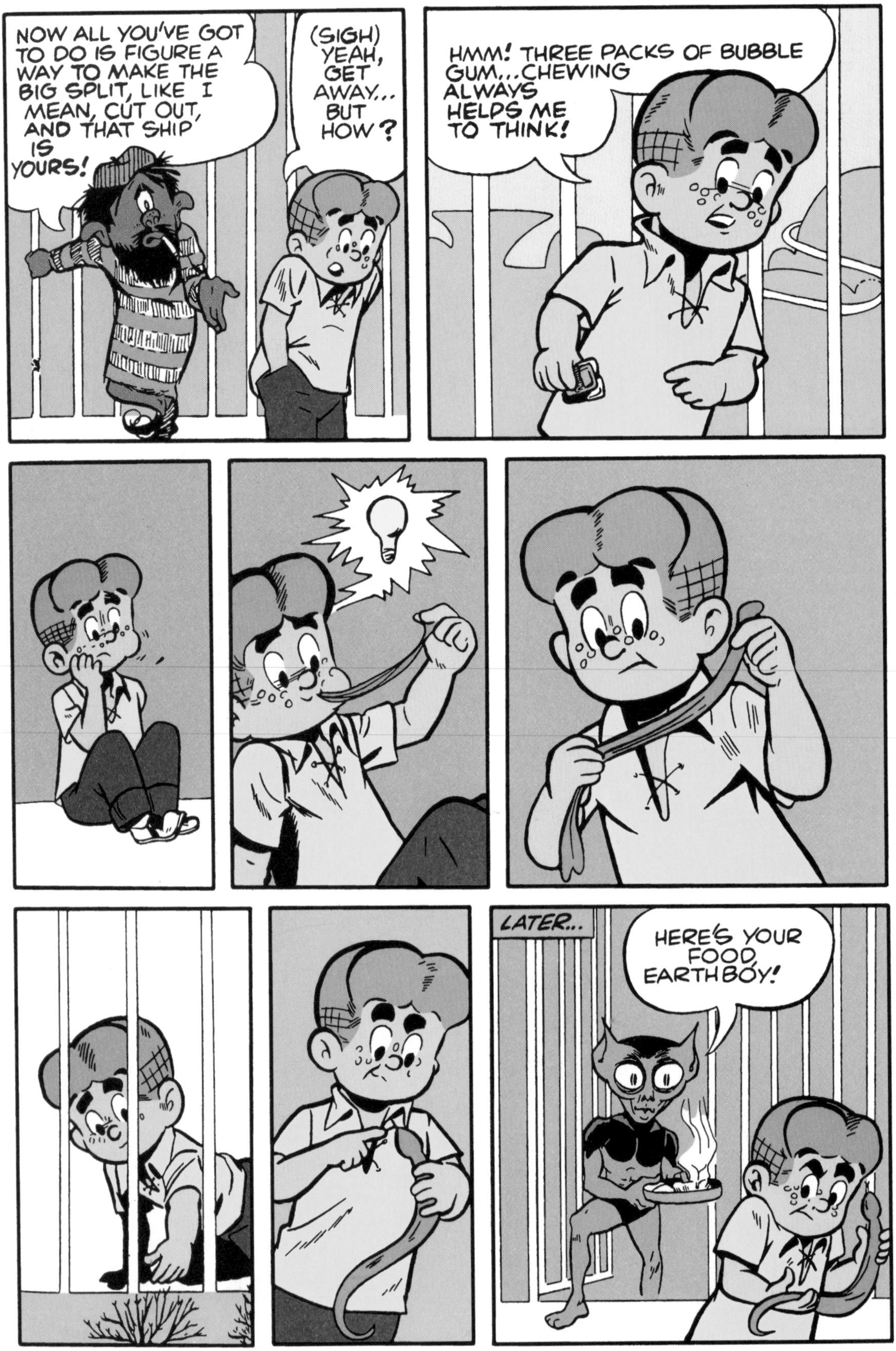
NOW ALL YOU'VE GOT TO DO IS FIGURE A WAY TO MAKE THE BIG SPLIT, LIKE I MEAN, CUT OUT, AND THAT SHIP IS YOURS!
(SIGH) YEAH, GET AWAY... BUT HOW?
HMM! THREE PACKS OF BUBBLE GUM...CHEWING ALWAYS HELPS ME TO THINK!
LATER...
HERE'S YOUR FOOD, EARTHBOY!

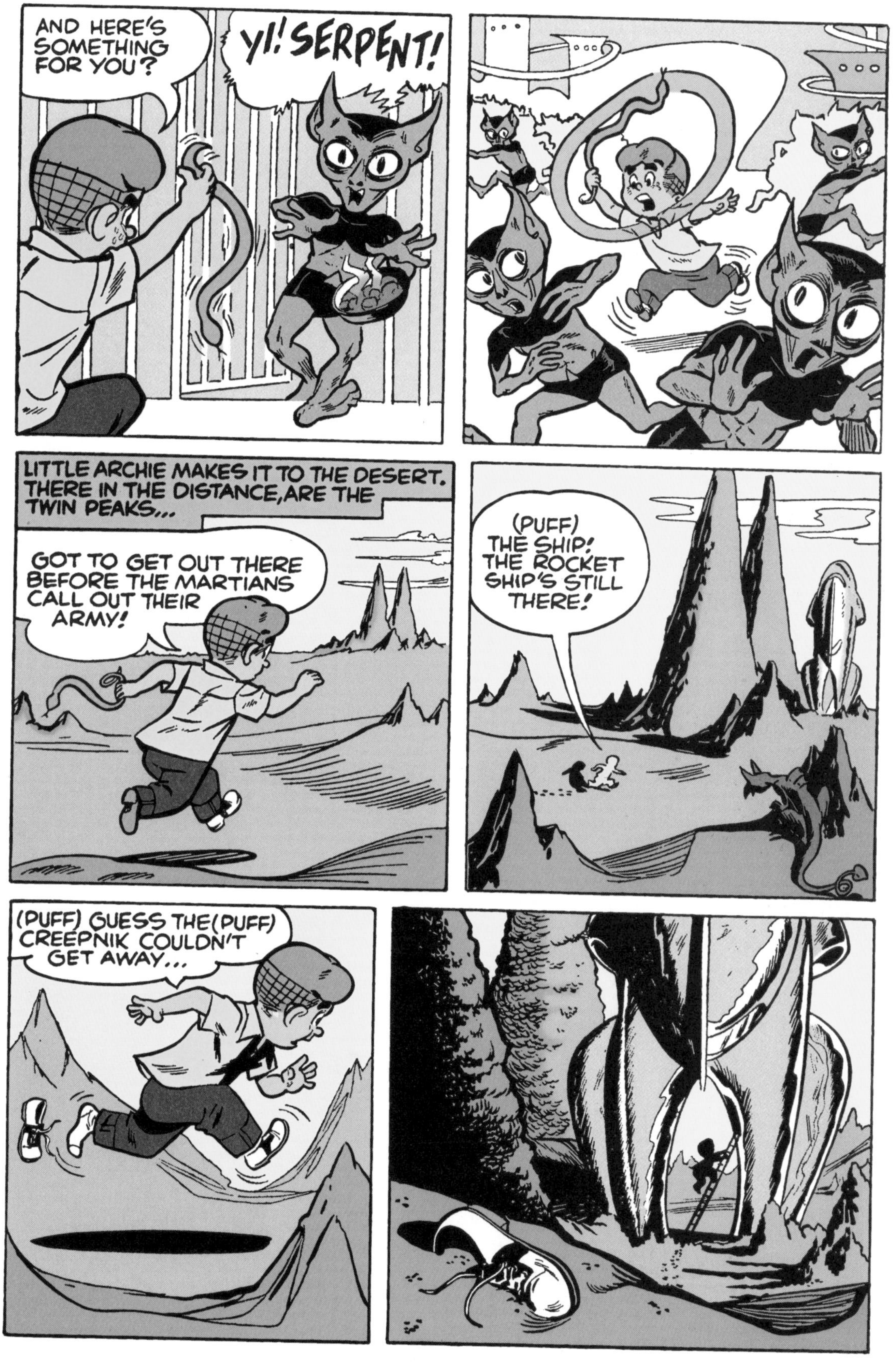
AND HERE'S SOMETHING FOR YOU?
YI! SERPENT!
LITTLE ARCHIE MAKES IT TO THE DESERT. THERE IN THE DISTANCE, ARE THE TWIN PEAKS...
GOT TO GET OUT THERE BEFORE THE MARTIANS CALL OUT THEIR ARMY!
(PUFF) THE SHIP! THE ROCKET SHIP'S STILL THERE!
(PUFF) GUESS THE (PUFF) CREEPNIK COULDN'T GET AWAY...

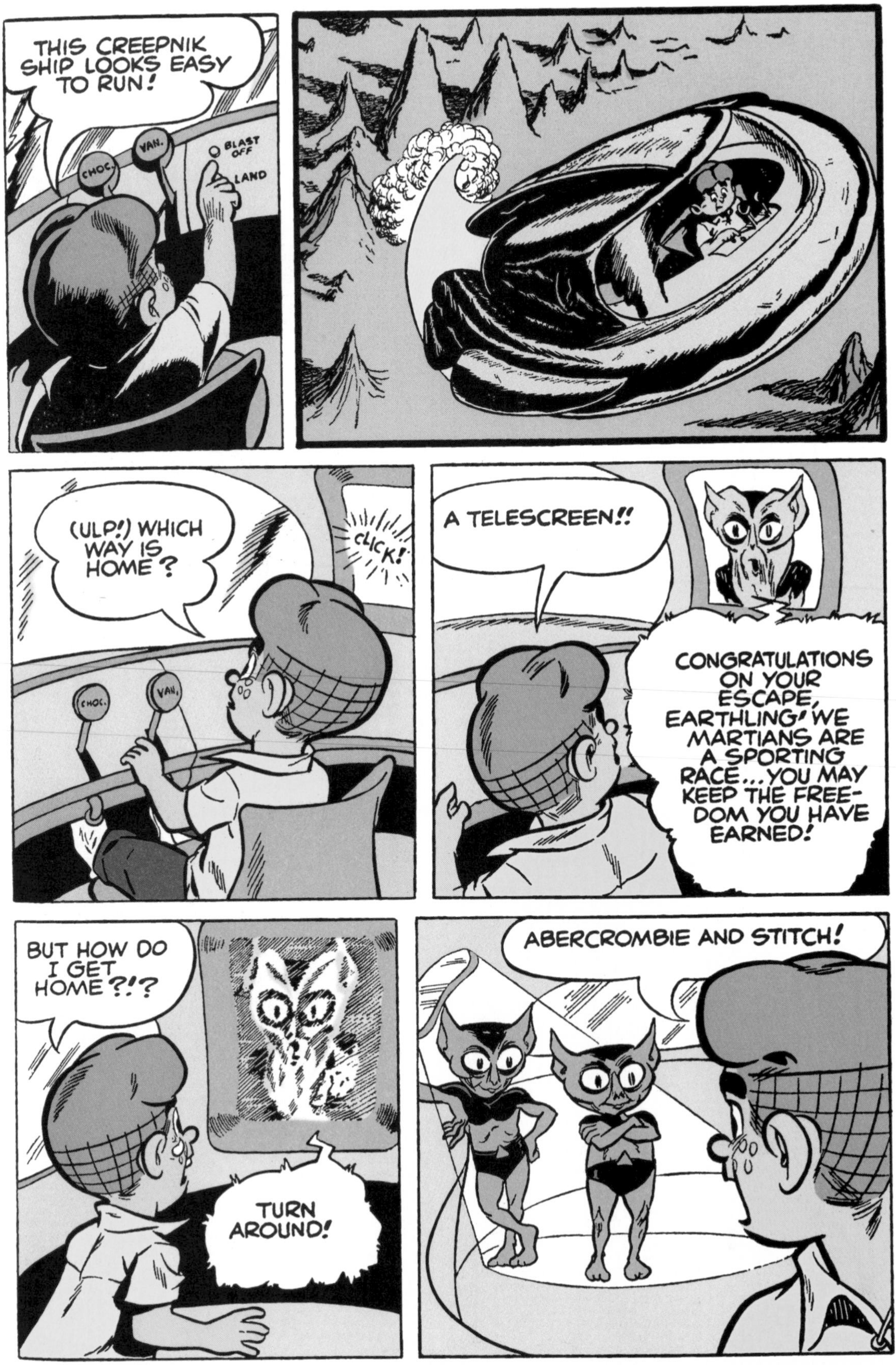
THIS CREEPNIK SHIP LOOKS EASY TO RUN!
CHOC.
VAN.
BLAST OFF
LAND
(ULP!) WHICH WAY IS HOME?
CLICK!
CHOC.
VAN.
A TELESCREEN!!
CONGRATULATIONS ON YOUR ESCAPE, EARTHLING! WE MARTIANS ARE A SPORTING RACE... YOU MAY KEEP THE FREE-DOM YOU HAVE EARNED!
BUT HOW DO I GET HOME?!?
TURN AROUND!
ABERCROMBIE AND STITCH!

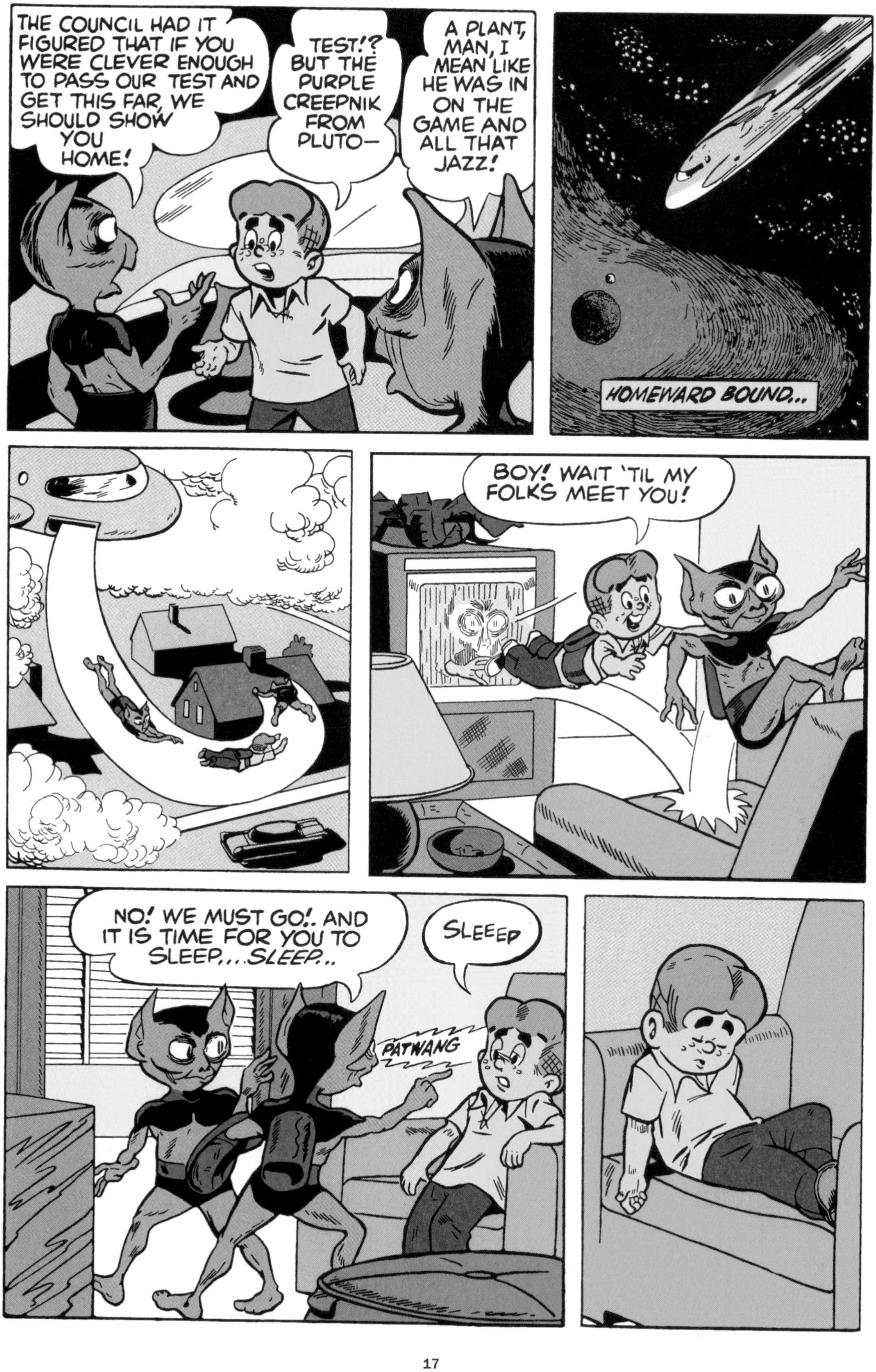
THE COUNCIL HAD IT FIGURED THAT IF YOU WERE CLEVER ENOUGH TO PASS OUR TEST AND GET THIS FAR, WE SHOULD SHOW YOU HOME!
TEST!? BUT THE PURPLE CREEPNIK FROM PLUTO—
A PLANT, MAN, I MEAN LIKE HE WAS IN ON THE GAME AND ALL THAT JAZZ!
HOMEWARD BOUND...
BOY! WAIT 'TIL MY FOLKS MEET YOU!
NO! WE MUST GO!. AND IT IS TIME FOR YOU TO SLEEP... SLEEP...
SLEEEP
PATWANG

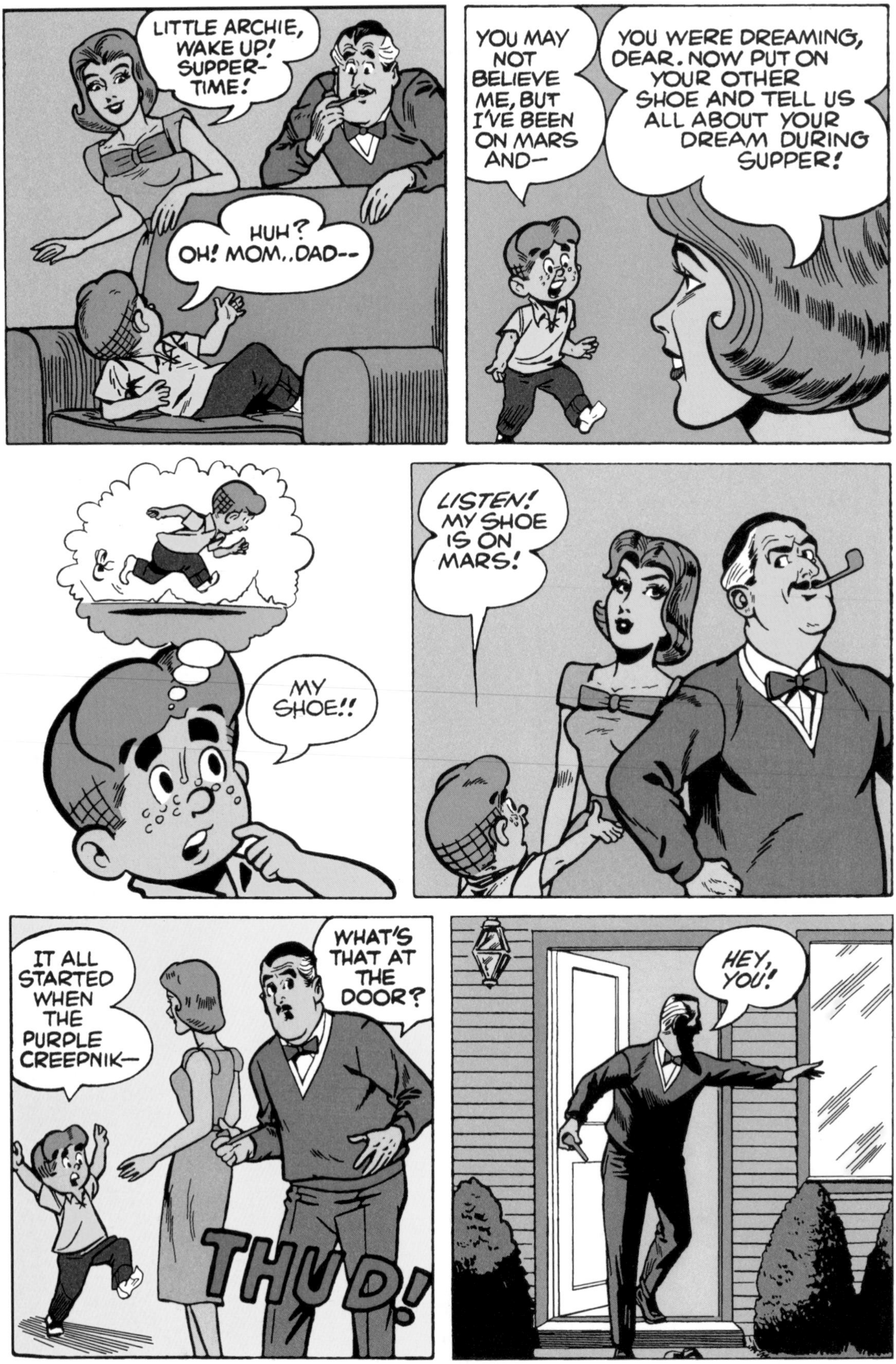
LITTLE ARCHIE, WAKE UP! SUPPER-TIME!
HUH? OH! MOM..DAD--
YOU MAY NOT BELIEVE ME, BUT I'VE BEEN ON MARS AND—
YOU WERE DREAMING, DEAR. NOW PUT ON YOUR OTHER SHOE AND TELL US ALL ABOUT YOUR DREAM DURING SUPPER!
MY SHOE!!
LISTEN! MY SHOE IS ON MARS!
IT ALL STARTED WHEN THE PURPLE CREEPNIK—
WHAT'S THAT AT THE DOOR?
THUD!
HEY, YOU!

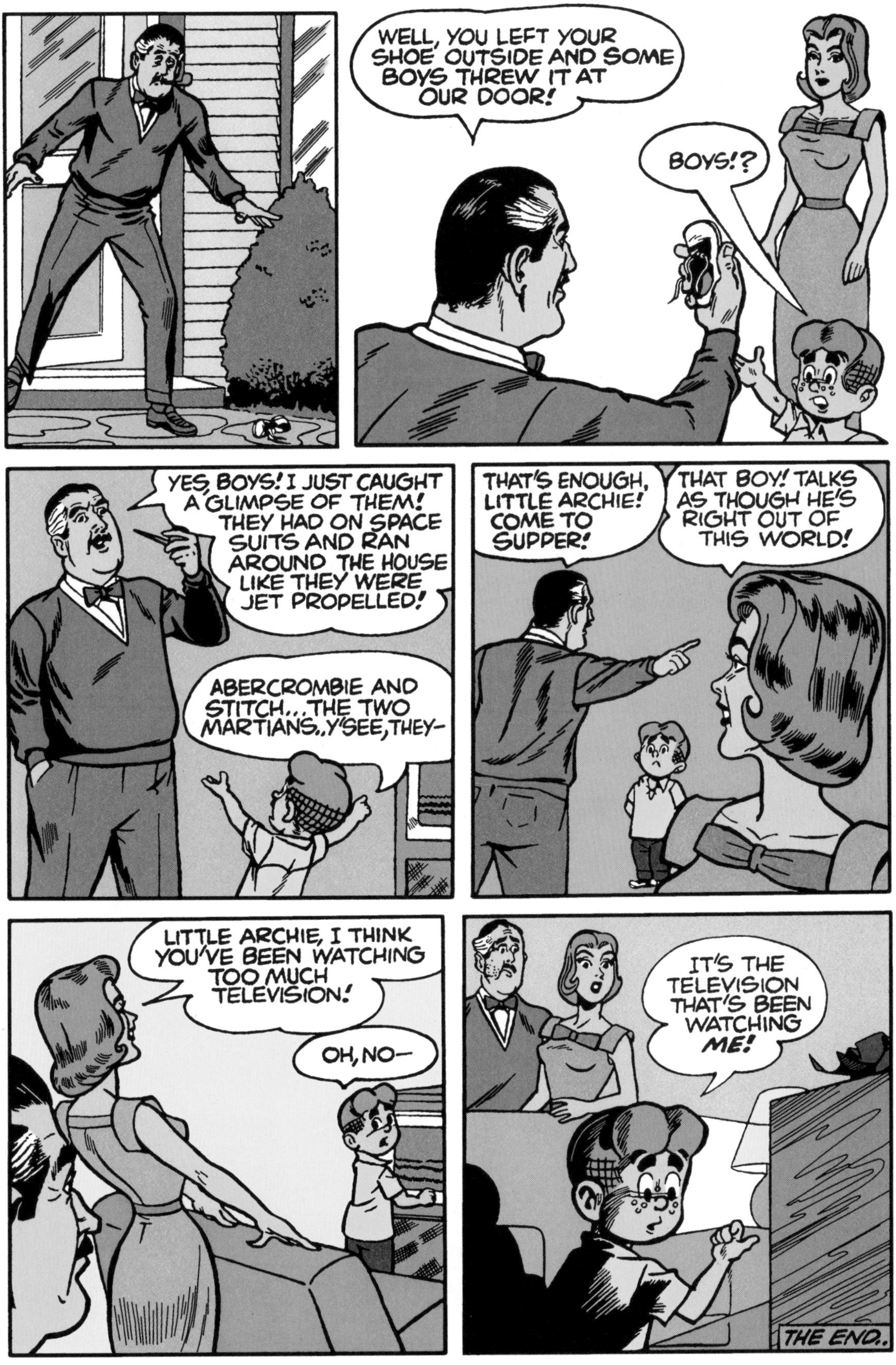
WELL, YOU LEFT YOUR SHOE OUTSIDE AND SOME BOYS THREW IT AT OUR DOOR!
BOYS!?
YES, BOYS! I JUST CAUGHT A GLIMPSE OF THEM! THEY HAD ON SPACE SUITS AND RAN AROUND THE HOUSE LIKE THEY WERE JET PROPELLED!
ABERCROMBIE AND STITCH... THE TWO MARTIANS.. Y'SEE, THEY-
THAT'S ENOUGH, LITTLE ARCHIE! COME TO SUPPER!
THAT BOY! TALKS AS THOUGH HE'S RIGHT OUT OF THIS WORLD!
LITTLE ARCHIE, I THINK YOU'VE BEEN WATCHING TOO MUCH TELEVISION!
OH, NO-
IT'S THE TELEVISION THAT'S BEEN WATCHING *ME!*
THE END.

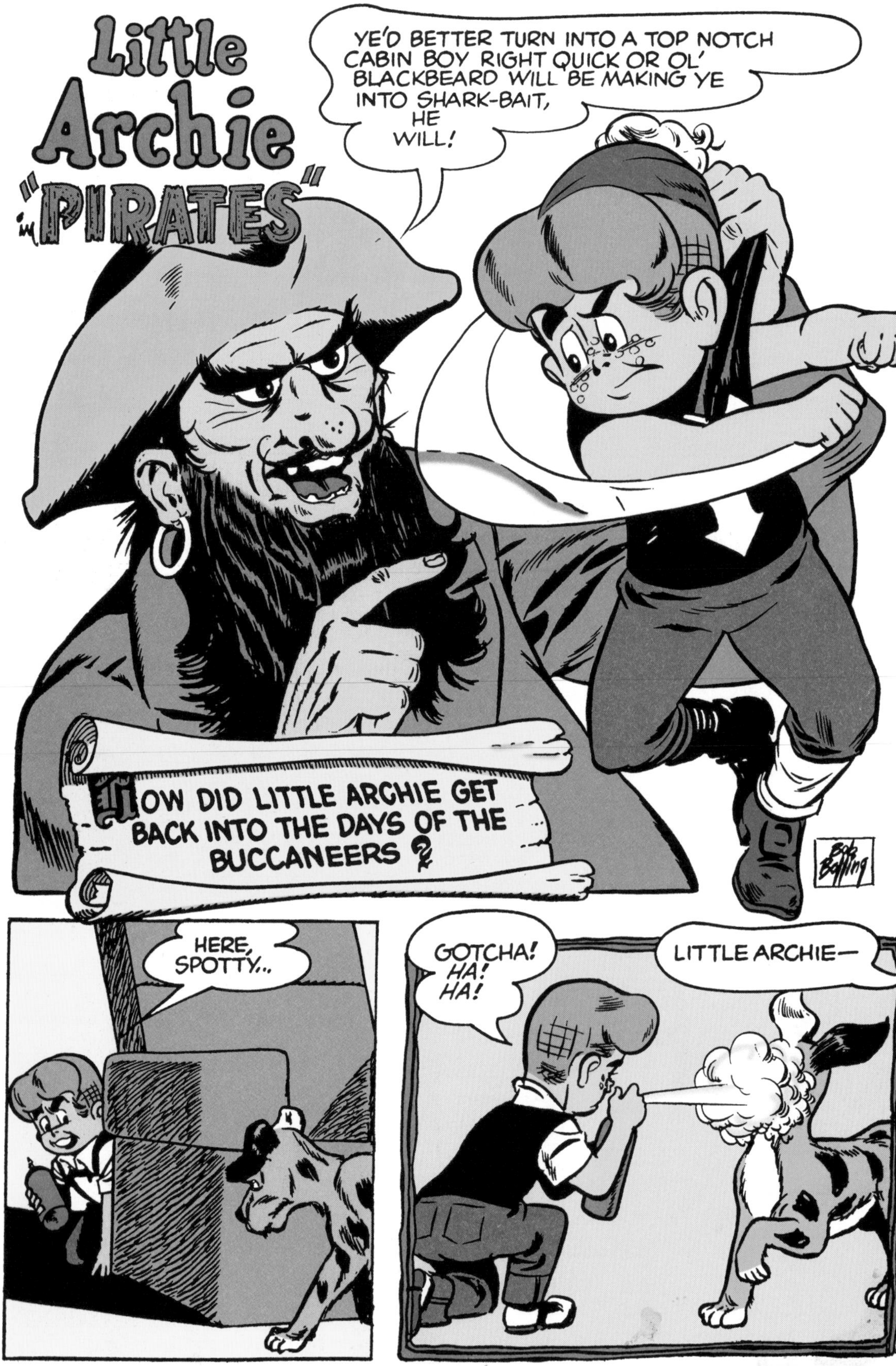
Little Archie
in "PIRATES"
YE'D BETTER TURN INTO A TOP NOTCH CABIN BOY RIGHT QUICK OR OL' BLACKBEARD WILL BE MAKING YE INTO SHARK-BAIT, HE WILL!
HOW DID LITTLE ARCHIE GET BACK INTO THE DAYS OF THE BUCCANEERS ?
Bob Bolling
HERE, SPOTTY...
GOTCHA! HA! HA!
LITTLE ARCHIE—

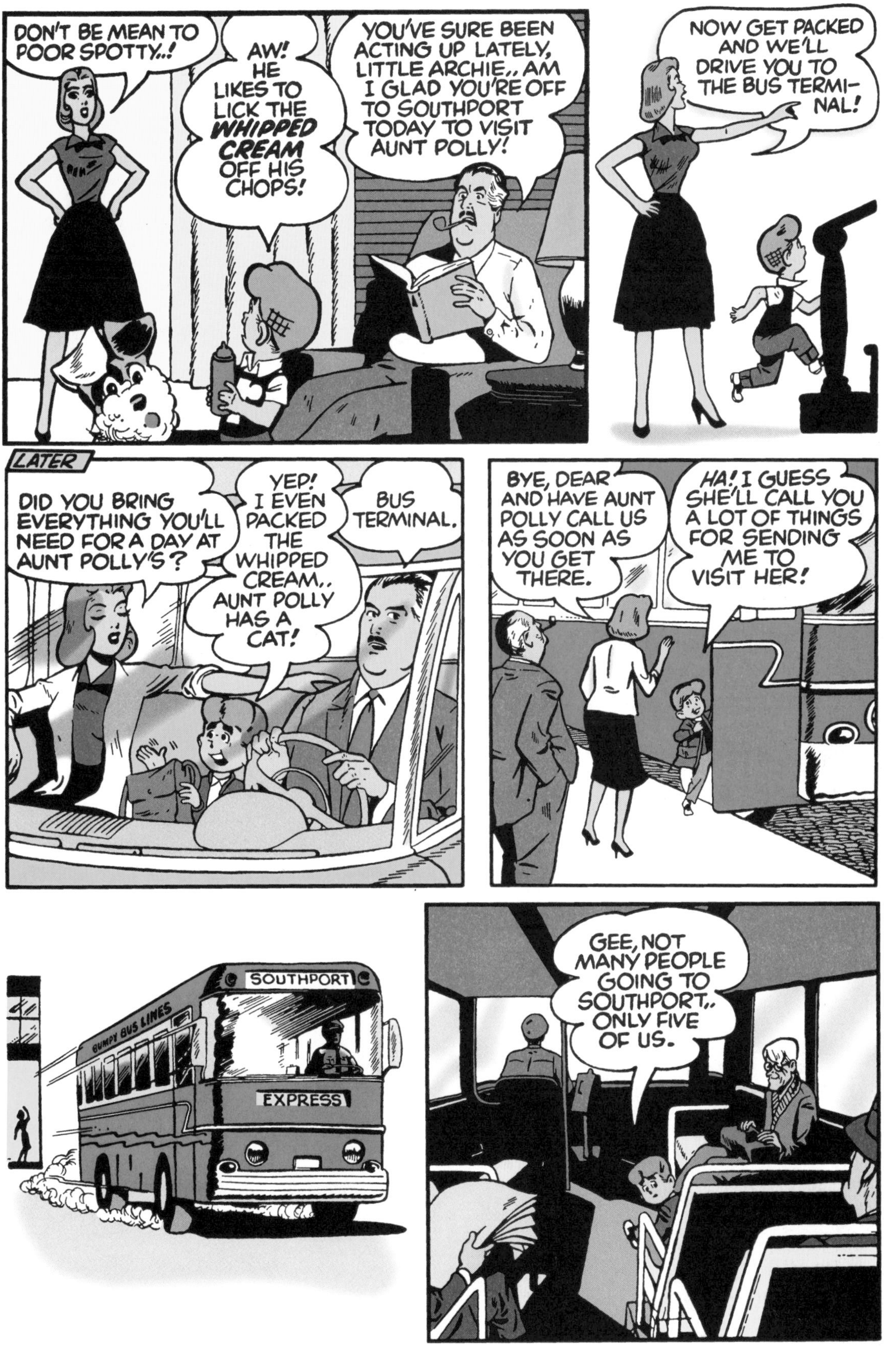
DON'T BE MEAN TO POOR SPOTTY..!
AW! HE LIKES TO LICK THE WHIPPED CREAM OFF HIS CHOPS!
YOU'VE SURE BEEN ACTING UP LATELY, LITTLE ARCHIE,. AM I GLAD YOU'RE OFF TO SOUTHPORT TODAY TO VISIT AUNT POLLY!
NOW GET PACKED AND WE'LL DRIVE YOU TO THE BUS TERMINAL!
LATER
DID YOU BRING EVERYTHING YOU'LL NEED FOR A DAY AT AUNT POLLY'S?
YEP! I EVEN PACKED THE WHIPPED CREAM,. AUNT POLLY HAS A CAT!
BUS TERMINAL.
BYE, DEAR AND HAVE AUNT POLLY CALL US AS SOON AS YOU GET THERE.
HA! I GUESS SHE'LL CALL YOU A LOT OF THINGS FOR SENDING ME TO VISIT HER!
SOUTHPORT
BUMPY BUS LINES
EXPRESS
GEE, NOT MANY PEOPLE GOING TO SOUTHPORT,. ONLY FIVE OF US.

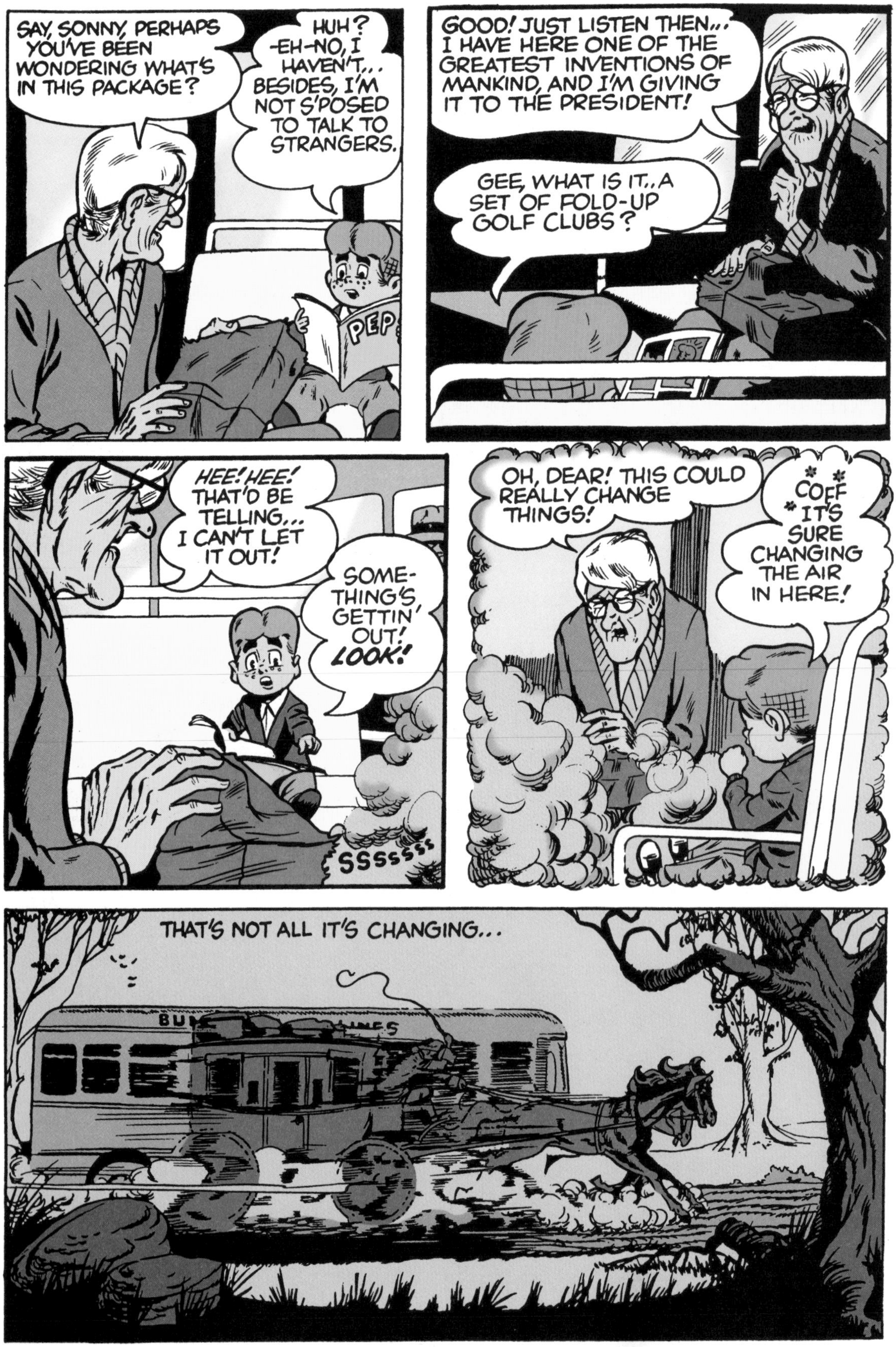
SAY, SONNY, PERHAPS YOU'VE BEEN WONDERING WHAT'S IN THIS PACKAGE?
HUH? -EH-NO, I HAVEN'T... BESIDES, I'M NOT S'POSED TO TALK TO STRANGERS.
PEP
GOOD! JUST LISTEN THEN... I HAVE HERE ONE OF THE GREATEST INVENTIONS OF MANKIND, AND I'M GIVING IT TO THE PRESIDENT!
GEE, WHAT IS IT.. A SET OF FOLD-UP GOLF CLUBS?
HEE! HEE! THAT'D BE TELLING... I CAN'T LET IT OUT!
SOME-THING'S GETTIN' OUT! LOOK!
SSSsssss
OH, DEAR! THIS COULD REALLY CHANGE THINGS!
* * COFF * IT'S SURE CHANGING THE AIR IN HERE!
THAT'S NOT ALL IT'S CHANGING...

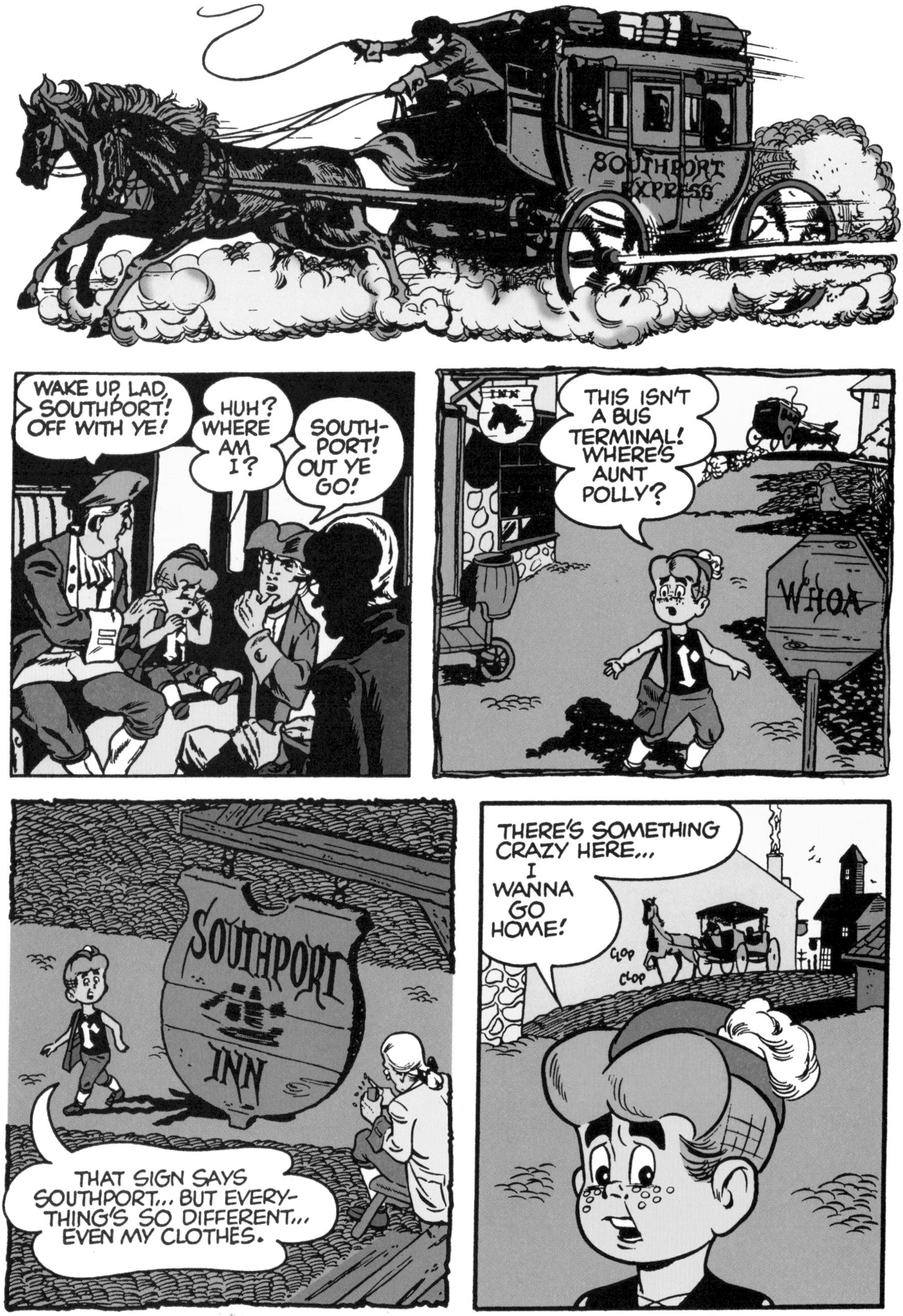
SOUTHPORT EXPRESS
WAKE UP, LAD, SOUTHPORT! OFF WITH YE!
HUH? WHERE AM I?
SOUTH-PORT! OUT YE GO!
INN
THIS ISN'T A BUS TERMINAL! WHERE'S AUNT POLLY?
WHOA
SOUTHPORT INN
THAT SIGN SAYS SOUTHPORT... BUT EVERY-THING'S SO DIFFERENT... EVEN MY CLOTHES.
THERE'S SOMETHING CRAZY HERE... I WANNA GO HOME!
CLOP CLOP

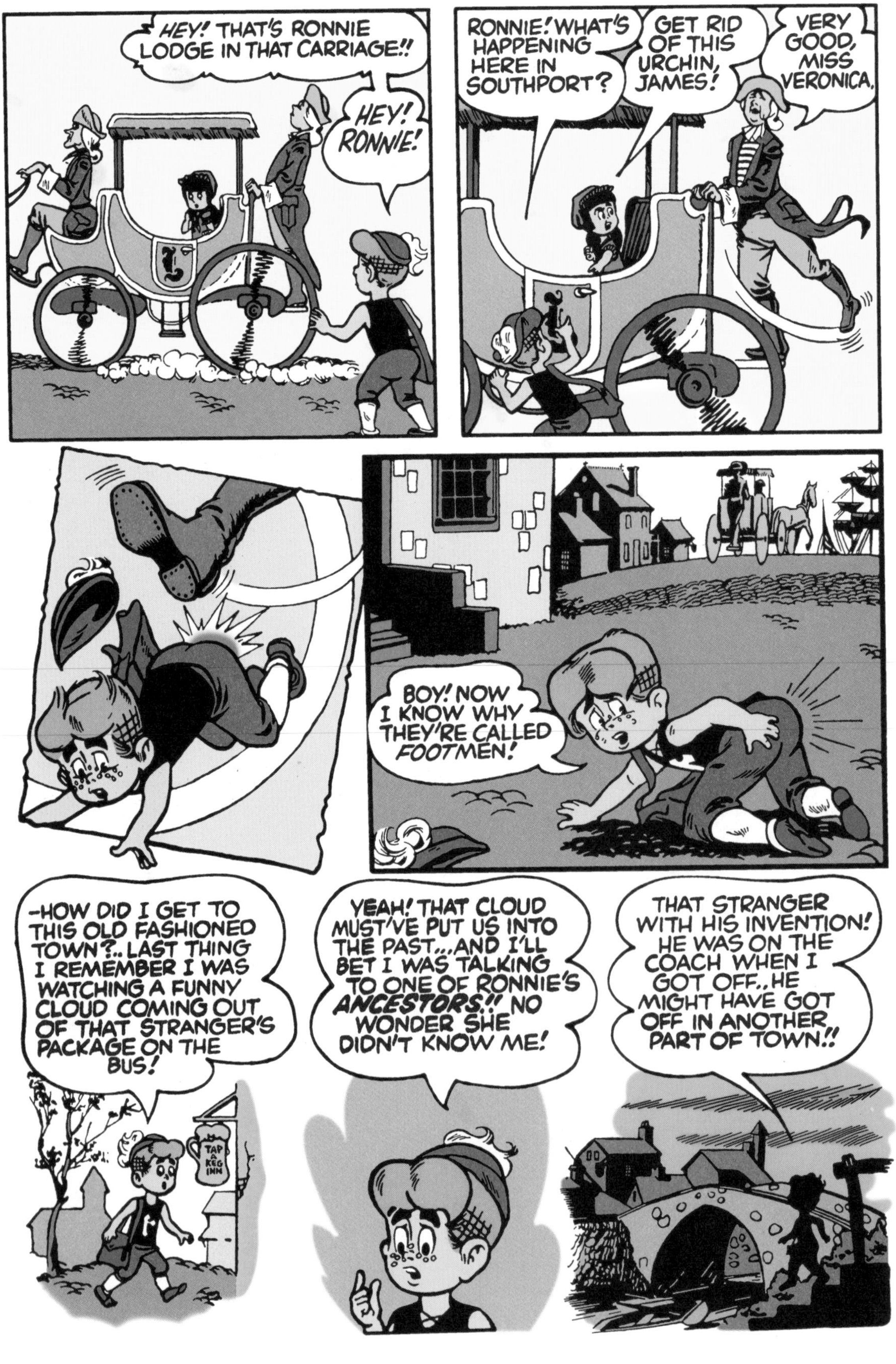
HEY! THAT'S RONNIE LODGE IN THAT CARRIAGE!!
HEY! RONNIE!
RONNIE! WHAT'S HAPPENING HERE IN SOUTHPORT?
GET RID OF THIS URCHIN, JAMES!
VERY GOOD, MISS VERONICA.
BOY! NOW I KNOW WHY THEY'RE CALLED FOOTMEN!
-HOW DID I GET TO THIS OLD FASHIONED TOWN?.. LAST THING I REMEMBER I WAS WATCHING A FUNNY CLOUD COMING OUT OF THAT STRANGER'S PACKAGE ON THE BUS!
YEAH! THAT CLOUD MUST'VE PUT US INTO THE PAST...AND I'LL BET I WAS TALKING TO ONE OF RONNIE'S ANCESTORS!! NO WONDER SHE DIDN'T KNOW ME!
THAT STRANGER WITH HIS INVENTION! HE WAS ON THE COACH WHEN I GOT OFF.. HE MIGHT HAVE GOT OFF IN ANOTHER PART OF TOWN!!

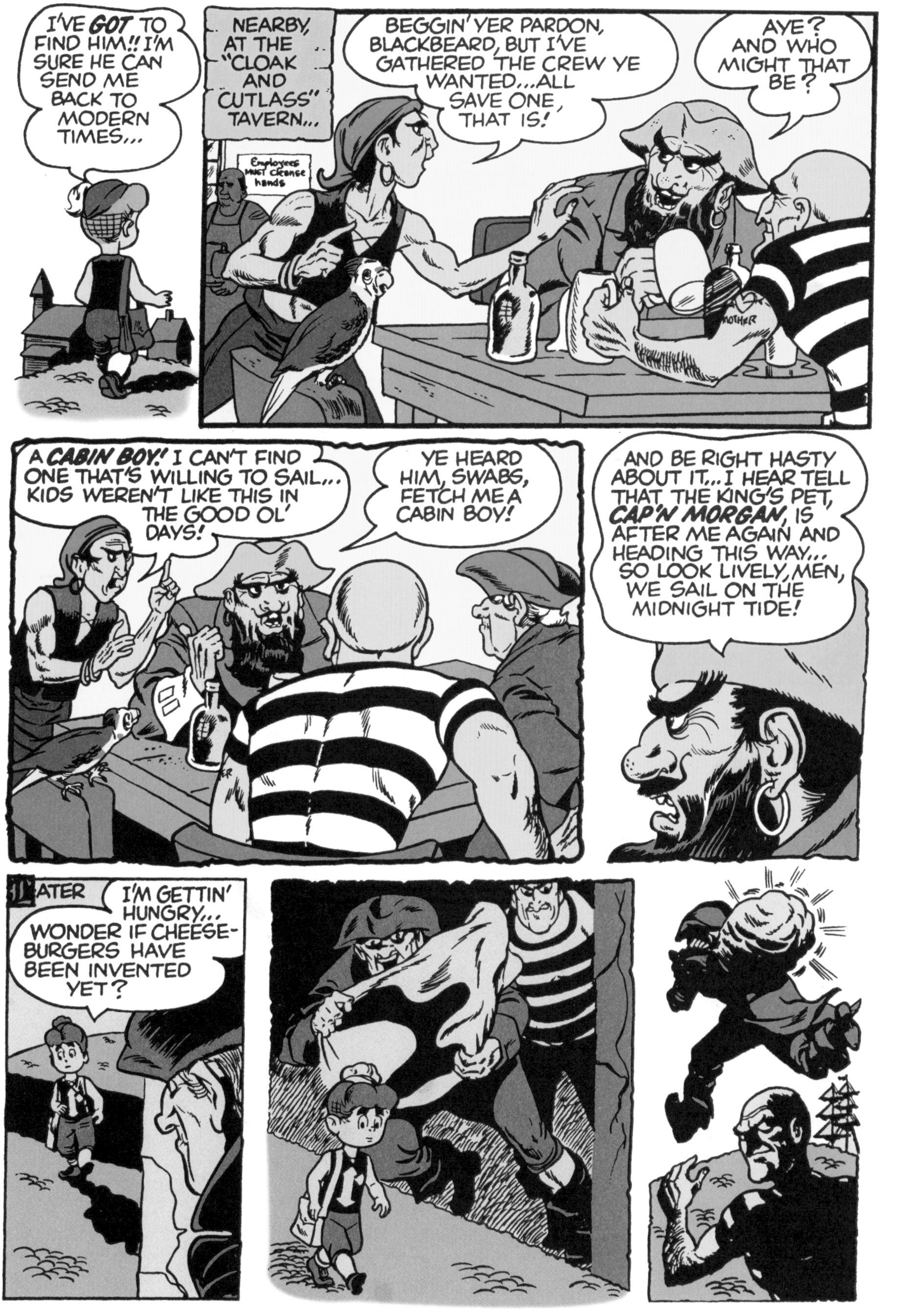
I'VE GOT TO FIND HIM!! I'M SURE HE CAN SEND ME BACK TO MODERN TIMES...
NEARBY, AT THE "CLOAK AND CUTLASS" TAVERN...
BEGGIN' YER PARDON, BLACKBEARD, BUT I'VE GATHERED THE CREW YE WANTED...ALL SAVE ONE, THAT IS!
AYE? AND WHO MIGHT THAT BE?
Employees MUST cleanse hands
MOTHER
A CABIN BOY! I CAN'T FIND ONE THAT'S WILLING TO SAIL... KIDS WEREN'T LIKE THIS IN THE GOOD OL' DAYS!
YE HEARD HIM, SWABS, FETCH ME A CABIN BOY!
AND BE RIGHT HASTY ABOUT IT... I HEAR TELL THAT THE KING'S PET, CAP'N MORGAN, IS AFTER ME AGAIN AND HEADING THIS WAY... SO LOOK LIVELY, MEN, WE SAIL ON THE MIDNIGHT TIDE!
LATER
I'M GETTIN' HUNGRY... WONDER IF CHEESE-BURGERS HAVE BEEN INVENTED YET?

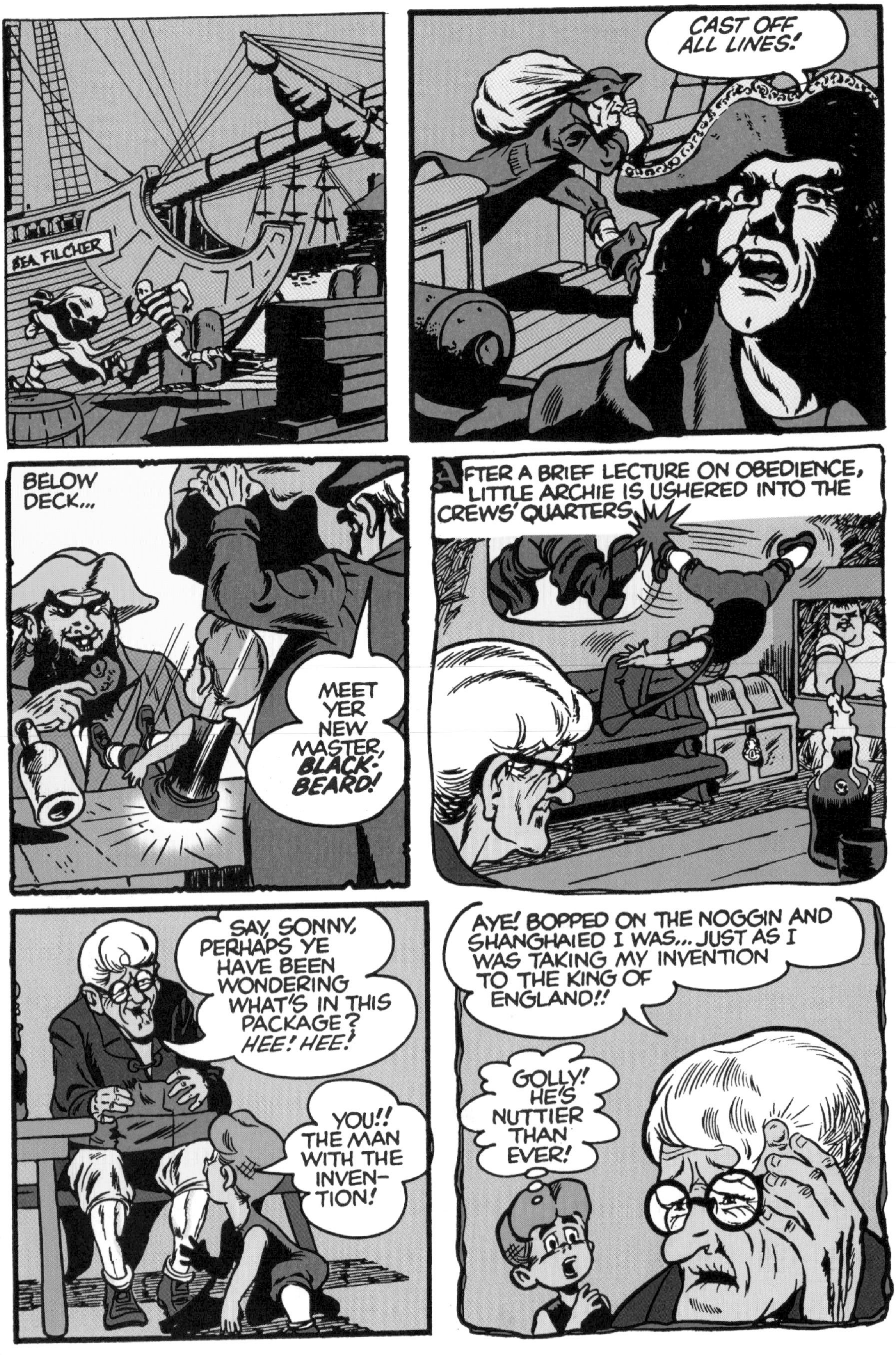
SEA FILCHER
CAST OFF ALL LINES!
BELOW DECK...
MEET YER NEW MASTER, BLACK-BEARD!
AFTER A BRIEF LECTURE ON OBEDIENCE, LITTLE ARCHIE IS USHERED INTO THE CREWS' QUARTERS
SAY, SONNY, PERHAPS YE HAVE BEEN WONDERING WHAT'S IN THIS PACKAGE? HEE! HEE!
YOU!! THE MAN WITH THE INVEN-TION!
AYE! BOPPED ON THE NOGGIN AND SHANGHAIED I WAS... JUST AS I WAS TAKING MY INVENTION TO THE KING OF ENGLAND!!
GOLLY! HE'S NUTTIER THAN EVER!

PLEASE! MAKE THAT CRAZY CLOUD COME AND GET US OUT OF HERE!!

KEEP BACK! THIS PACKAGE IS FOR THE KING!.. OR SHALL I BE PUTTING A PISTOL-BALL INTO YE?

LEAVE HIM BE, LAD,... HE'S DAFT!

AND SO LITTLE ARCHIE IS FORCED TO WAIT ON BLACKBEARD HAND AND FOOT FOR THE NEXT FEW WEEKS AS THE "SEA FILCHER" GOES FROM PORT TO PORT LOOTING AND PLUNDERING...

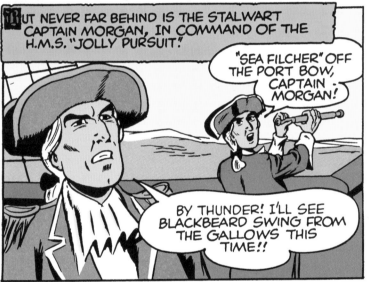

BUT NEVER FAR BEHIND IS THE STALWART CAPTAIN MORGAN, IN COMMAND OF THE H.M.S. "JOLLY PURSUIT!"

"SEA FILCHER" OFF THE PORT BOW, CAPTAIN MORGAN!

BY THUNDER! I'LL SEE BLACKBEARD SWING FROM THE GALLOWS THIS TIME!!

BUT A HEAVY FOG ROLLS IN AND THE "SEA FILCHER" IS LOST FROM SIGHT,...ONCE MORE BLACKBEARD ESCAPES THE HANGMAN'S NOOSE...

WEEKS LATER, AS THE "SEA FILCHER" APPROACHES A SOUTH-SEA ISLE AT TWILIGHT,...

SAIL HO!

WHERE AWAY?

IN YONDER COVE! IT'S THE "JOLLY PURSUIT!" THEY HAVEN'T SEEN US... THEY'RE HAVIN' TEA!

HA! WE'LL BE SAFE 'TIL SUNUP...THEN I'LL HAVE A SURPRISE FOR MORGAN, I WILL!

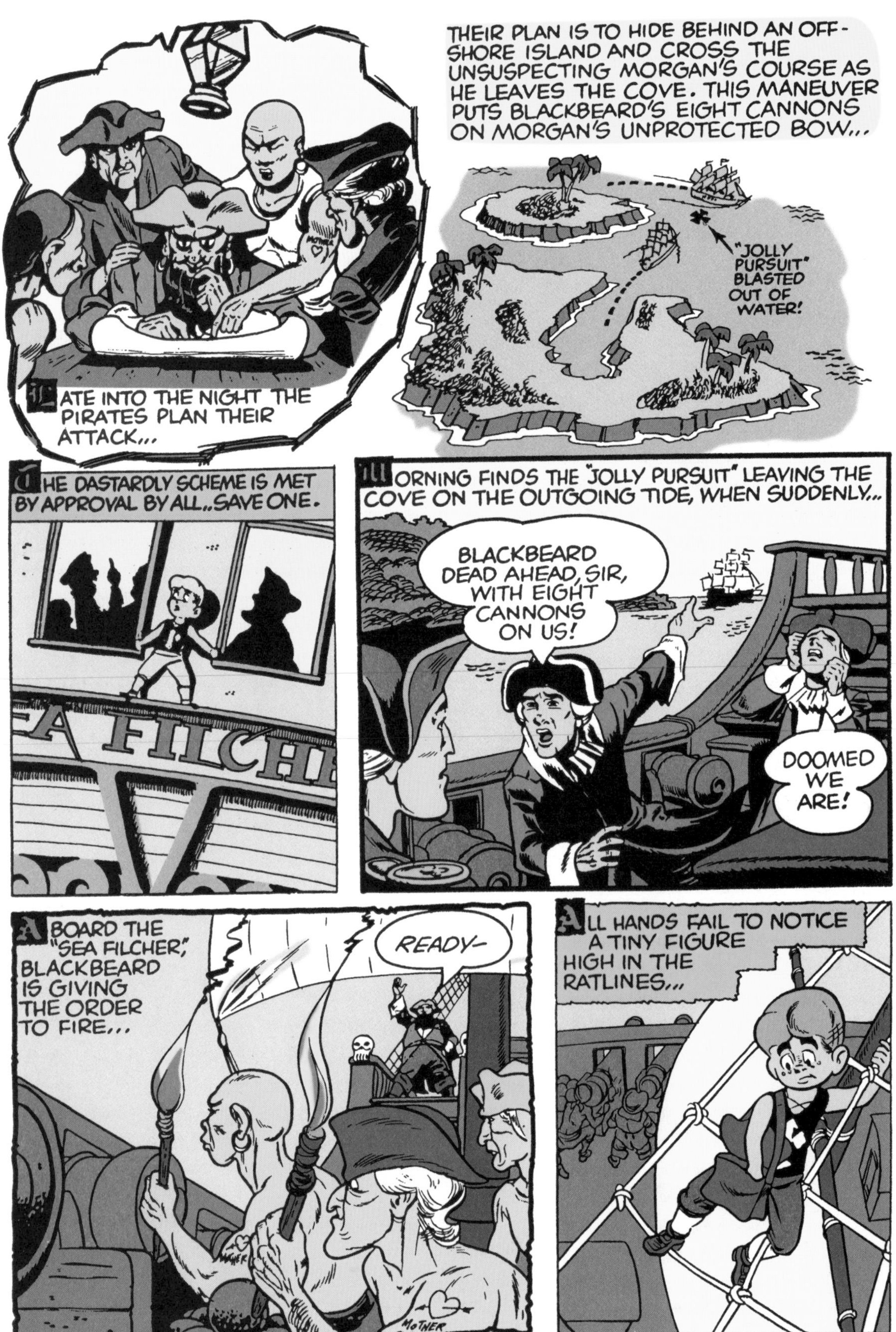
LATE INTO THE NIGHT THE PIRATES PLAN THEIR ATTACK...
MOTHER
THEIR PLAN IS TO HIDE BEHIND AN OFF-SHORE ISLAND AND CROSS THE UNSUSPECTING MORGAN'S COURSE AS HE LEAVES THE COVE. THIS MANEUVER PUTS BLACKBEARD'S EIGHT CANNONS ON MORGAN'S UNPROTECTED BOW...
"JOLLY PURSUIT" BLASTED OUT OF WATER!
THE DASTARDLY SCHEME IS MET BY APPROVAL BY ALL.. SAVE ONE.
EA FILCHE
MORNING FINDS THE "JOLLY PURSUIT" LEAVING THE COVE ON THE OUTGOING TIDE, WHEN SUDDENLY...
BLACKBEARD DEAD AHEAD, SIR, WITH EIGHT CANNONS ON US!
DOOMED WE ARE!
ABOARD THE "SEA FILCHER," BLACKBEARD IS GIVING THE ORDER TO FIRE...
READY-
MOTHER
ALL HANDS FAIL TO NOTICE A TINY FIGURE HIGH IN THE RATLINES...

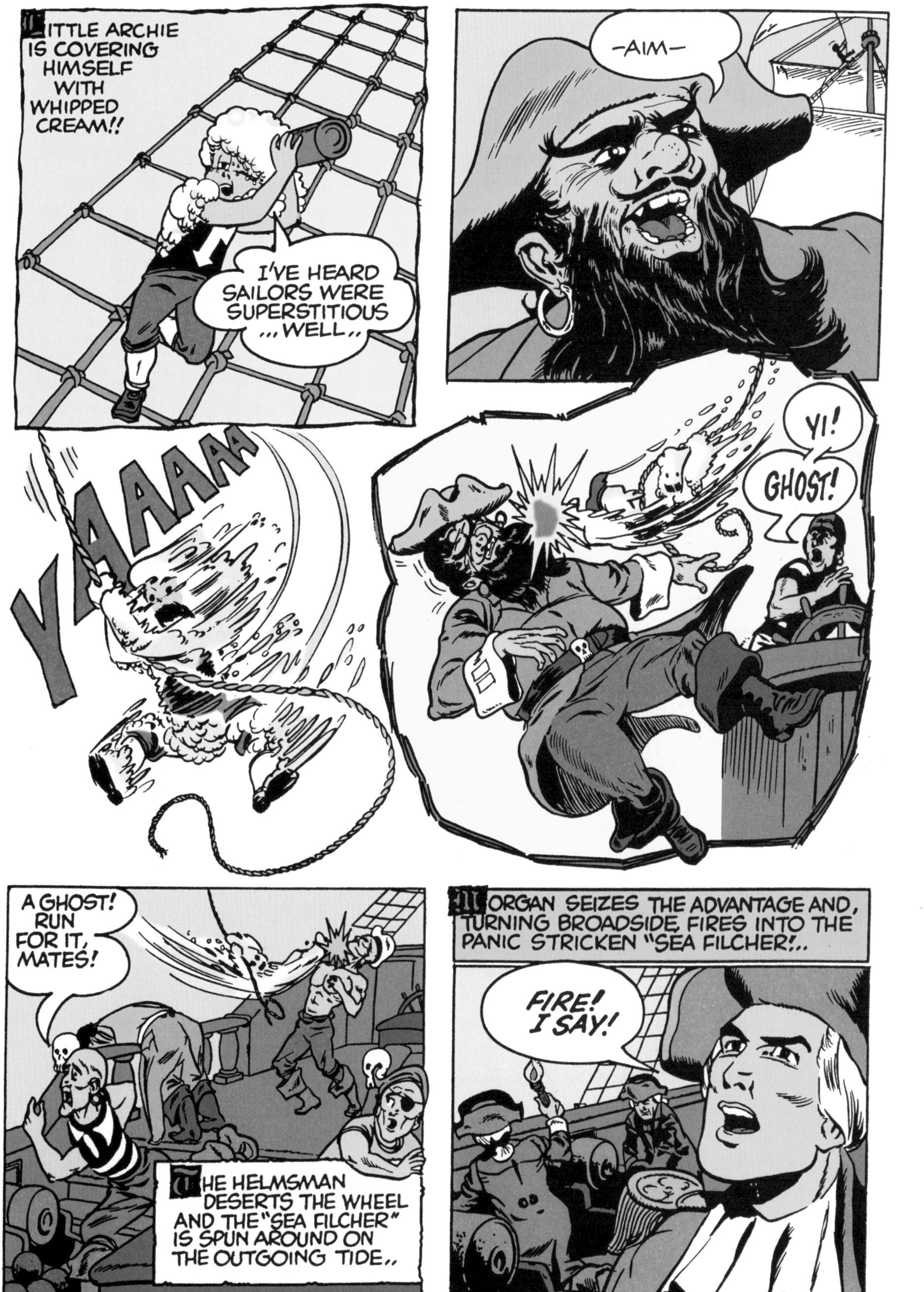
LITTLE ARCHIE IS COVERING HIMSELF WITH WHIPPED CREAM!!
I'VE HEARD SAILORS WERE SUPERSTITIOUS ...WELL..
-AIM-
YAAAAA
YI! GHOST!
A GHOST! RUN FOR IT, MATES!
THE HELMSMAN DESERTS THE WHEEL AND THE "SEA FILCHER" IS SPUN AROUND ON THE OUTGOING TIDE..
MORGAN SEIZES THE ADVANTAGE AND, TURNING BROADSIDE, FIRES INTO THE PANIC STRICKEN "SEA FILCHER"..
FIRE! I SAY!

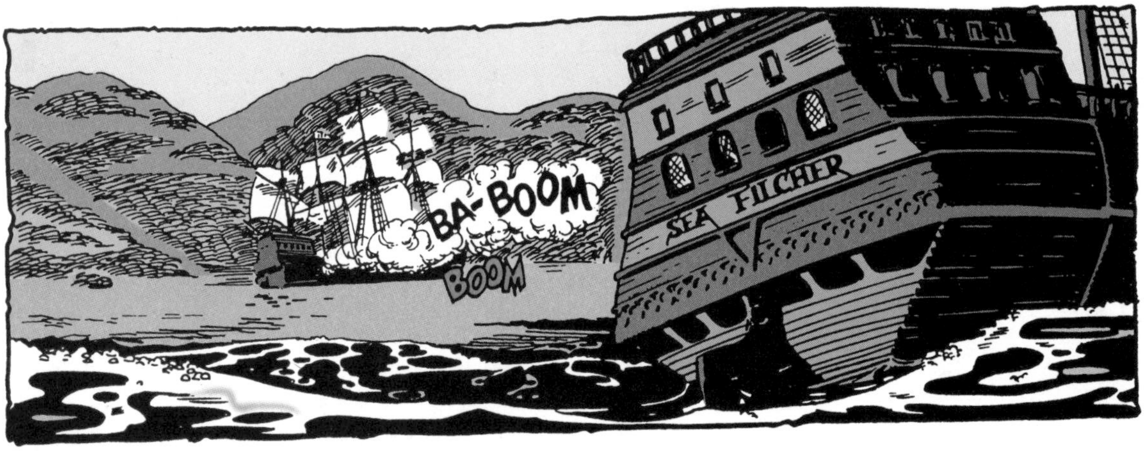

BA-BOOM
BOOM
SEA FILCHER

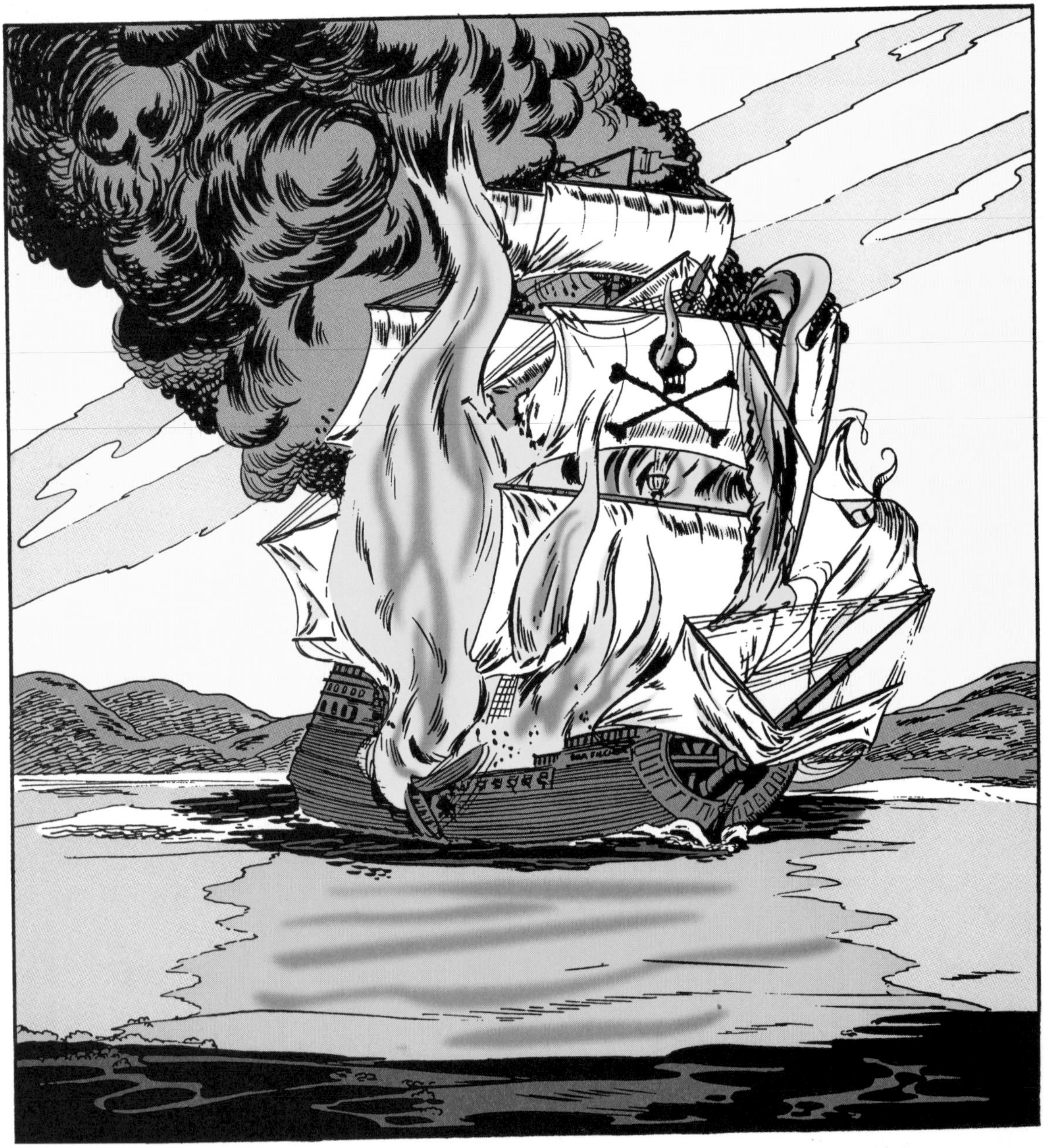

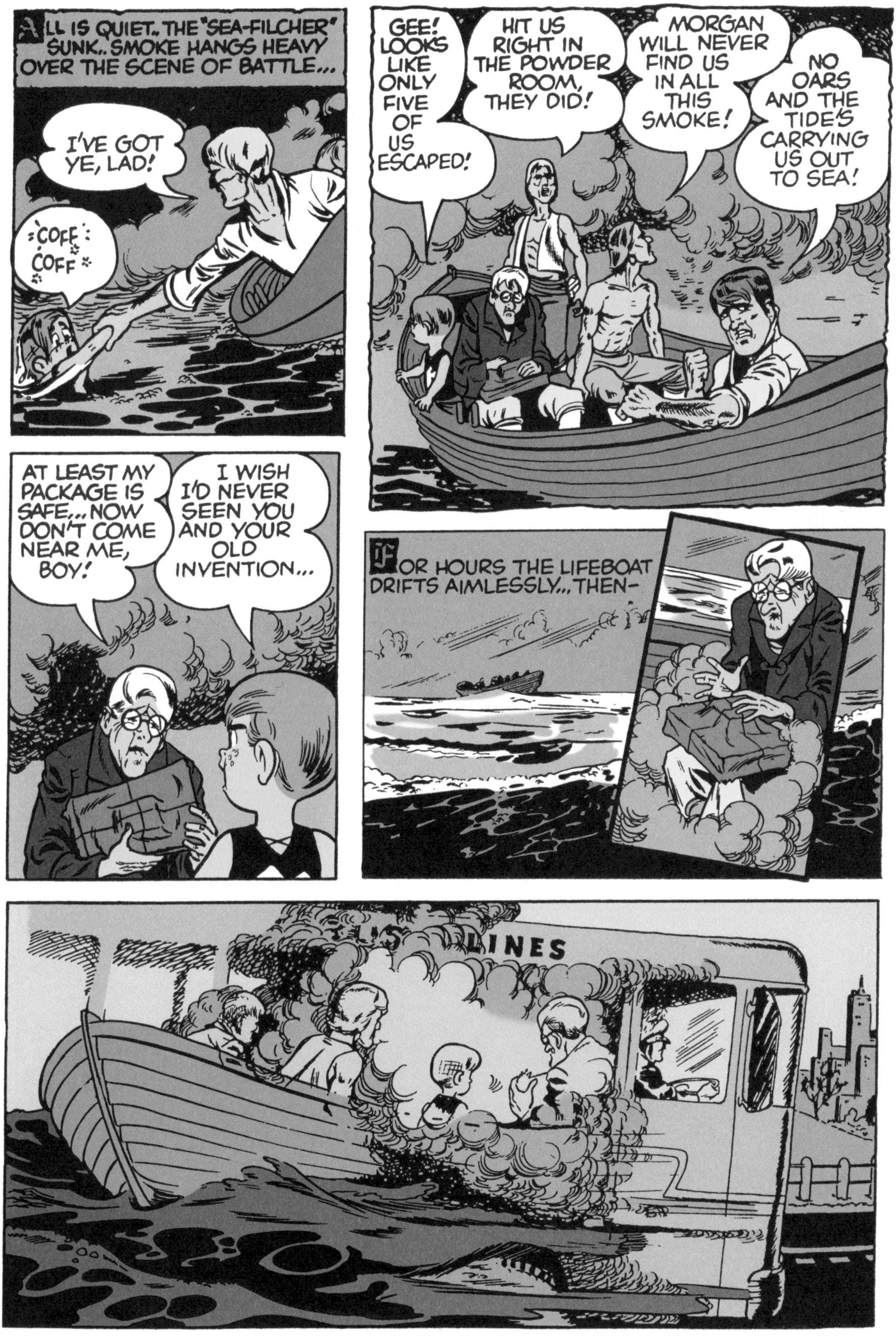
ALL IS QUIET.. THE "SEA-FILCHER" SUNK.. SMOKE HANGS HEAVY OVER THE SCENE OF BATTLE...
I'VE GOT YE, LAD!
COFF COFF
GEE! LOOKS LIKE ONLY FIVE OF US ESCAPED!
HIT US RIGHT IN THE POWDER ROOM, THEY DID!
MORGAN WILL NEVER FIND US IN ALL THIS SMOKE!
NO OARS AND THE TIDE'S CARRYING US OUT TO SEA!
AT LEAST MY PACKAGE IS SAFE... NOW DON'T COME NEAR ME, BOY!
I WISH I'D NEVER SEEN YOU AND YOUR OLD INVENTION...
FOR HOURS THE LIFEBOAT DRIFTS AIMLESSLY... THEN-
LINES

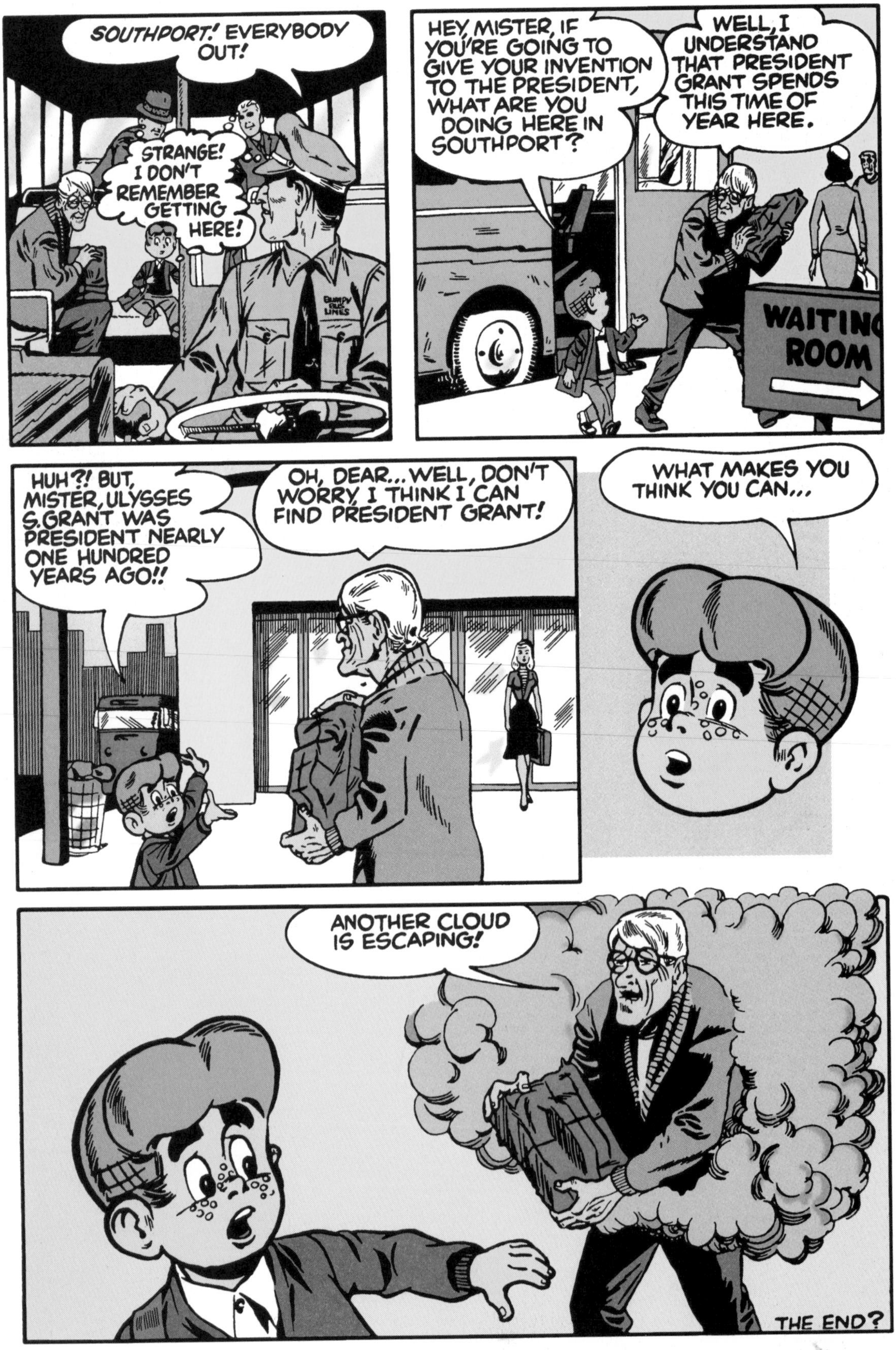
SOUTHPORT! EVERYBODY OUT!
STRANGE! I DON'T REMEMBER GETTING HERE!
BUMPY BUS LINES
HEY, MISTER, IF YOU'RE GOING TO GIVE YOUR INVENTION TO THE PRESIDENT, WHAT ARE YOU DOING HERE IN SOUTHPORT?
WELL, I UNDERSTAND THAT PRESIDENT GRANT SPENDS THIS TIME OF YEAR HERE.
WAITING ROOM
HUH?! BUT, MISTER, ULYSSES S. GRANT WAS PRESIDENT NEARLY ONE HUNDRED YEARS AGO!!
OH, DEAR... WELL, DON'T WORRY, I THINK I CAN FIND PRESIDENT GRANT!
WHAT MAKES YOU THINK YOU CAN...
ANOTHER CLOUD IS ESCAPING!
THE END?

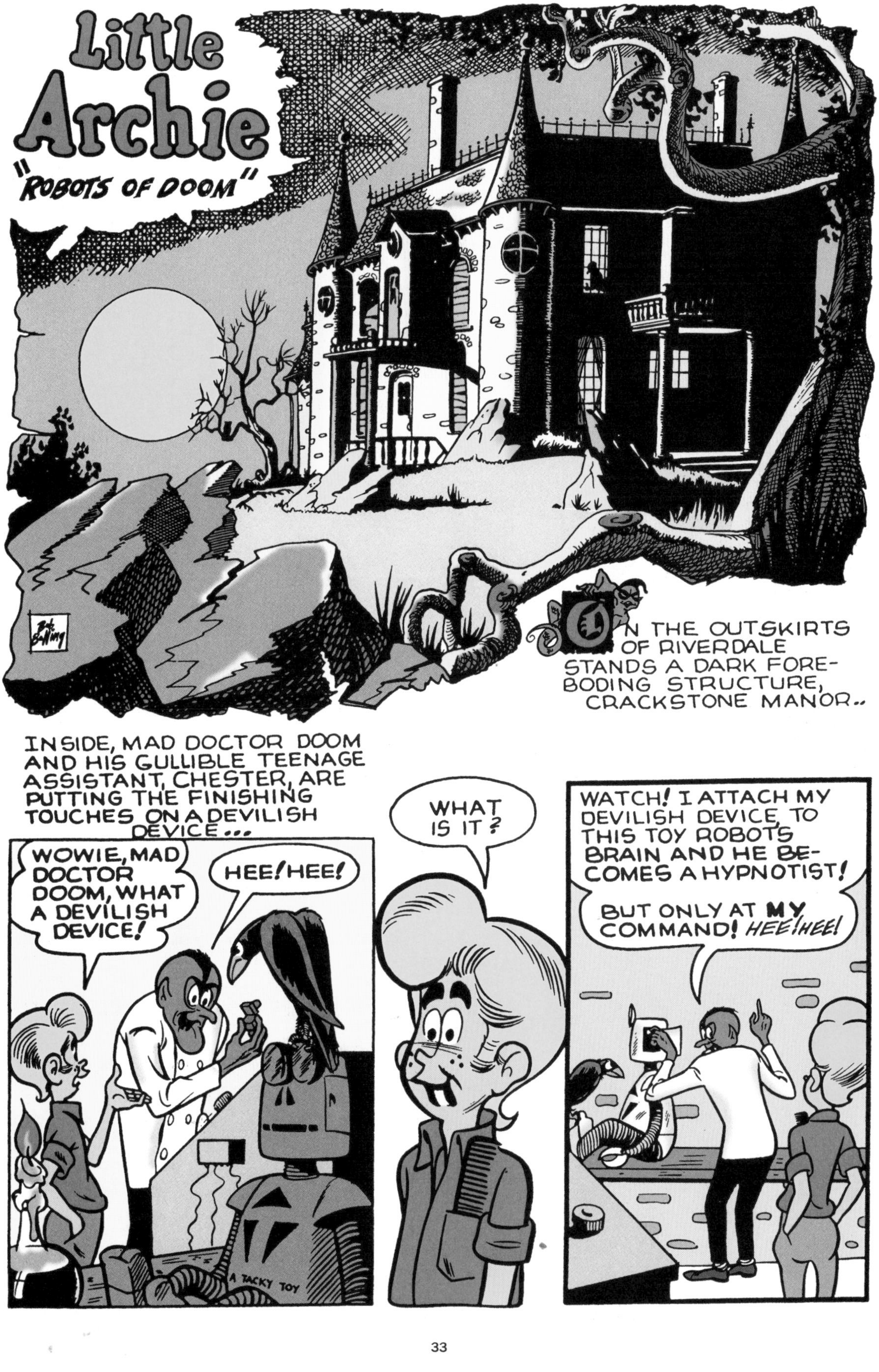
Little Archie
"ROBOTS OF DOOM"
ON THE OUTSKIRTS OF RIVERDALE STANDS A DARK FOREBODING STRUCTURE, CRACKSTONE MANOR..
INSIDE, MAD DOCTOR DOOM AND HIS GULLIBLE TEENAGE ASSISTANT, CHESTER, ARE PUTTING THE FINISHING TOUCHES ON A DEVILISH DEVICE...
WOWIE, MAD DOCTOR DOOM, WHAT A DEVILISH DEVICE!
HEE! HEE!
A TACKY TOY
WHAT IS IT?
WATCH! I ATTACH MY DEVILISH DEVICE, TO THIS TOY ROBOTS BRAIN AND HE BECOMES A HYPNOTIST!
BUT ONLY AT MY COMMAND! HEE! HEE!

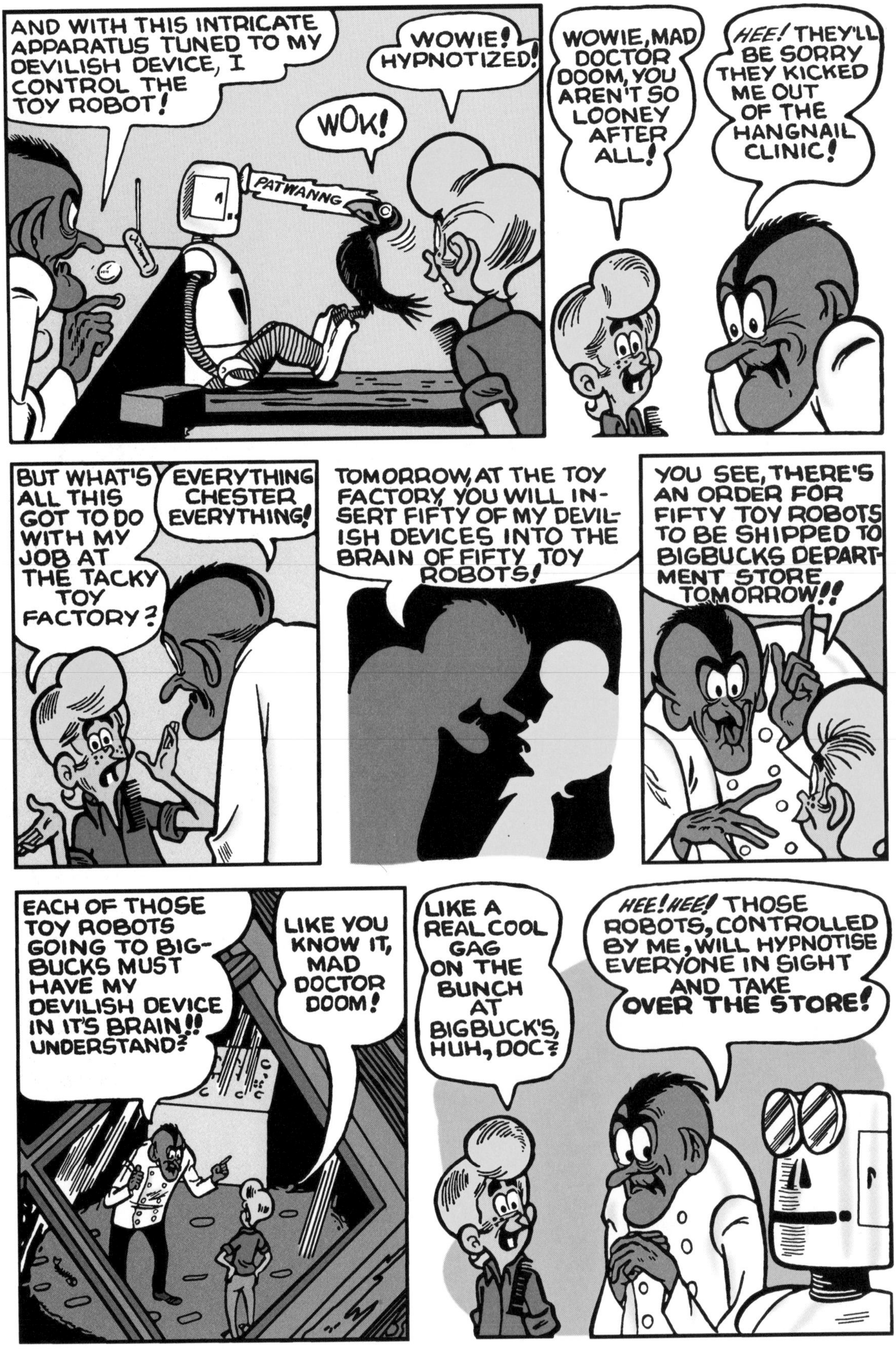
AND WITH THIS INTRICATE APPARATUS TUNED TO MY DEVILISH DEVICE, I CONTROL THE TOY ROBOT!
WOWIE! HYPNOTIZED!
WOK!
PATWANNG
WOWIE, MAD DOCTOR DOOM, YOU AREN'T SO LOONEY AFTER ALL!
HEE! THEY'LL BE SORRY THEY KICKED ME OUT OF THE HANGNAIL CLINIC!
BUT WHAT'S ALL THIS GOT TO DO WITH MY JOB AT THE TACKY TOY FACTORY?
EVERYTHING CHESTER EVERYTHING!
TOMORROW, AT THE TOY FACTORY, YOU WILL INSERT FIFTY OF MY DEVILISH DEVICES INTO THE BRAIN OF FIFTY TOY ROBOTS!
YOU SEE, THERE'S AN ORDER FOR FIFTY TOY ROBOTS TO BE SHIPPED TO BIGBUCKS DEPARTMENT STORE TOMORROW!!
EACH OF THOSE TOY ROBOTS GOING TO BIGBUCKS MUST HAVE MY DEVILISH DEVICE IN IT'S BRAIN!! UNDERSTAND?
LIKE YOU KNOW IT, MAD DOCTOR DOOM!
LIKE A REAL COOL GAG ON THE BUNCH AT BIGBUCK'S, HUH, DOC?
HEE! HEE! THOSE ROBOTS, CONTROLLED BY ME, WILL HYPNOTISE EVERYONE IN SIGHT AND TAKE OVER THE STORE!

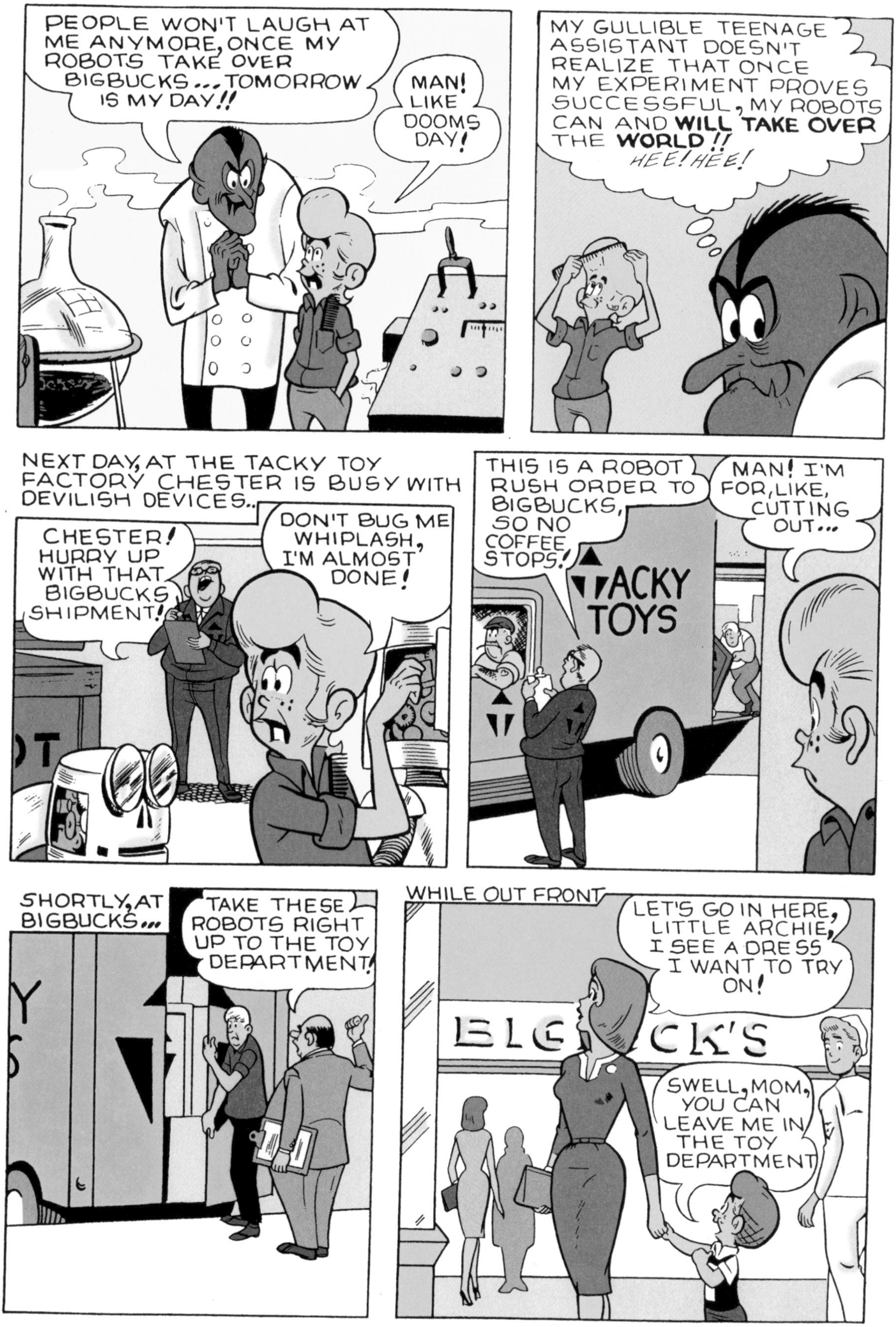
PEOPLE WON'T LAUGH AT ME ANYMORE, ONCE MY ROBOTS TAKE OVER BIGBUCKS... TOMORROW IS MY DAY!!
MAN! LIKE DOOMS DAY!
MY GULLIBLE TEENAGE ASSISTANT DOESN'T REALIZE THAT ONCE MY EXPERIMENT PROVES SUCCESSFUL, MY ROBOTS CAN AND WILL TAKE OVER THE WORLD!!
HEE! HEE!
NEXT DAY, AT THE TACKY TOY FACTORY CHESTER IS BUSY WITH DEVILISH DEVICES..
CHESTER! HURRY UP WITH THAT BIGBUCKS SHIPMENT!
DON'T BUG ME WHIPLASH, I'M ALMOST DONE!
THIS IS A ROBOT RUSH ORDER TO BIGBUCKS, SO NO COFFEE STOPS!
MAN! I'M FOR, LIKE, CUTTING OUT...
ACKY TOYS
SHORTLY, AT BIGBUCKS...
TAKE THESE ROBOTS RIGHT UP TO THE TOY DEPARTMENT!
WHILE OUT FRONT
LET'S GO IN HERE, LITTLE ARCHIE, I SEE A DRESS I WANT TO TRY ON!
SWELL, MOM, YOU CAN LEAVE ME IN THE TOY DEPARTMENT

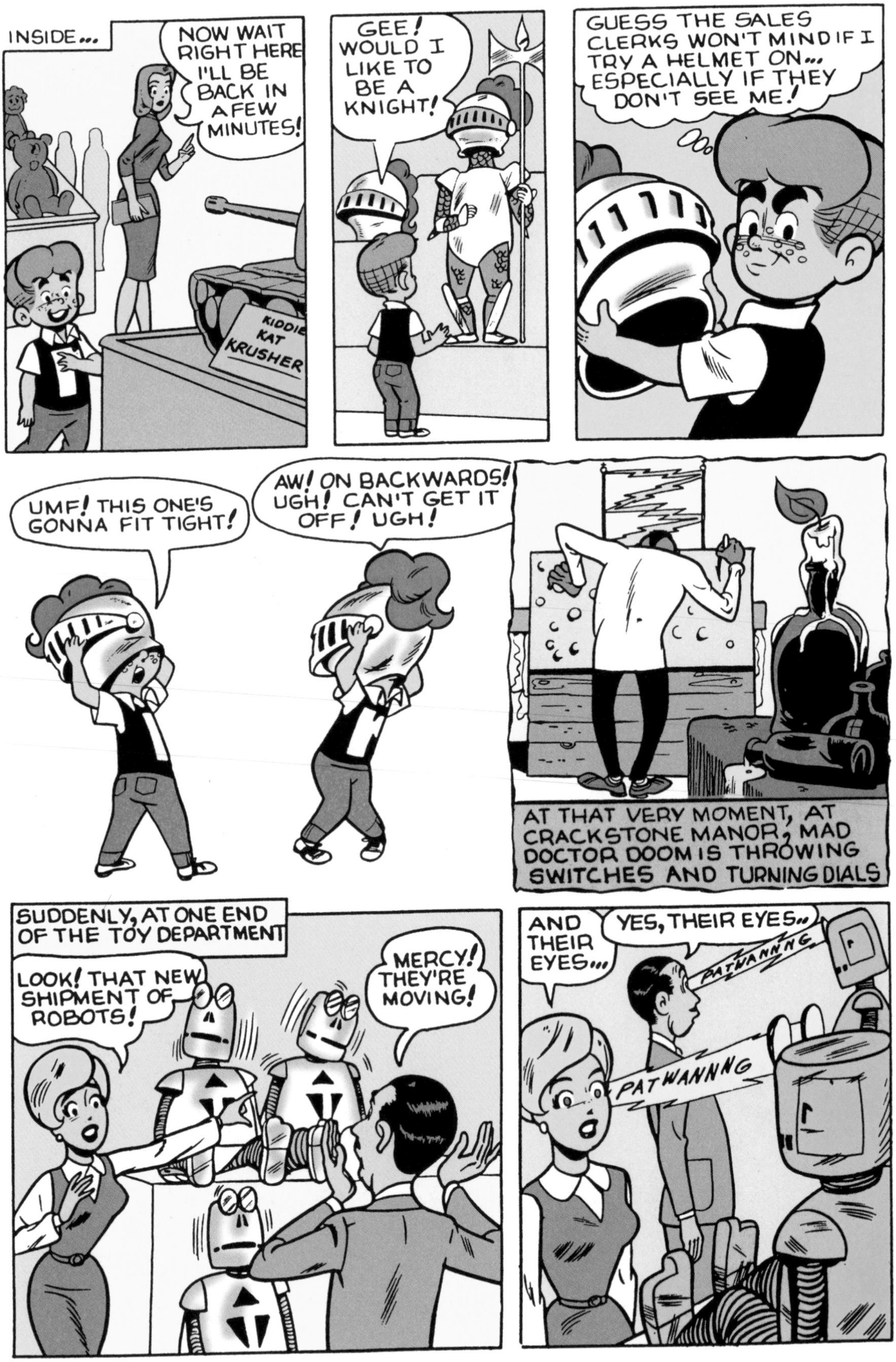
INSIDE...
NOW WAIT RIGHT HERE I'LL BE BACK IN A FEW MINUTES!
KIDDIE KAT KRUSHER
GEE! WOULD I LIKE TO BE A KNIGHT!
GUESS THE SALES CLERKS WON'T MIND IF I TRY A HELMET ON... ESPECIALLY IF THEY DON'T SEE ME!
UMF! THIS ONE'S GONNA FIT TIGHT!
AW! ON BACKWARDS! UGH! CAN'T GET IT OFF! UGH!
AT THAT VERY MOMENT, AT CRACKSTONE MANOR, MAD DOCTOR DOOM IS THROWING SWITCHES AND TURNING DIALS
SUDDENLY, AT ONE END OF THE TOY DEPARTMENT
LOOK! THAT NEW SHIPMENT OF ROBOTS!
MERCY! THEY'RE MOVING!
AND THEIR EYES...
YES, THEIR EYES..
PATWANNNG
PATWANNNG

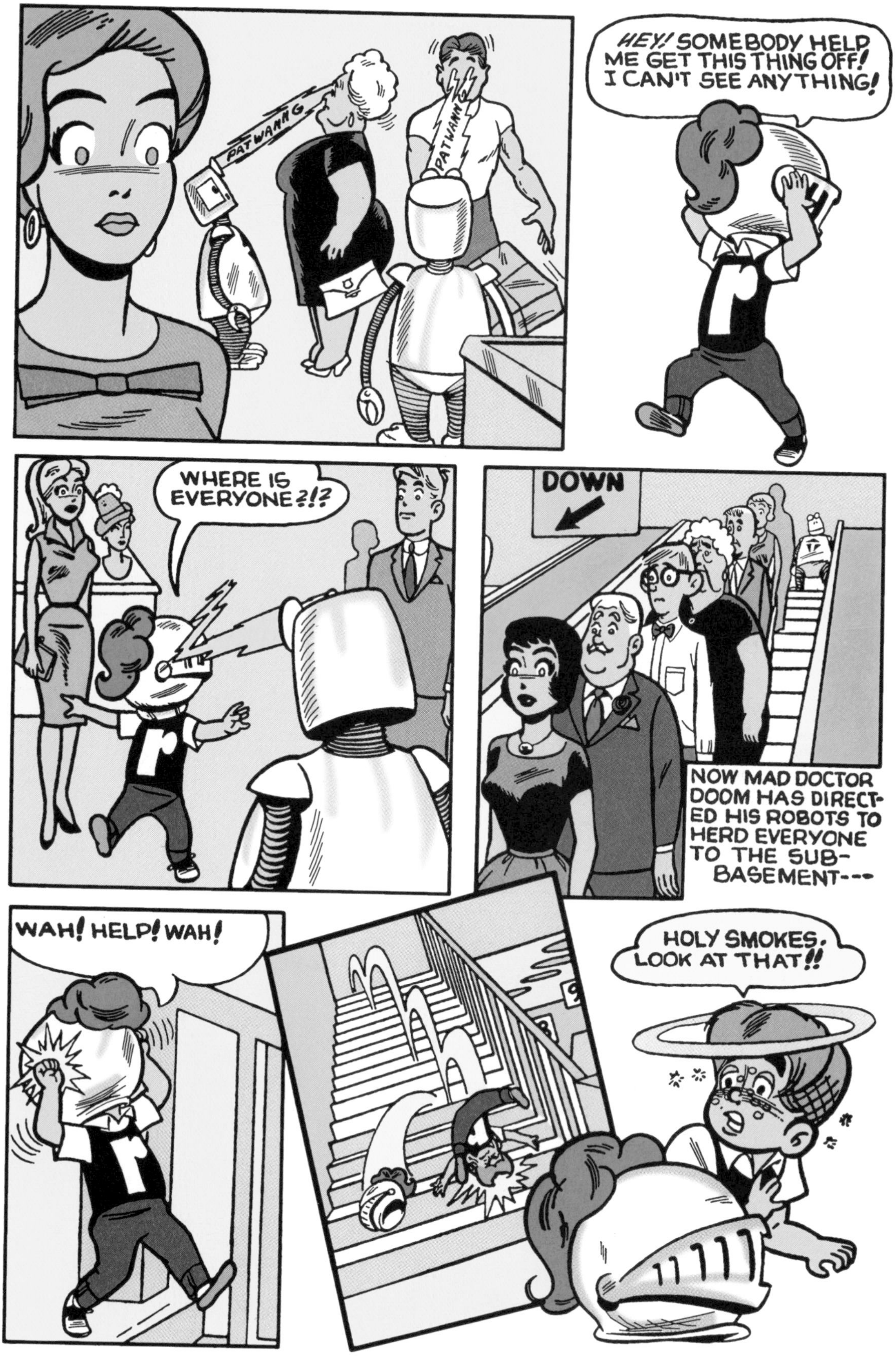
PATWANNG
PATWANN
HEY! SOMEBODY HELP ME GET THIS THING OFF! I CAN'T SEE ANYTHING!
WHERE IS EVERYONE ?!?
DOWN
NOW MAD DOCTOR DOOM HAS DIRECTED HIS ROBOTS TO HERD EVERYONE TO THE SUB-BASEMENT---
WAH! HELP! WAH!
HOLY SMOKES. LOOK AT THAT!!

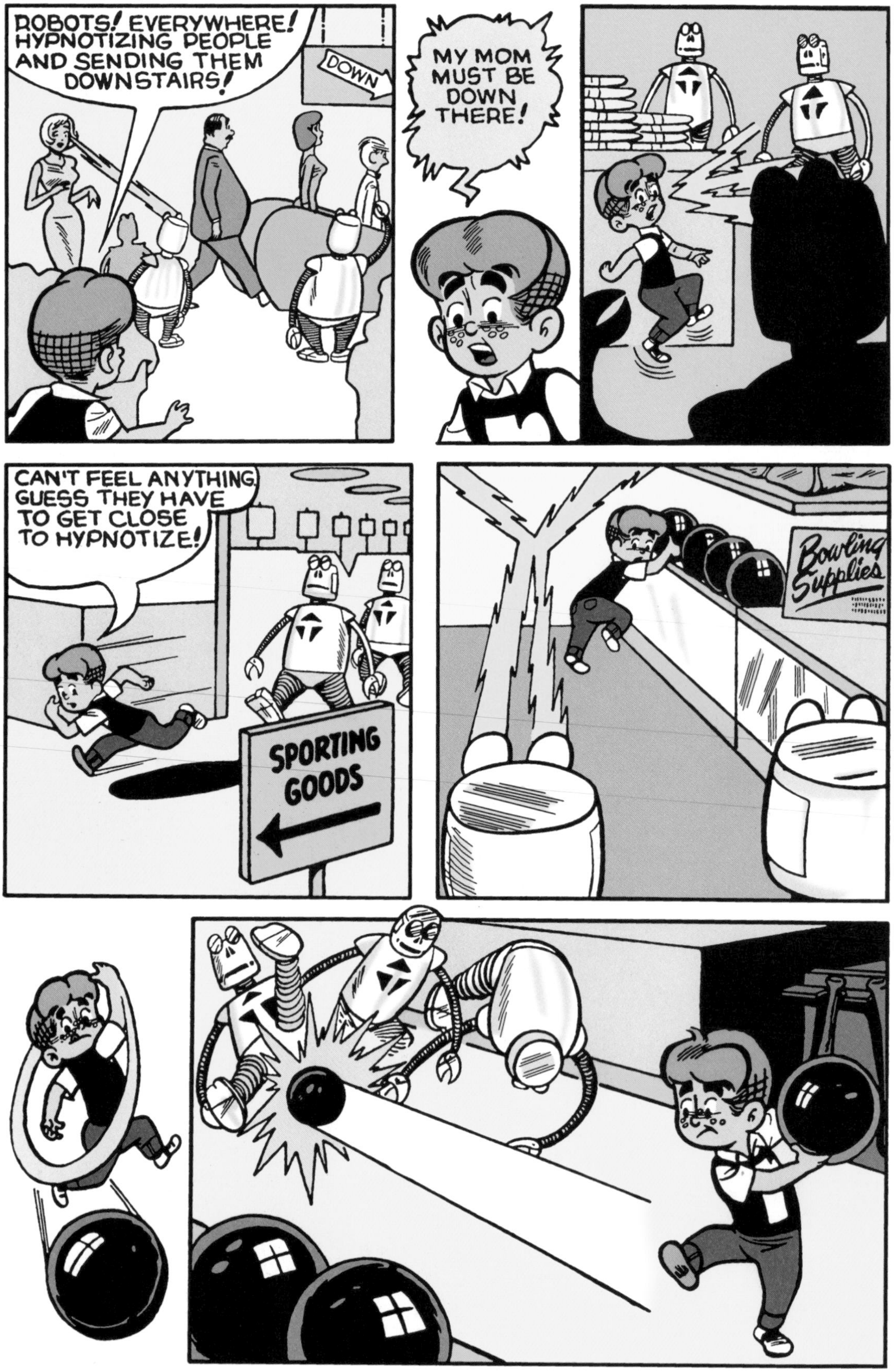
ROBOTS! EVERYWHERE! HYPNOTIZING PEOPLE AND SENDING THEM DOWNSTAIRS!
DOWN
MY MOM MUST BE DOWN THERE!
CAN'T FEEL ANYTHING. GUESS THEY HAVE TO GET CLOSE TO HYPNOTIZE!
SPORTING GOODS
Bowling Supplies

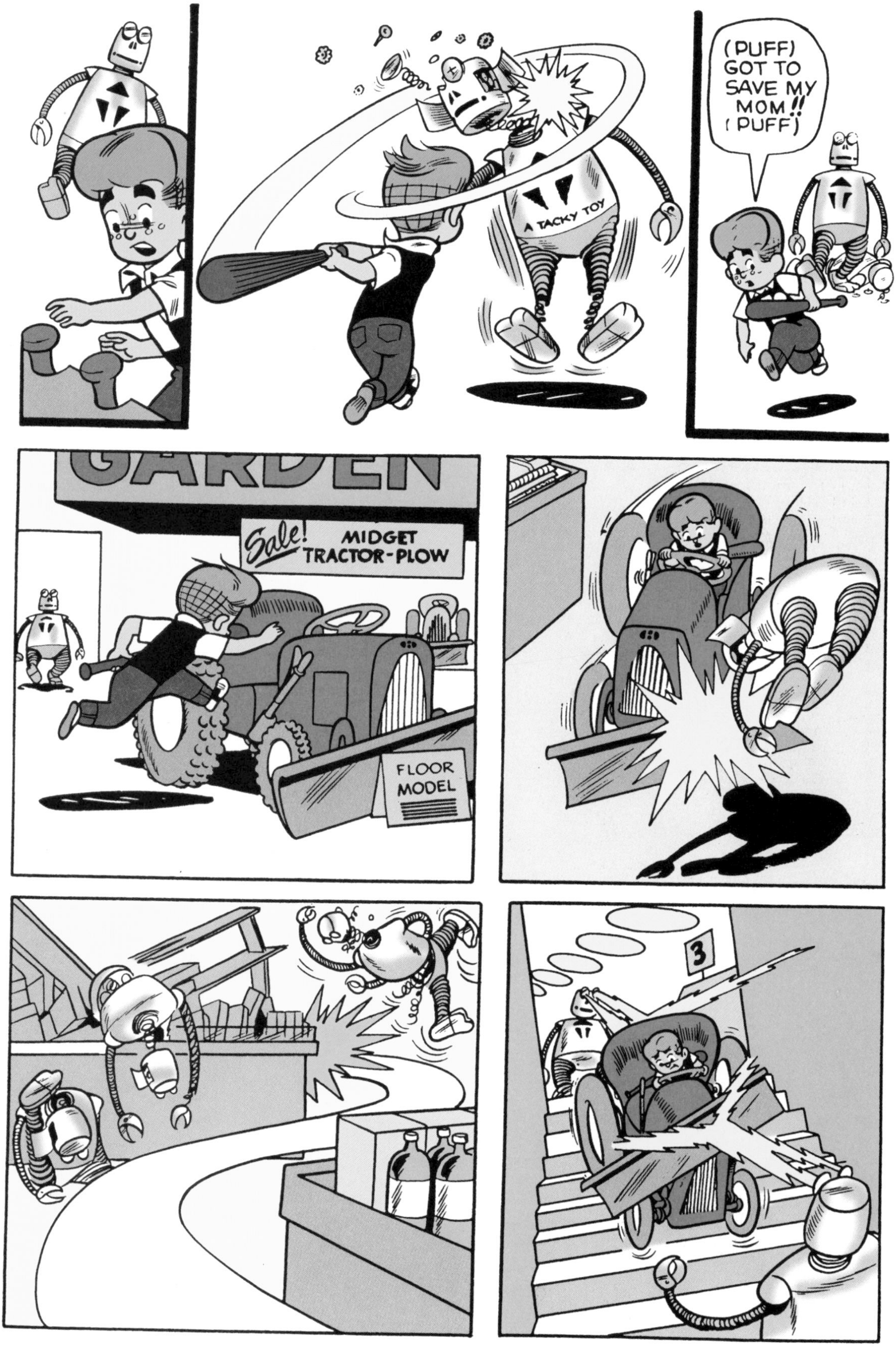
A TACKY TOY
(PUFF) GOT TO SAVE MY MOM!! (PUFF)
GARDEN
Sale! MIDGET TRACTOR-PLOW
FLOOR MODEL
3

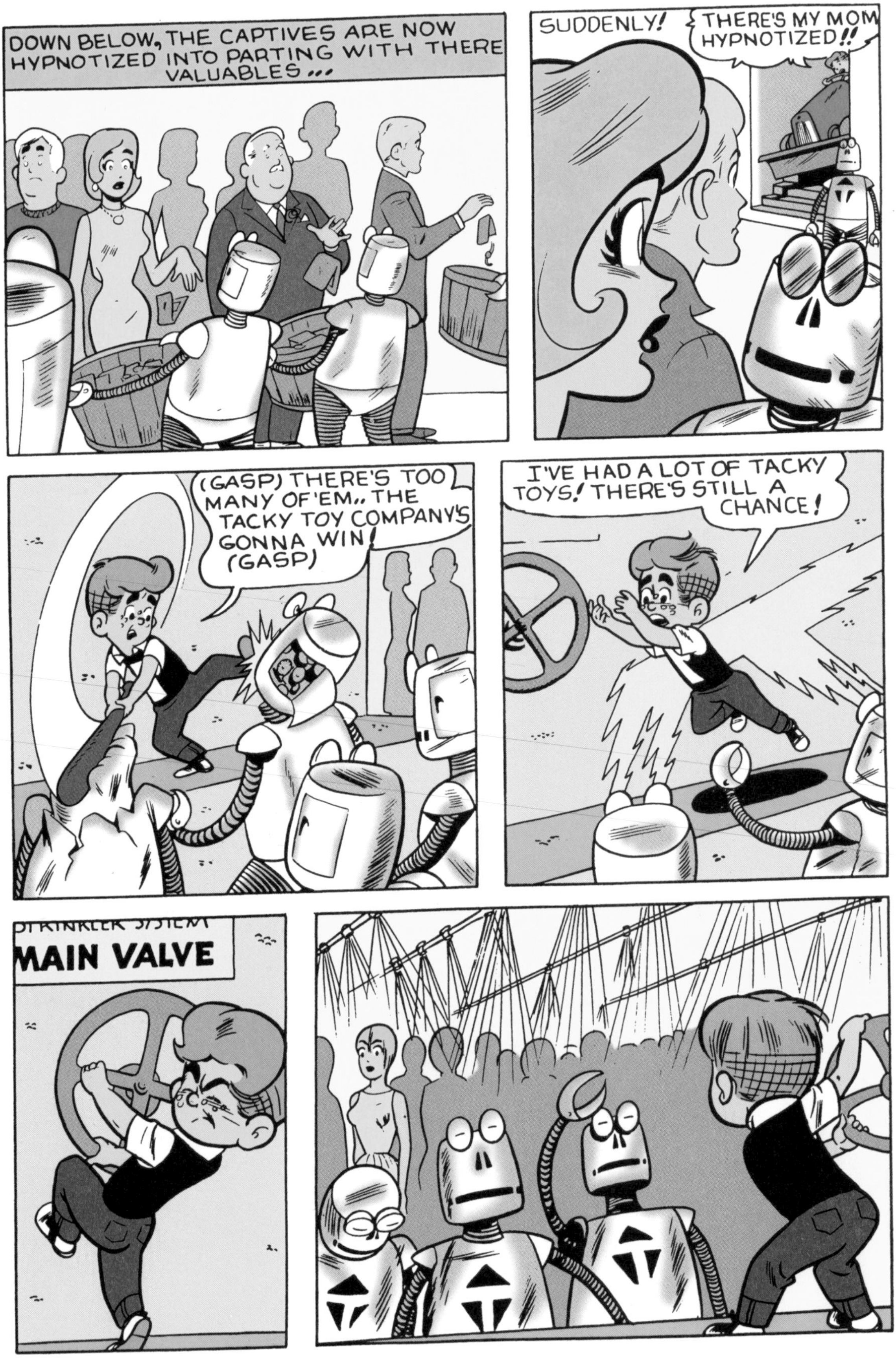
DOWN BELOW, THE CAPTIVES ARE NOW HYPNOTIZED INTO PARTING WITH THERE VALUABLES...
SUDDENLY!
THERE'S MY MOM HYPNOTIZED!!
(GASP) THERE'S TOO MANY OF 'EM.. THE TACKY TOY COMPANY'S GONNA WIN! (GASP)
I'VE HAD A LOT OF TACKY TOYS! THERE'S STILL A CHANCE!
MAIN VALVE

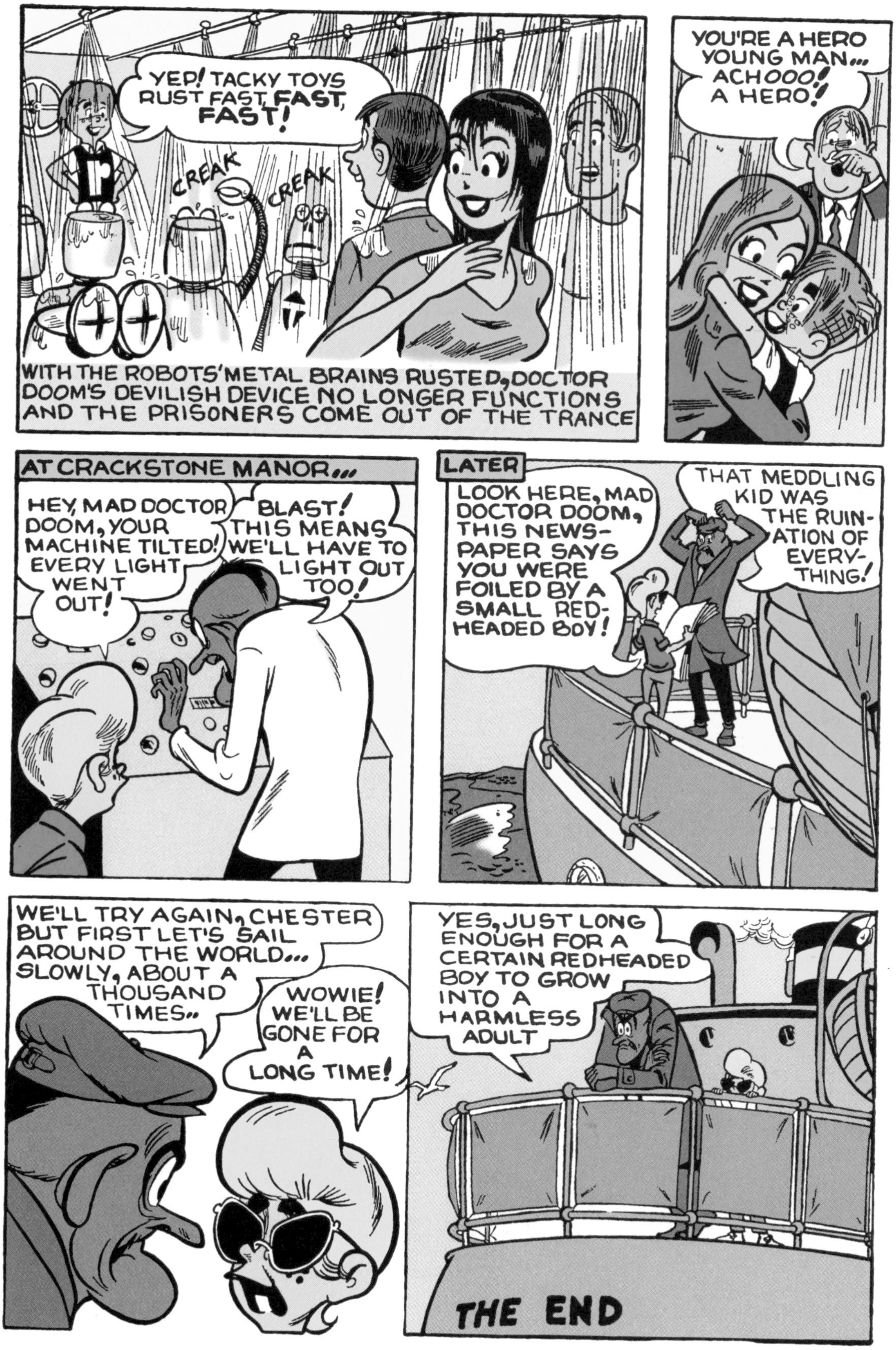
YEP! TACKY TOYS RUST FAST, FAST, FAST!
CREAK
CREAK
WITH THE ROBOTS' METAL BRAINS RUSTED, DOCTOR DOOM'S DEVILISH DEVICE NO LONGER FUNCTIONS AND THE PRISONERS COME OUT OF THE TRANCE
YOU'RE A HERO YOUNG MAN... ACHOOO! A HERO!
AT CRACKSTONE MANOR...
HEY, MAD DOCTOR DOOM, YOUR MACHINE TILTED! EVERY LIGHT WENT OUT!
BLAST! THIS MEANS WE'LL HAVE TO LIGHT OUT TOO!
LATER
LOOK HERE, MAD DOCTOR DOOM, THIS NEWS-PAPER SAYS YOU WERE FOILED BY A SMALL RED-HEADED BOY!
THAT MEDDLING KID WAS THE RUIN-ATION OF EVERY-THING!
WE'LL TRY AGAIN, CHESTER BUT FIRST LET'S SAIL AROUND THE WORLD... SLOWLY, ABOUT A THOUSAND TIMES..
WOWIE! WE'LL BE GONE FOR A LONG TIME!
YES, JUST LONG ENOUGH FOR A CERTAIN REDHEADED BOY TO GROW INTO A HARMLESS ADULT
THE END

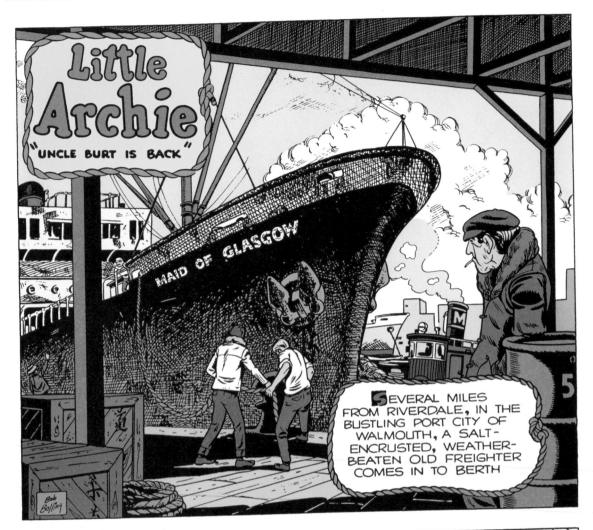

Little Archie

"UNCLE BURT IS BACK"

MAID OF GLASGOW

Bob Bolling

SEVERAL MILES FROM RIVERDALE, IN THE BUSTLING PORT CITY OF WALMOUTH, A SALT-ENCRUSTED, WEATHER-BEATEN OLD FREIGHTER COMES IN TO BERTH

IT'S UNCLE BURT!! HIS SHIP'S DOCKED IN WALMOUTH FOR THREE DAYS!

UNCLE BURT?! OH, NO!

OH, BOY! UNCLE BURT!

NOW CATCH THE NEXT BUS RIGHT OUT HERE!

MY UNCLE'S A REAL HERO!

(GROAN) THAT SEAFARING YARN SPINNER!

BUGS NIP S

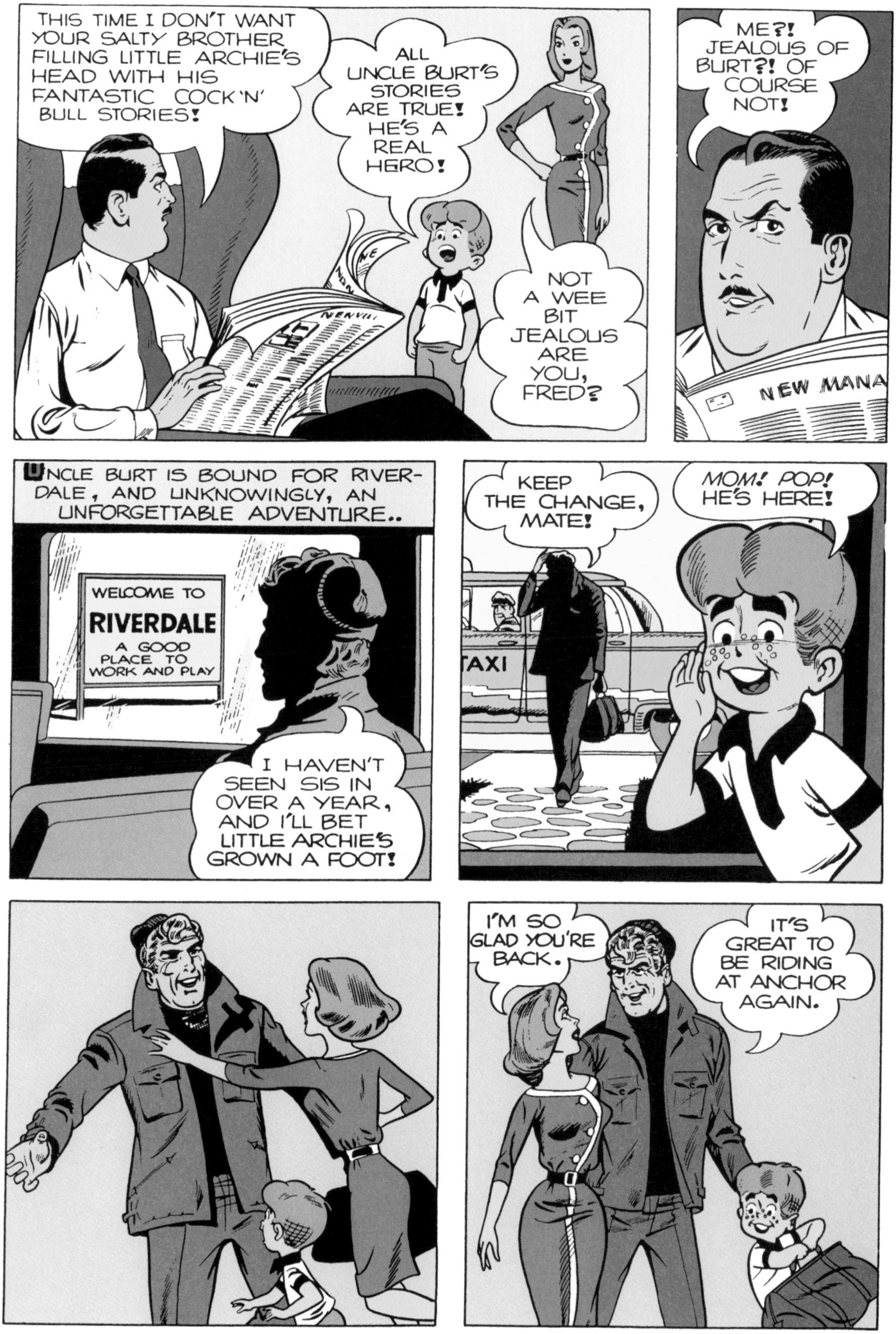
THIS TIME I DON'T WANT YOUR SALTY BROTHER FILLING LITTLE ARCHIE'S HEAD WITH HIS FANTASTIC COCK 'N' BULL STORIES!
ALL UNCLE BURT'S STORIES ARE TRUE! HE'S A REAL HERO!
NOT A WEE BIT JEALOUS ARE YOU, FRED?
ME?! JEALOUS OF BURT?! OF COURSE NOT!
NEW MANA
UNCLE BURT IS BOUND FOR RIVER-DALE, AND UNKNOWINGLY, AN UNFORGETTABLE ADVENTURE..
WELCOME TO RIVERDALE A GOOD PLACE TO WORK AND PLAY
I HAVEN'T SEEN SIS IN OVER A YEAR, AND I'LL BET LITTLE ARCHIE'S GROWN A FOOT!
KEEP THE CHANGE, MATE!
MOM! POP! HE'S HERE!
TAXI
I'M SO GLAD YOU'RE BACK.
IT'S GREAT TO BE RIDING AT ANCHOR AGAIN.

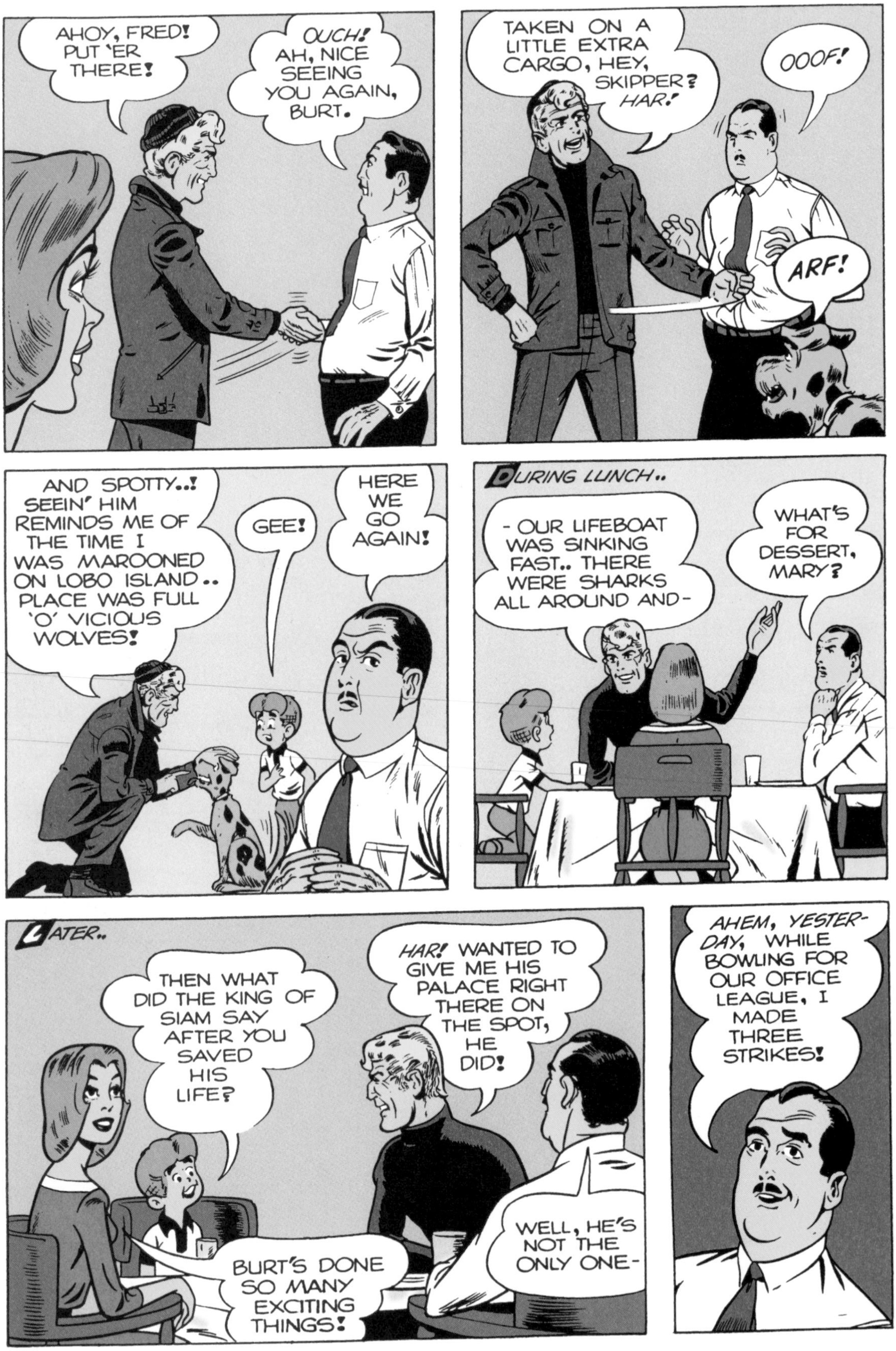
AHOY, FRED! PUT 'ER THERE!
OUCH! AH, NICE SEEING YOU AGAIN, BURT.
TAKEN ON A LITTLE EXTRA CARGO, HEY, SKIPPER? HAR!
OOOF!
ARF!
AND SPOTTY..! SEEIN' HIM REMINDS ME OF THE TIME I WAS MAROONED ON LOBO ISLAND.. PLACE WAS FULL 'O' VICIOUS WOLVES!
GEE!
HERE WE GO AGAIN!
DURING LUNCH..
- OUR LIFEBOAT WAS SINKING FAST.. THERE WERE SHARKS ALL AROUND AND-
WHAT'S FOR DESSERT, MARY?
LATER..
THEN WHAT DID THE KING OF SIAM SAY AFTER YOU SAVED HIS LIFE?
HAR! WANTED TO GIVE ME HIS PALACE RIGHT THERE ON THE SPOT, HE DID!
BURT'S DONE SO MANY EXCITING THINGS!
WELL, HE'S NOT THE ONLY ONE-
AHEM, YESTER-DAY, WHILE BOWLING FOR OUR OFFICE LEAGUE, I MADE THREE STRIKES!

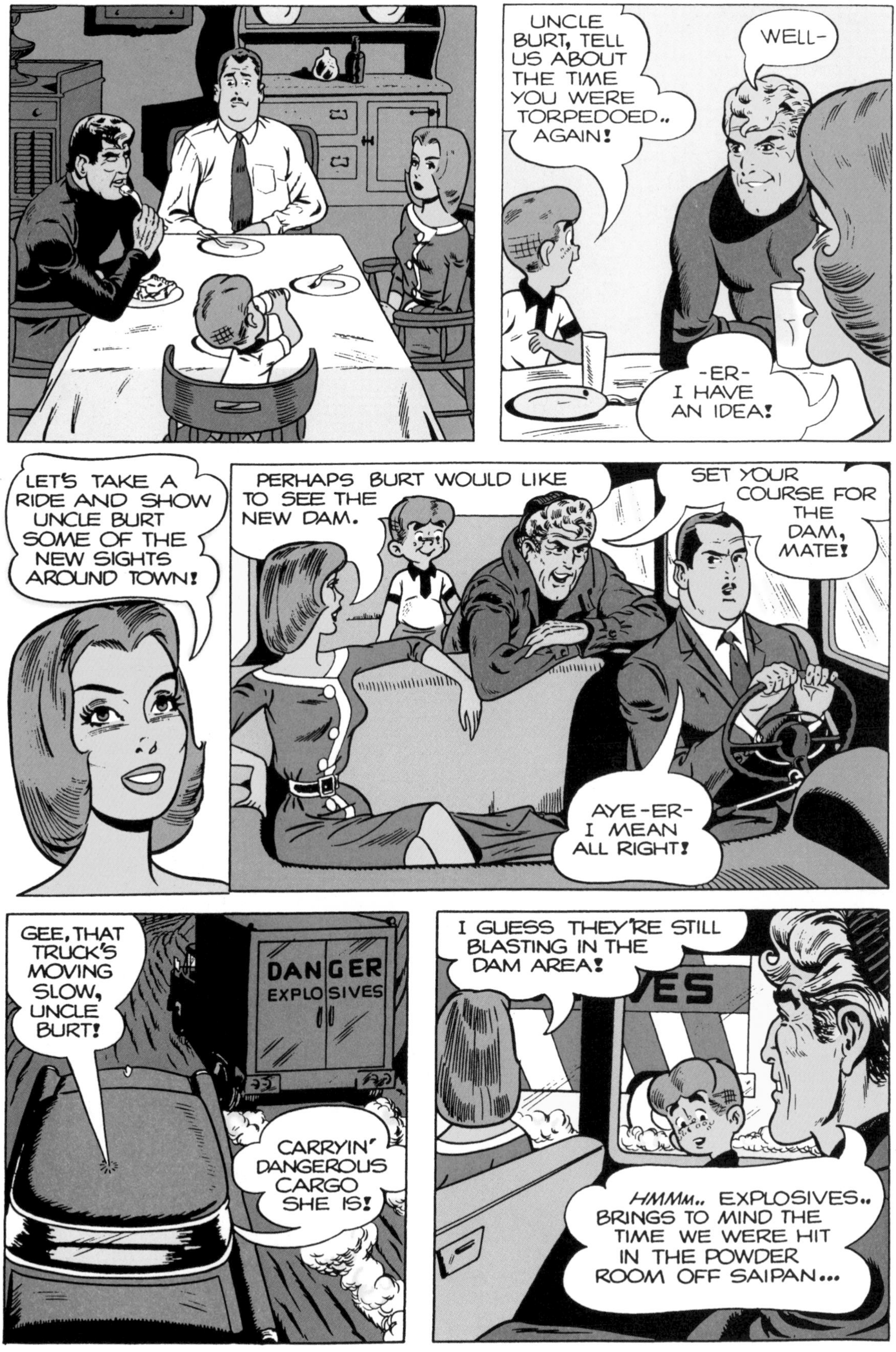
UNCLE BURT, TELL US ABOUT THE TIME YOU WERE TORPEDOED.. AGAIN!
WELL-
-ER- I HAVE AN IDEA!
LET'S TAKE A RIDE AND SHOW UNCLE BURT SOME OF THE NEW SIGHTS AROUND TOWN!
PERHAPS BURT WOULD LIKE TO SEE THE NEW DAM.
SET YOUR COURSE FOR THE DAM, MATE!
AYE-ER- I MEAN ALL RIGHT!
GEE, THAT TRUCK'S MOVING SLOW, UNCLE BURT!
DANGER EXPLOSIVES
CARRYIN' DANGEROUS CARGO SHE IS!
I GUESS THEY'RE STILL BLASTING IN THE DAM AREA!
HMMM.. EXPLOSIVES.. BRINGS TO MIND THE TIME WE WERE HIT IN THE POWDER ROOM OFF SAIPAN...

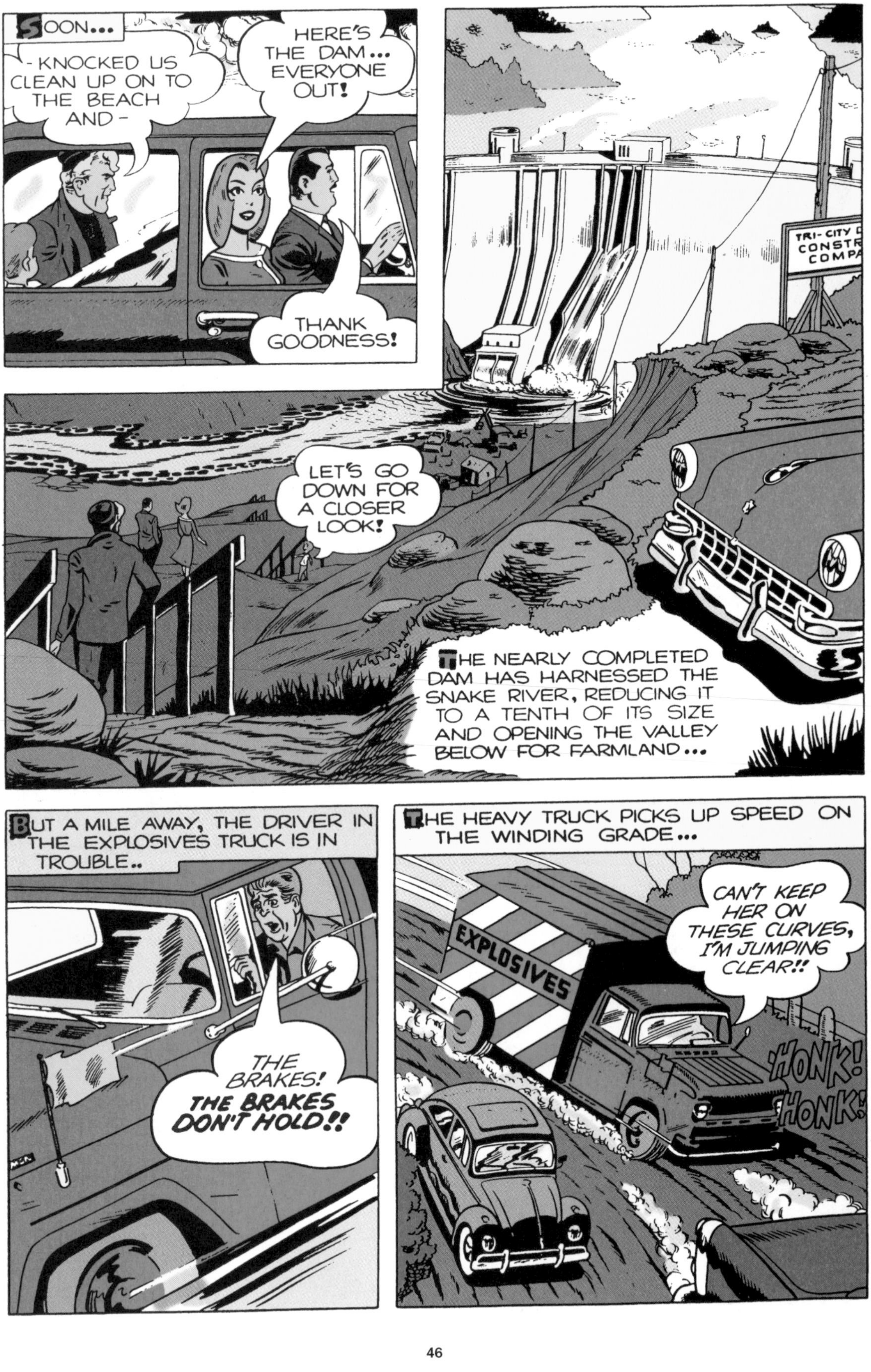
SOON...
-KNOCKED US CLEAN UP ON TO THE BEACH AND-
HERE'S THE DAM... EVERYONE OUT!
THANK GOODNESS!
TRI-CITY
CONSTR
COMPA
LET'S GO DOWN FOR A CLOSER LOOK!
THE NEARLY COMPLETED DAM HAS HARNESSED THE SNAKE RIVER, REDUCING IT TO A TENTH OF ITS SIZE AND OPENING THE VALLEY BELOW FOR FARMLAND...
BUT A MILE AWAY, THE DRIVER IN THE EXPLOSIVES TRUCK IS IN TROUBLE..
THE BRAKES! THE BRAKES DON'T HOLD!!
THE HEAVY TRUCK PICKS UP SPEED ON THE WINDING GRADE...
EXPLOSIVES
CAN'T KEEP HER ON THESE CURVES, I'M JUMPING CLEAR!!
HONK! HONK!

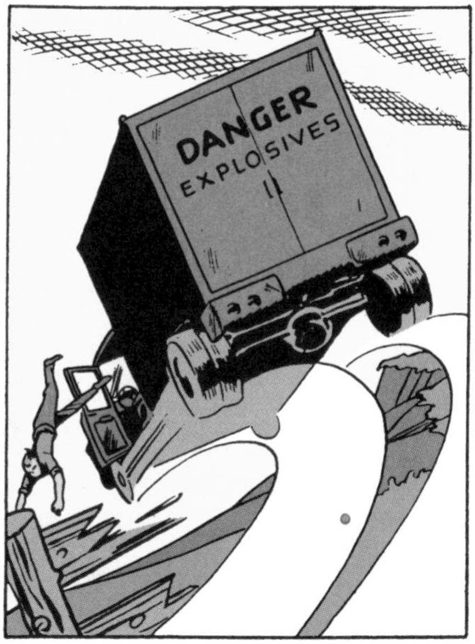
DANGER
EXPLOSIVES

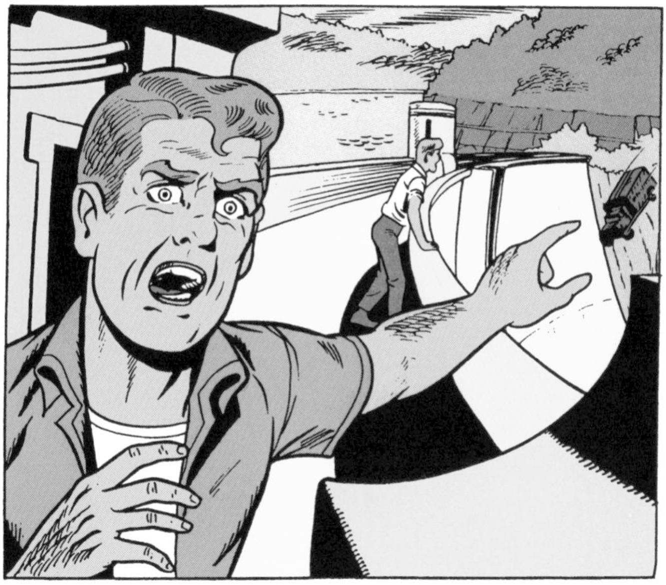

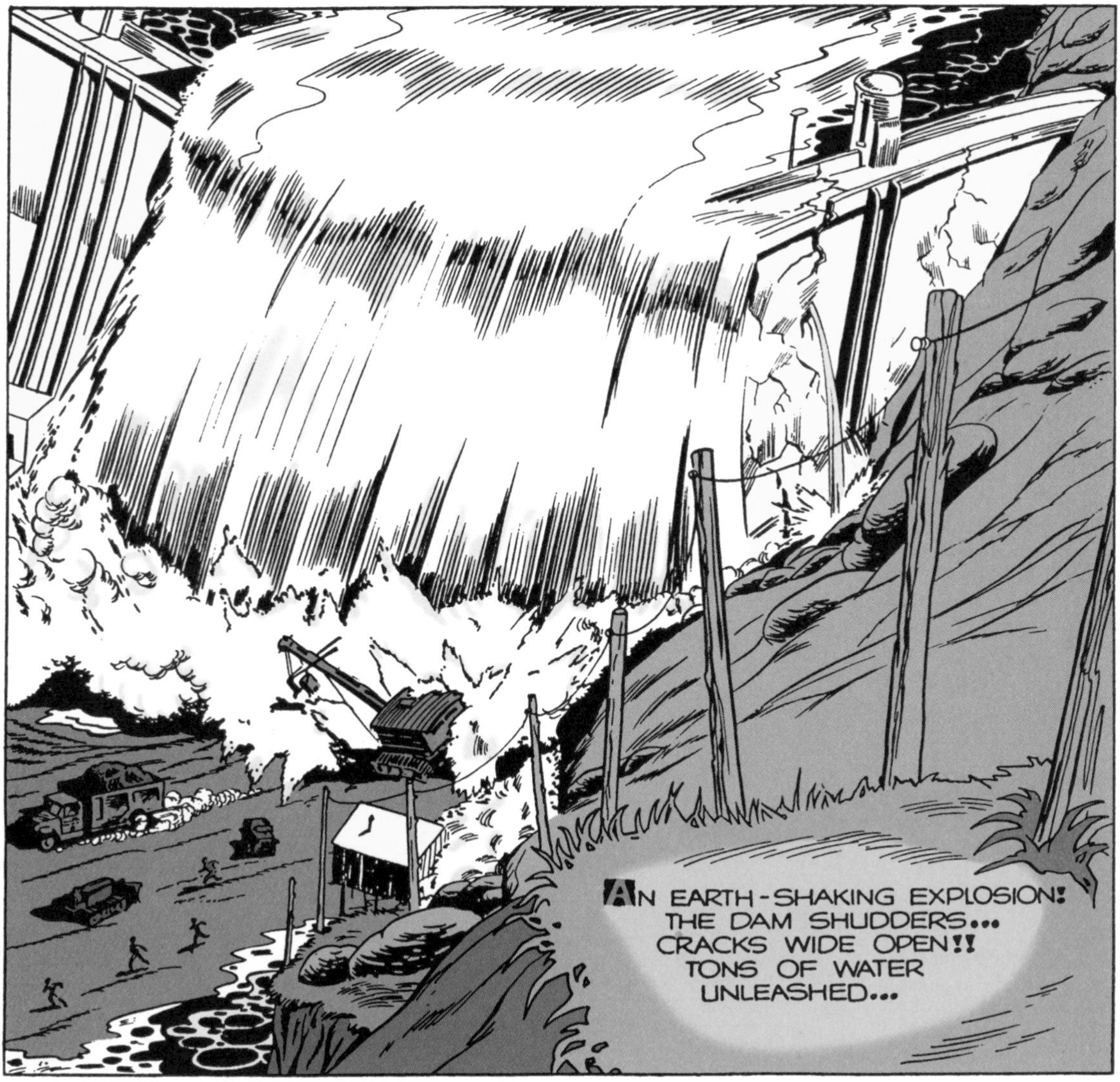
AN EARTH-SHAKING EXPLOSION! THE DAM SHUDDERS... CRACKS WIDE OPEN!! TONS OF WATER UNLEASHED...

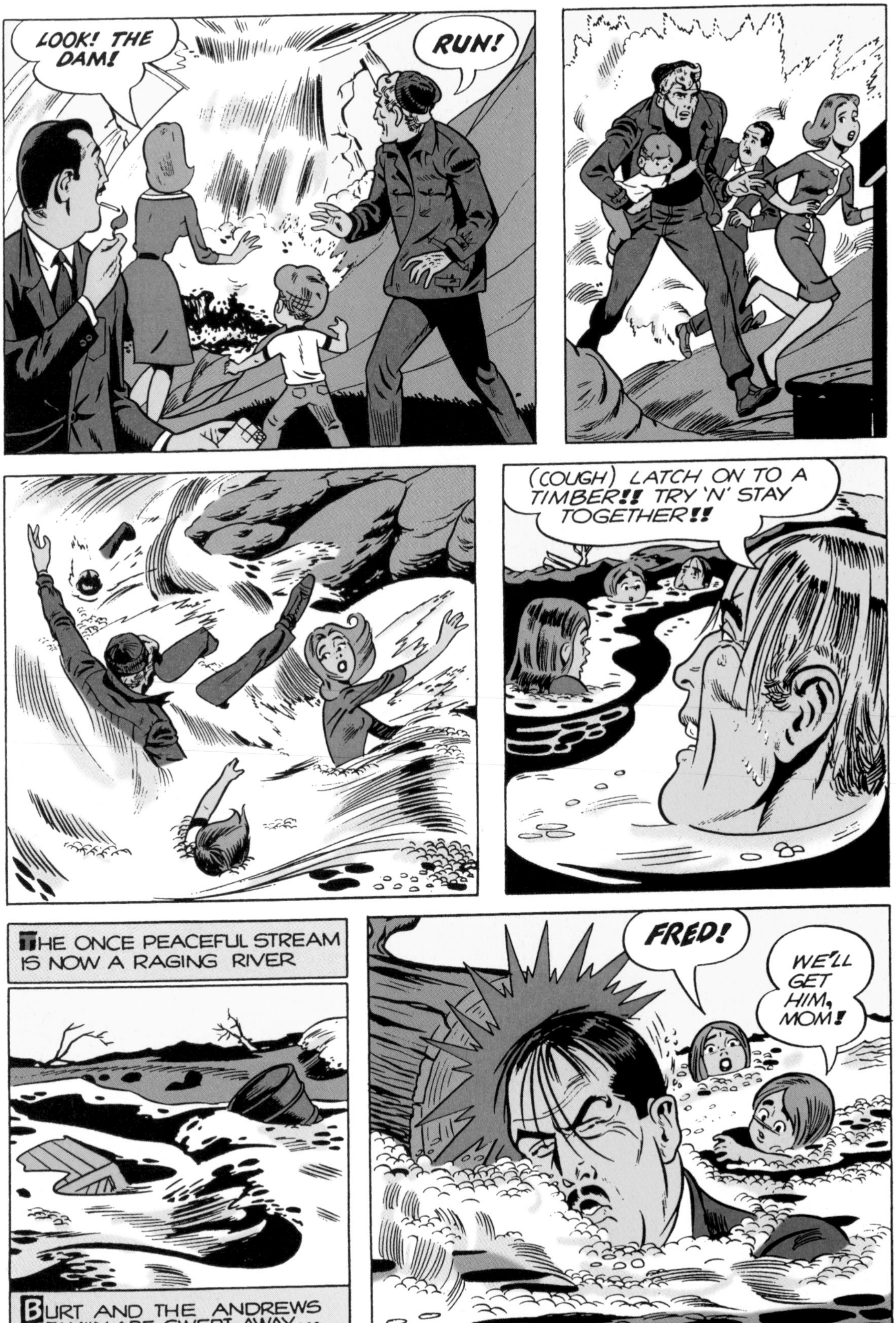
LOOK! THE DAM!
RUN!
(COUGH) LATCH ON TO A TIMBER!! TRY 'N' STAY TOGETHER!!
THE ONCE PEACEFUL STREAM IS NOW A RAGING RIVER
BURT AND THE ANDREWS FAMILY ARE SWEPT AWAY...
FRED!
WE'LL GET HIM, MOM!

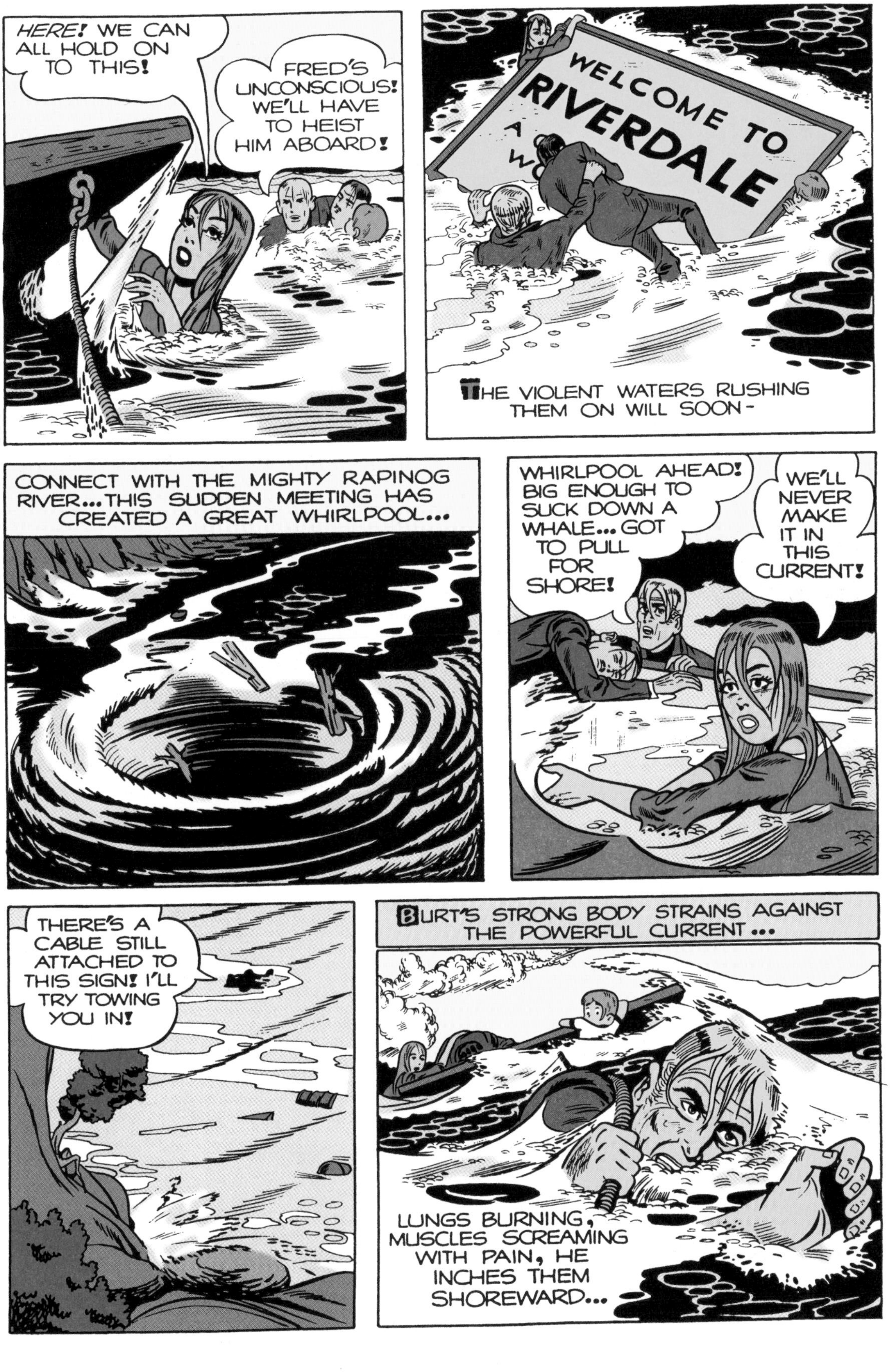
HERE! WE CAN ALL HOLD ON TO THIS!
FRED'S UNCONSCIOUS! WE'LL HAVE TO HEIST HIM ABOARD!
WELCOME TO RIVERDALE
THE VIOLENT WATERS RUSHING THEM ON WILL SOON-
CONNECT WITH THE MIGHTY RAPINOG RIVER... THIS SUDDEN MEETING HAS CREATED A GREAT WHIRLPOOL...
WHIRLPOOL AHEAD! BIG ENOUGH TO SUCK DOWN A WHALE... GOT TO PULL FOR SHORE!
WE'LL NEVER MAKE IT IN THIS CURRENT!
THERE'S A CABLE STILL ATTACHED TO THIS SIGN! I'LL TRY TOWING YOU IN!
BURT'S STRONG BODY STRAINS AGAINST THE POWERFUL CURRENT...
LUNGS BURNING, MUSCLES SCREAMING WITH PAIN, HE INCHES THEM SHOREWARD...

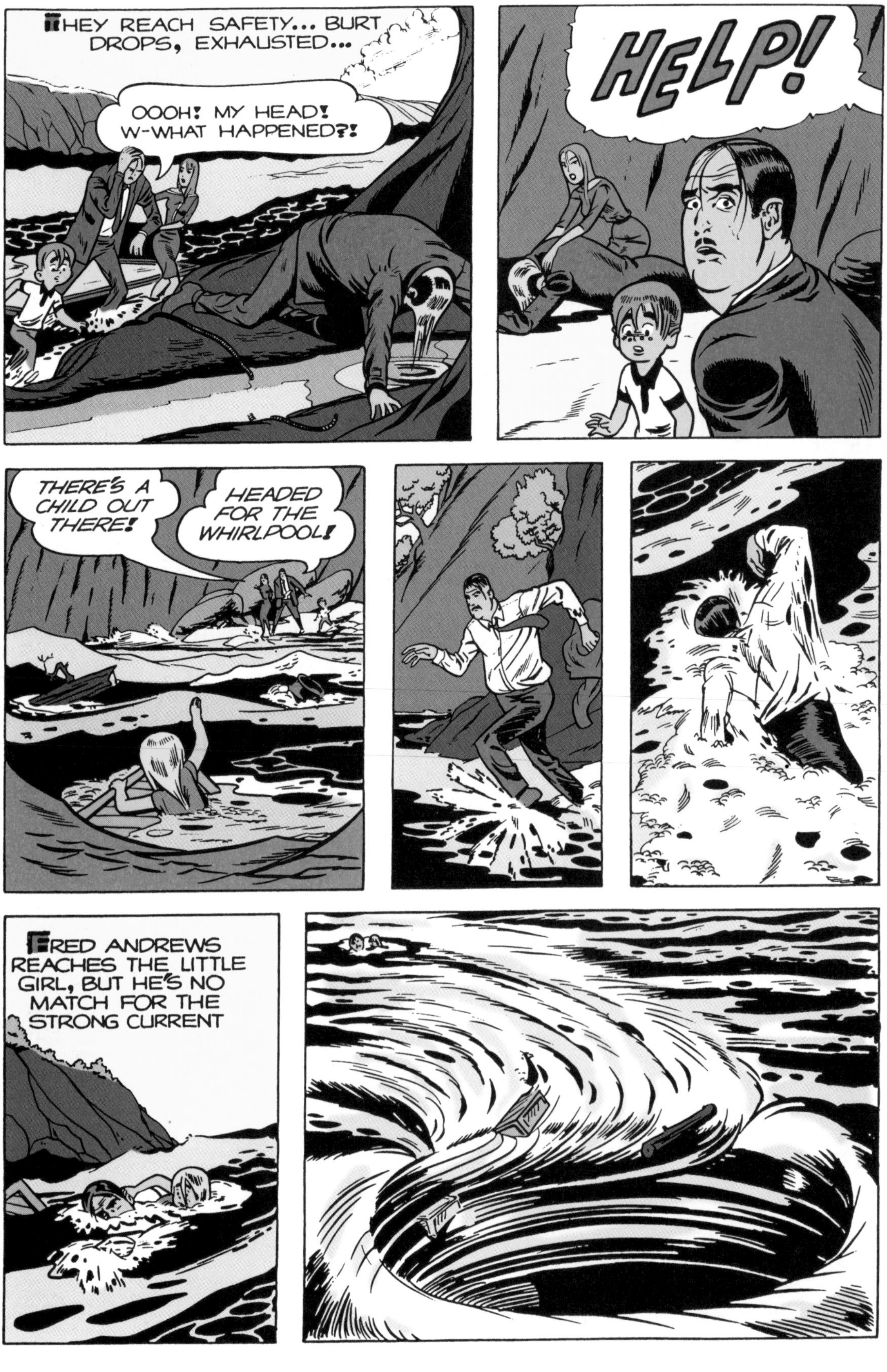
THEY REACH SAFETY... BURT DROPS, EXHAUSTED...
OOOH! MY HEAD! W-WHAT HAPPENED?!
HELP!
THERE'S A CHILD OUT THERE!
HEADED FOR THE WHIRLPOOL!
FRED ANDREWS REACHES THE LITTLE GIRL, BUT HE'S NO MATCH FOR THE STRONG CURRENT

SUDDENLY, THE BANK HIGH ABOVE THE SWOLLEN RIVER BEGINS TO TREMBLE...

THE VIOLENT ONRUSH OF FLOOD WATERS HAS UNDERCUT THE BANK, WEAKENING IT AND CAUSING -

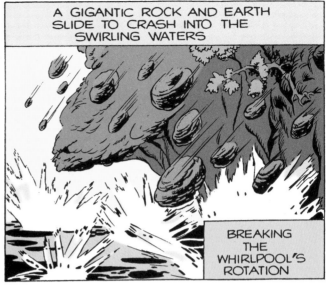

A GIGANTIC ROCK AND EARTH SLIDE TO CRASH INTO THE SWIRLING WATERS

BREAKING THE WHIRLPOOL'S ROTATION

THE WHIRLPOOL'S INTENDED VICTIMS ARE QUICKLY BORNE OUT ON TO THE BROAD RAPINOG RIVER, WHERE -

A RESCUE CRAFT, HURRYING TO THE SCENE OF THE DISTASTER, PICKS THEM UP

LATER, WHEN ALL ARE REUNITED...

SON, YOUR DAD MAY BE A QUIET MAN, BUT HE HAS A HEAP 'O' COURAGE IN HIM THAT COMES BUSTIN' OUT WHEN-EVER HE NEEDS IT!

THERE'S MIGHTY FEW MEN THAT ARE WILLIN' TO TAKE ON A WHIRLPOOL!

AND IT'S MIGHTY FEW KIDS THAT'S GOT A REAL LIVE HERO FOR A FATHER!

THE END

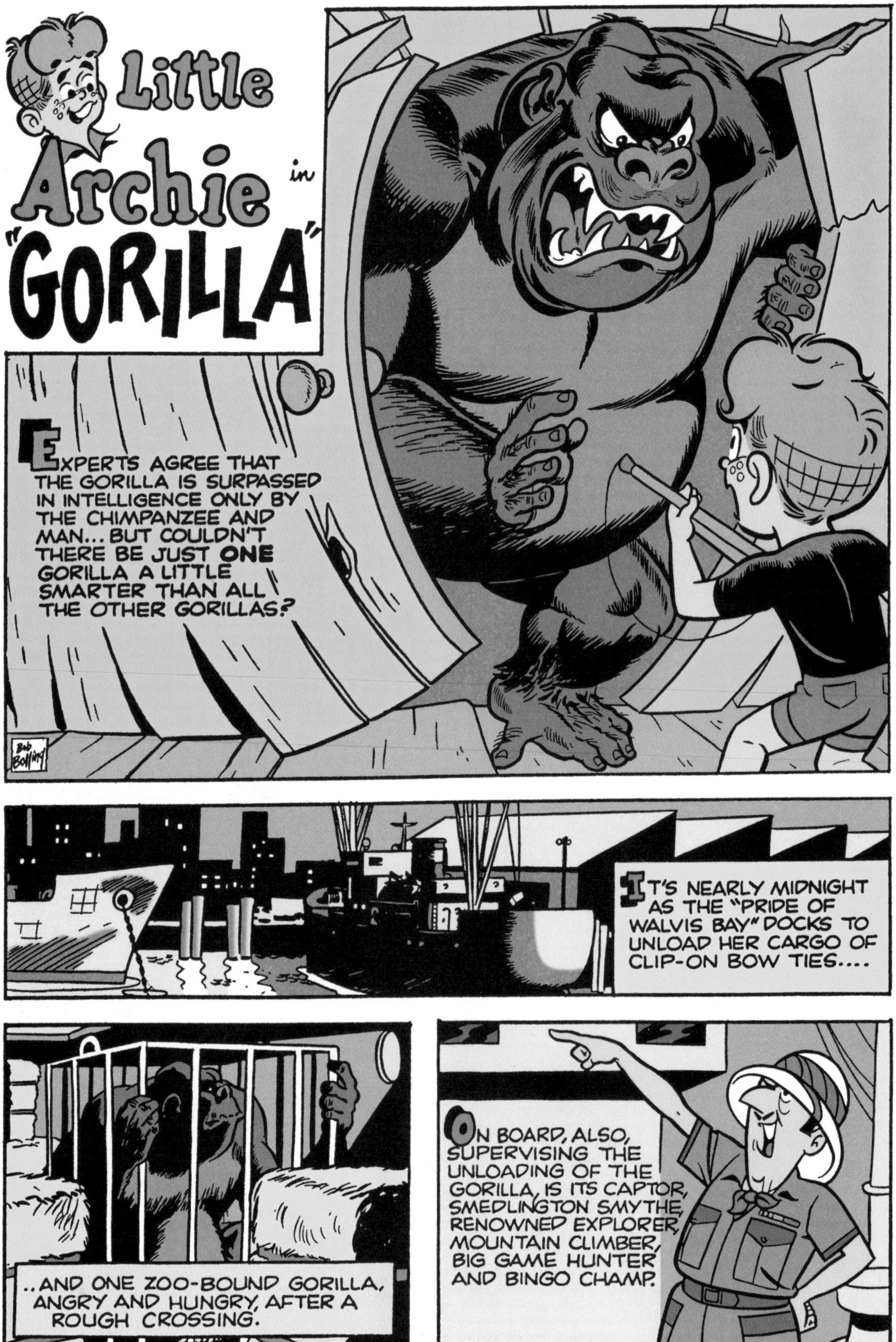
Little Archie in
"GORILLA"
EXPERTS AGREE THAT THE GORILLA IS SURPASSED IN INTELLIGENCE ONLY BY THE CHIMPANZEE AND MAN... BUT COULDN'T THERE BE JUST ONE GORILLA A LITTLE SMARTER THAN ALL THE OTHER GORILLAS?
Bob Bolling
IT'S NEARLY MIDNIGHT AS THE "PRIDE OF WALVIS BAY" DOCKS TO UNLOAD HER CARGO OF CLIP-ON BOW TIES....
..AND ONE ZOO-BOUND GORILLA, ANGRY AND HUNGRY, AFTER A ROUGH CROSSING.
ON BOARD, ALSO, SUPERVISING THE UNLOADING OF THE GORILLA, IS ITS CAPTOR, SMEDLINGTON SMYTHE, RENOWNED EXPLORER, MOUNTAIN CLIMBER, BIG GAME HUNTER AND BINGO CHAMP.

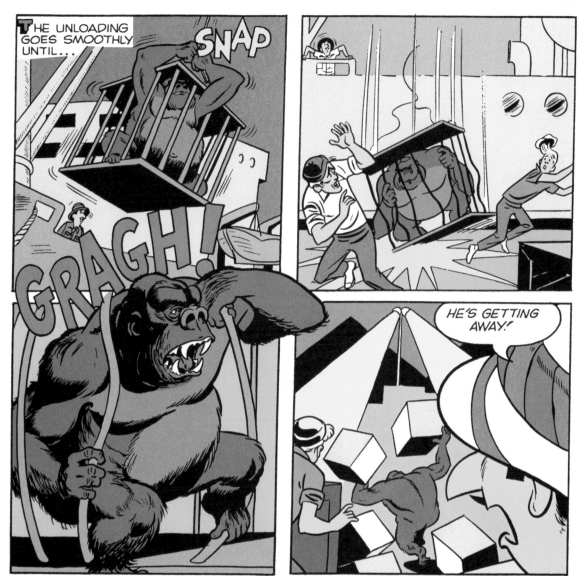

THE UNLOADING GOES SMOOTHLY UNTIL...

SNAP

GRAGH!

HE'S GETTING AWAY!

EARLY, NEXT DAY...

GOLLY, LITTLE ARCHIE, YOU SURE GET HUNGRY WHEN YOU'RE EXPLORING AFRICA!

JUGGY! LET'S GO UP TO OUR TREE HUT AND EAT OUR LUNCH! WE'LL BE SAFE FROM HIPPOS THERE!

2.

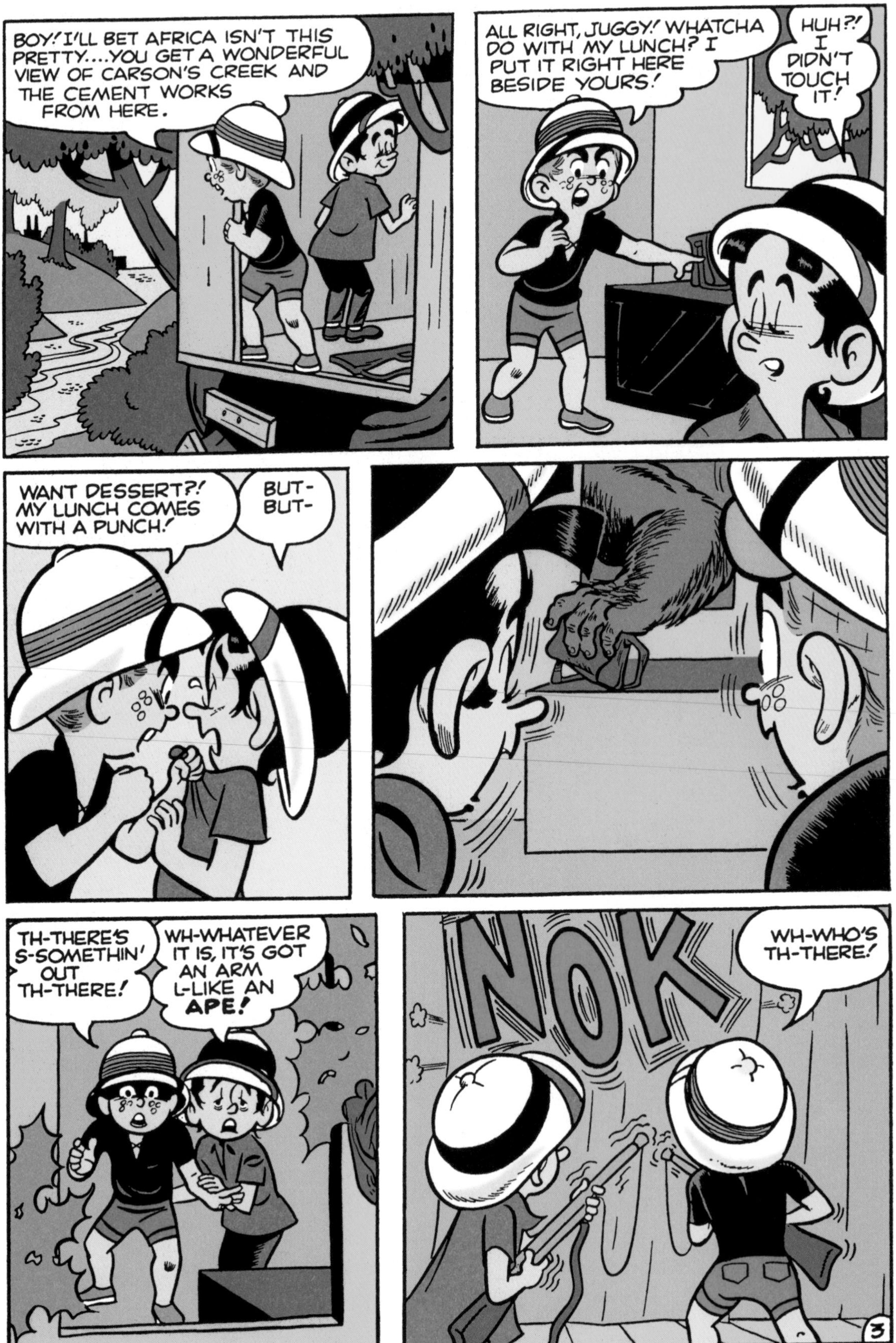
BOY! I'LL BET AFRICA ISN'T THIS PRETTY....YOU GET A WONDERFUL VIEW OF CARSON'S CREEK AND THE CEMENT WORKS FROM HERE.
ALL RIGHT, JUGGY! WHATCHA DO WITH MY LUNCH? I PUT IT RIGHT HERE BESIDE YOURS!
HUH?! I DIDN'T TOUCH IT!
WANT DESSERT?! MY LUNCH COMES WITH A PUNCH!
BUT- BUT-
TH-THERE'S S-SOMETHIN' OUT TH-THERE!
WH-WHATEVER IT IS, IT'S GOT AN ARM L-LIKE AN APE!
NOK
WH-WHO'S TH-THERE!
3

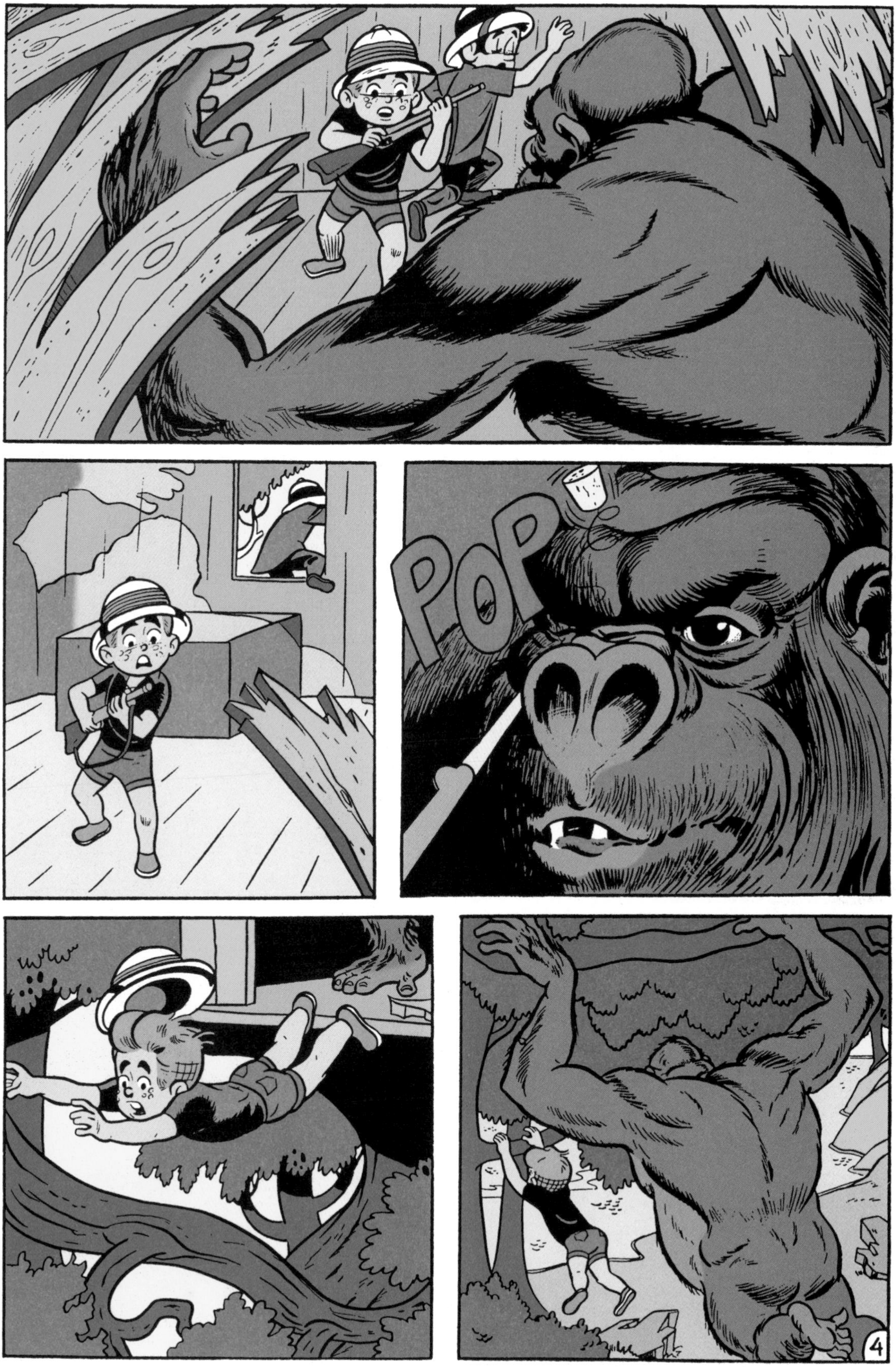
POP
4

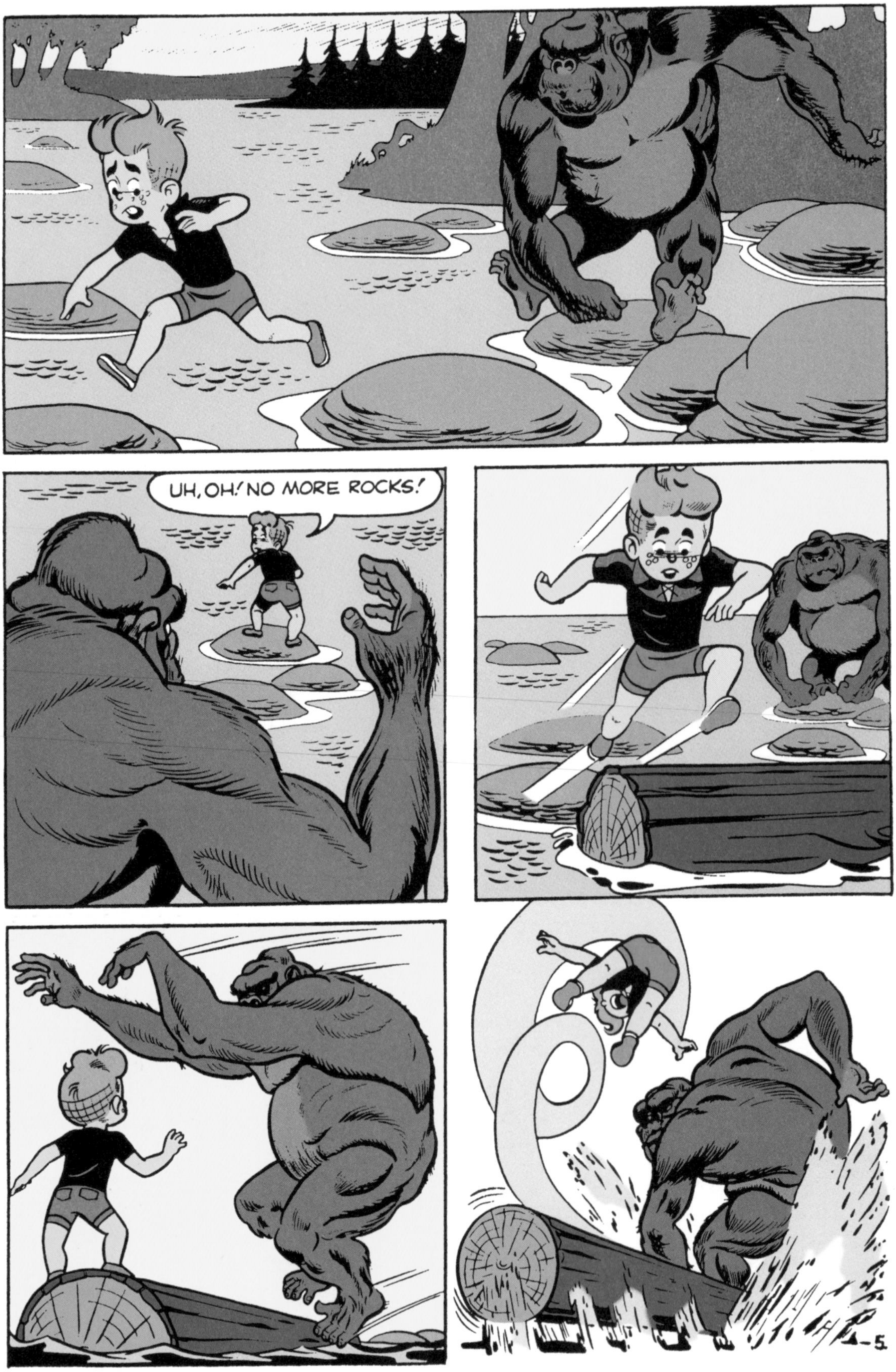
UH, OH! NO MORE ROCKS!

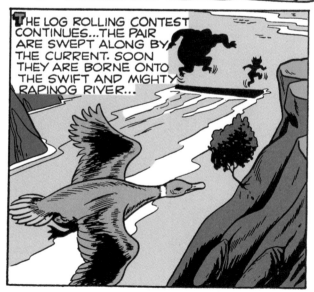

THE LOG ROLLING CONTEST CONTINUES...THE PAIR ARE SWEPT ALONG BY THE CURRENT. SOON THEY ARE BORNE ONTO THE SWIFT AND MIGHTY RAPINOG RIVER...

PAST THE CEMENT WORKS, PAST THE DOCKS-

6.

—AND PAST SMEDLINGTON SMYTHE ABOARD THE *PRIDE OF WALVIS BAY.*

HALLOoooo! OUT THERE!

I BELIEVE THAT'S MY GORILLA YOU HAVE THERE!

(PUFF) COME 'N' GET 'EM! I CAN'T (PUFF) HOLD OUT MUCH LONGER!!

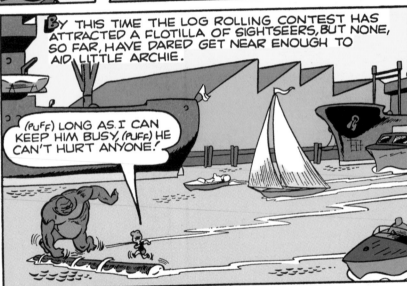

BY THIS TIME THE LOG ROLLING CONTEST HAS ATTRACTED A FLOTILLA OF SIGHTSEERS, BUT NONE, SO FAR, HAVE DARED GET NEAR ENOUGH TO AID LITTLE ARCHIE.

(PUFF) LONG AS I CAN KEEP HIM BUSY, (PUFF) HE CAN'T HURT ANYONE!

BUT NOW, SMEDLINGTON SMYTHE HAS COMMANDEERED A PASSING VESSEL.

FOLLOW THAT LOG, YAWL!

THINK WE CAN KETCH 'EM?

ARE YOU GOING TO **SHOOT** THE GORILLA, MISTER?

NO! THIS IS A **CAPTURE** GUN! IT SHOOTS DARTS CONTAINING A PARALYZING POTION THAT WILL PUT THE BEAST TO SLEEP!

WE'RE GAINING ON THEM! BUT WHERE'D ALL THE OTHER BOATS GO?

THEY'VE TURNED BACK! LOOK OVER THERE... **FOG** ROLLING IN!

GROAN

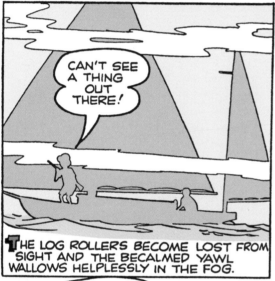

CAN'T SEE A THING OUT THERE!

THE LOG ROLLERS BECOME LOST FROM SIGHT AND THE BECALMED YAWL WALLOWS HELPLESSLY IN THE FOG.

Y!!

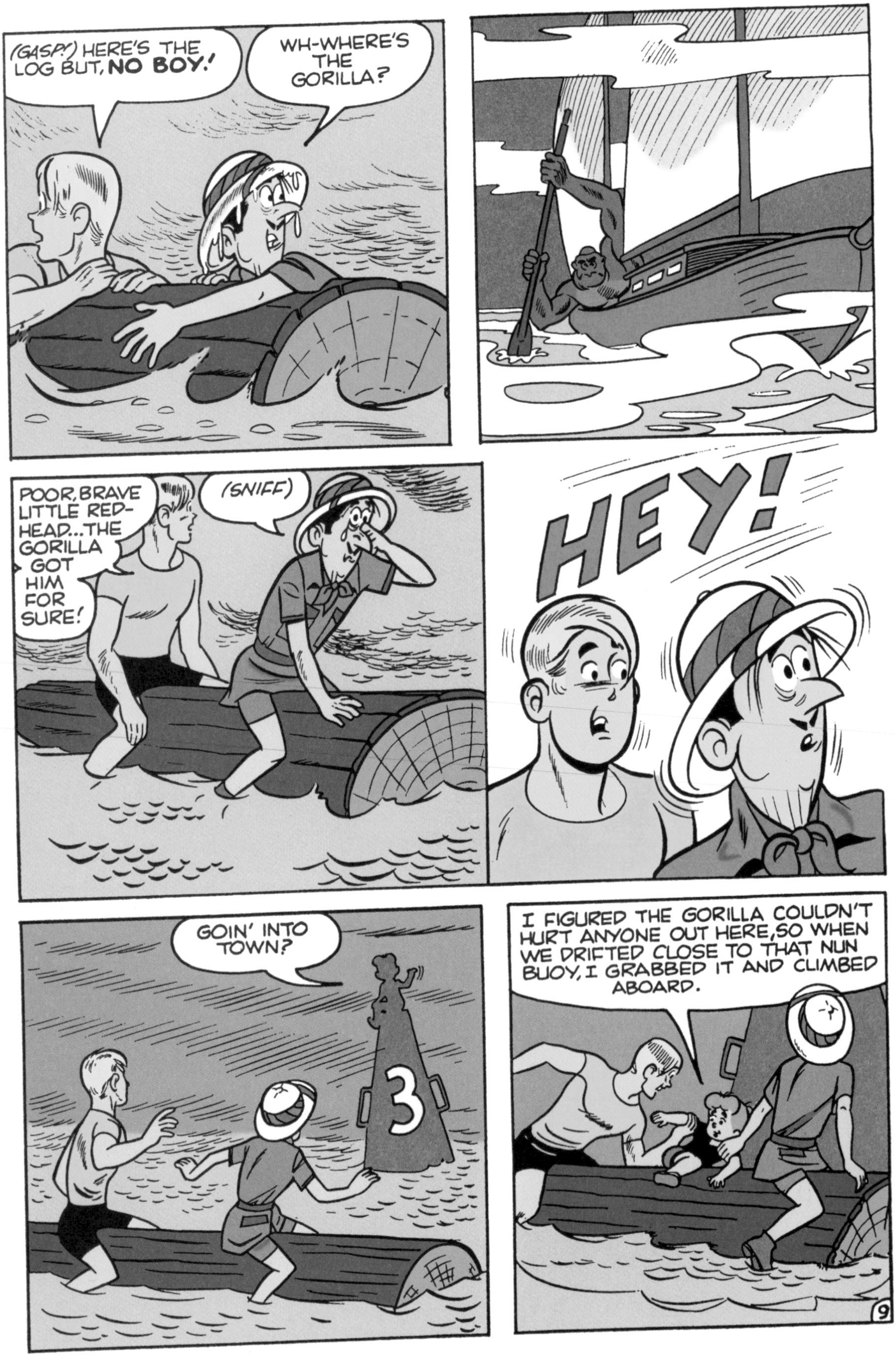
(GASP!) HERE'S THE LOG BUT, NO BOY!
WH-WHERE'S THE GORILLA?
POOR, BRAVE LITTLE RED-HEAD... THE GORILLA GOT HIM FOR SURE!
(SNIFF)
HEY!
GOIN' INTO TOWN?
3
I FIGURED THE GORILLA COULDN'T HURT ANYONE OUT HERE, SO WHEN WE DRIFTED CLOSE TO THAT NUN BUOY, I GRABBED IT AND CLIMBED ABOARD.
9

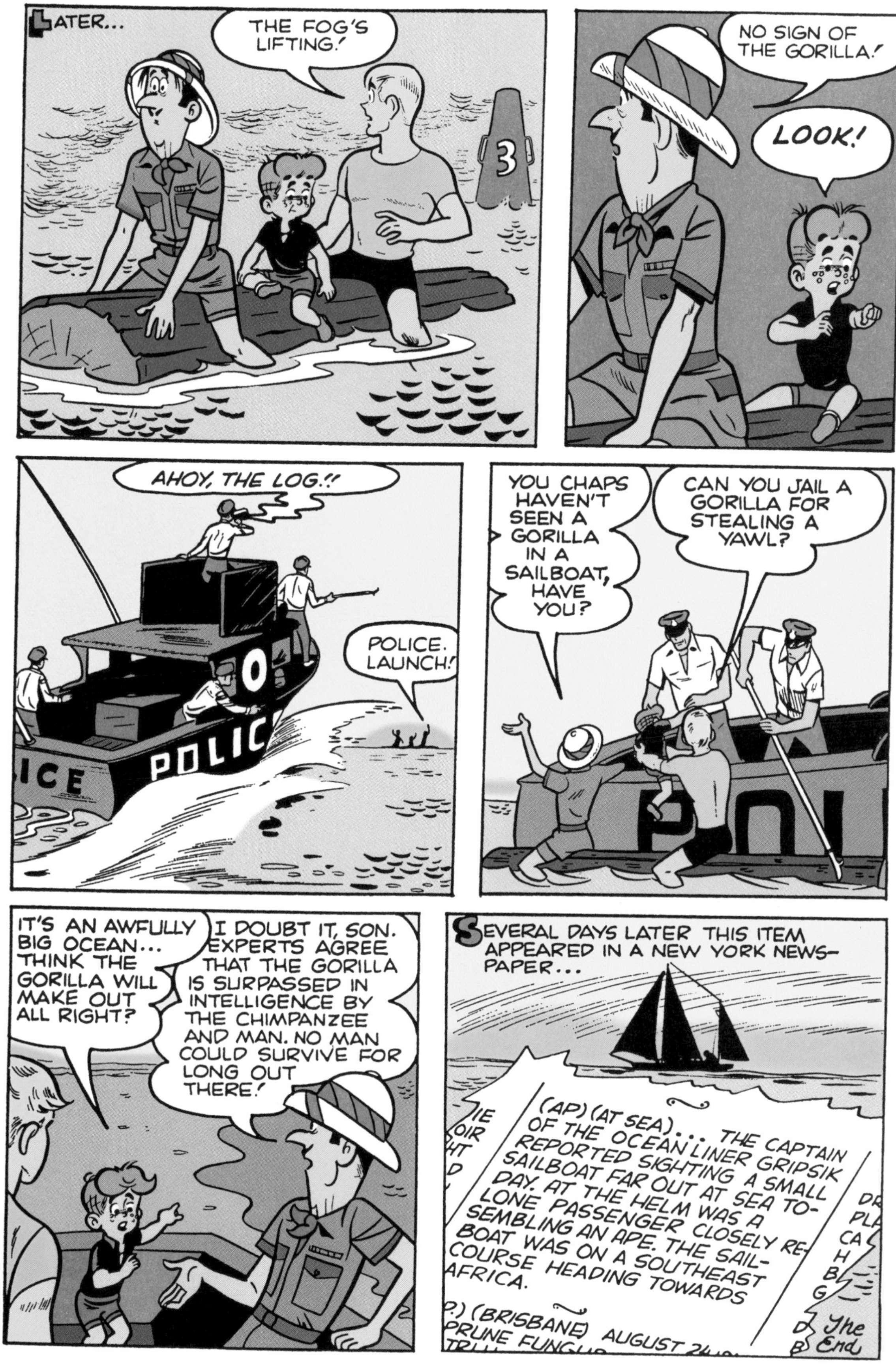
LATER...
THE FOG'S LIFTING!
3
NO SIGN OF THE GORILLA!
LOOK!
AHOY, THE LOG!!
POLICE. LAUNCH!
POLIC
ICE
YOU CHAPS HAVEN'T SEEN A GORILLA IN A SAILBOAT, HAVE YOU?
CAN YOU JAIL A GORILLA FOR STEALING A YAWL?
IT'S AN AWFULLY BIG OCEAN... THINK THE GORILLA WILL MAKE OUT ALL RIGHT?
I DOUBT IT, SON. EXPERTS AGREE THAT THE GORILLA IS SURPASSED IN INTELLIGENCE BY THE CHIMPANZEE AND MAN. NO MAN COULD SURVIVE FOR LONG OUT THERE!
SEVERAL DAYS LATER THIS ITEM APPEARED IN A NEW YORK NEWS-PAPER...
(AP) (AT SEA)... THE CAPTAIN OF THE OCEAN LINER GRIPSIK REPORTED SIGHTING A SMALL SAILBOAT FAR OUT AT SEA TO-DAY. AT THE HELM WAS A LONE PASSENGER CLOSELY RE-SEMBLING AN APE. THE SAIL-BOAT WAS ON A SOUTHEAST COURSE HEADING TOWARDS AFRICA.
(BRISBANE) AUGUST 24
The End

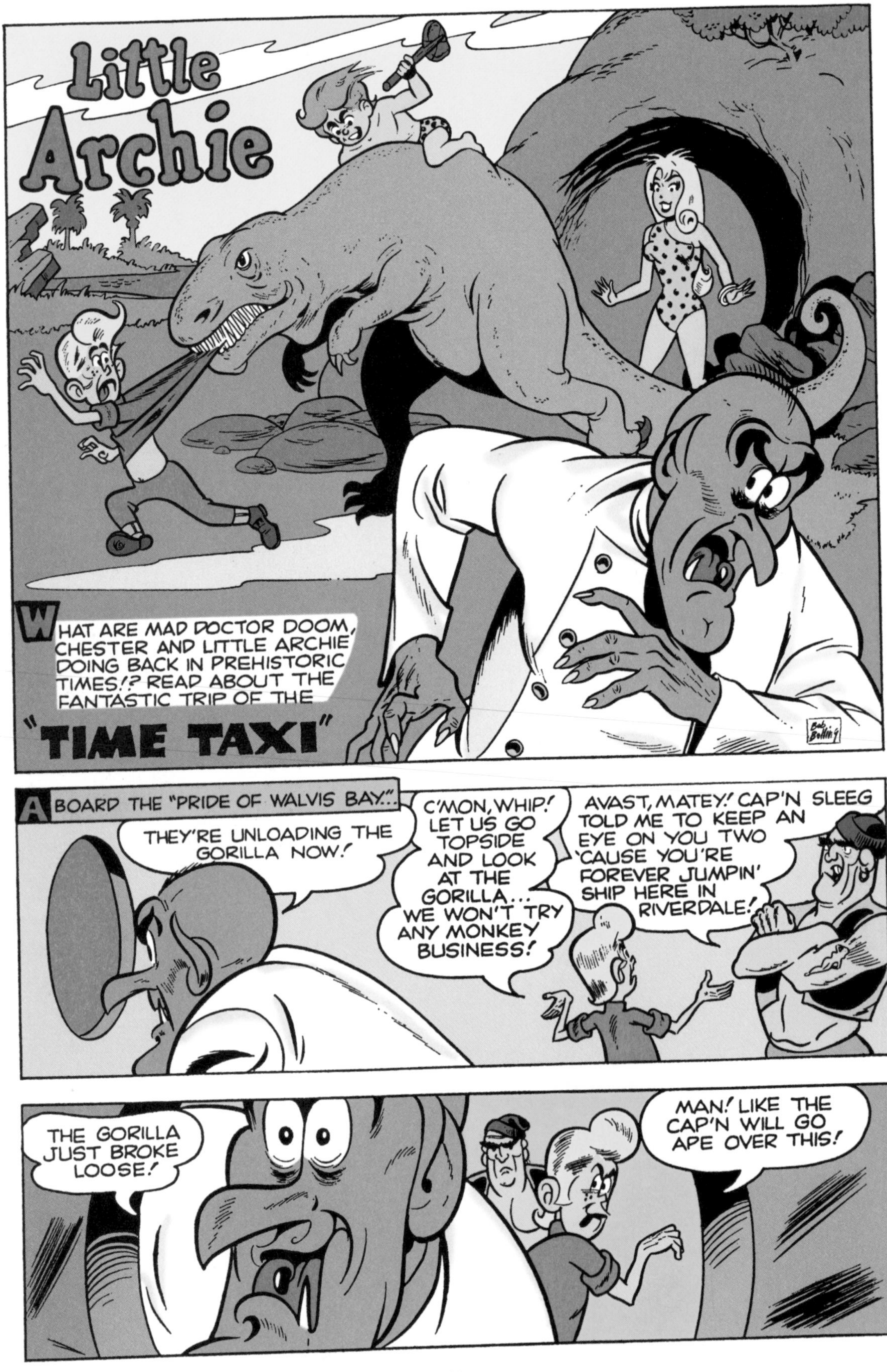
Little Archie
WHAT ARE MAD DOCTOR DOOM, CHESTER AND LITTLE ARCHIE DOING BACK IN PREHISTORIC TIMES!? READ ABOUT THE FANTASTIC TRIP OF THE
"TIME TAXI"
Bob Bolling
ABOARD THE "PRIDE OF WALVIS BAY."..
THEY'RE UNLOADING THE GORILLA NOW!
C'MON, WHIP! LET US GO TOPSIDE AND LOOK AT THE GORILLA... WE WON'T TRY ANY MONKEY BUSINESS!
AVAST, MATEY! CAP'N SLEEG TOLD ME TO KEEP AN EYE ON YOU TWO 'CAUSE YOU'RE FOREVER JUMPIN' SHIP HERE IN RIVERDALE!
THE GORILLA JUST BROKE LOOSE!
MAN! LIKE THE CAP'N WILL GO APE OVER THIS!

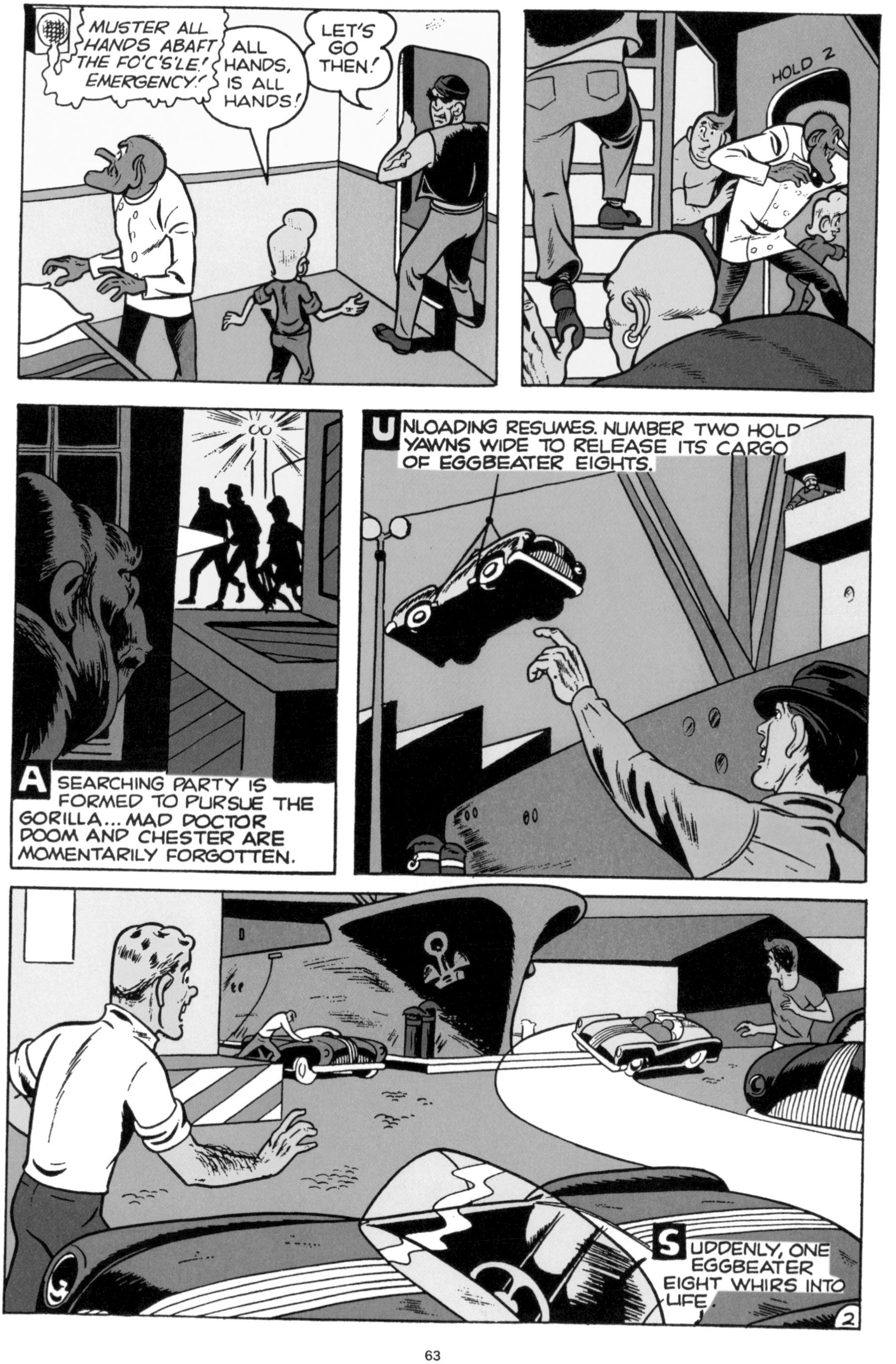
MUSTER ALL HANDS ABAFT THE FO'C'S'LE! EMERGENCY!
ALL HANDS, IS ALL HANDS!
LET'S GO THEN!
HOLD 2
A SEARCHING PARTY IS FORMED TO PURSUE THE GORILLA... MAD DOCTOR DOOM AND CHESTER ARE MOMENTARILY FORGOTTEN.
UNLOADING RESUMES. NUMBER TWO HOLD YAWNS WIDE TO RELEASE ITS CARGO OF EGGBEATER EIGHTS.
SUDDENLY, ONE EGGBEATER EIGHT WHIRS INTO LIFE.
2

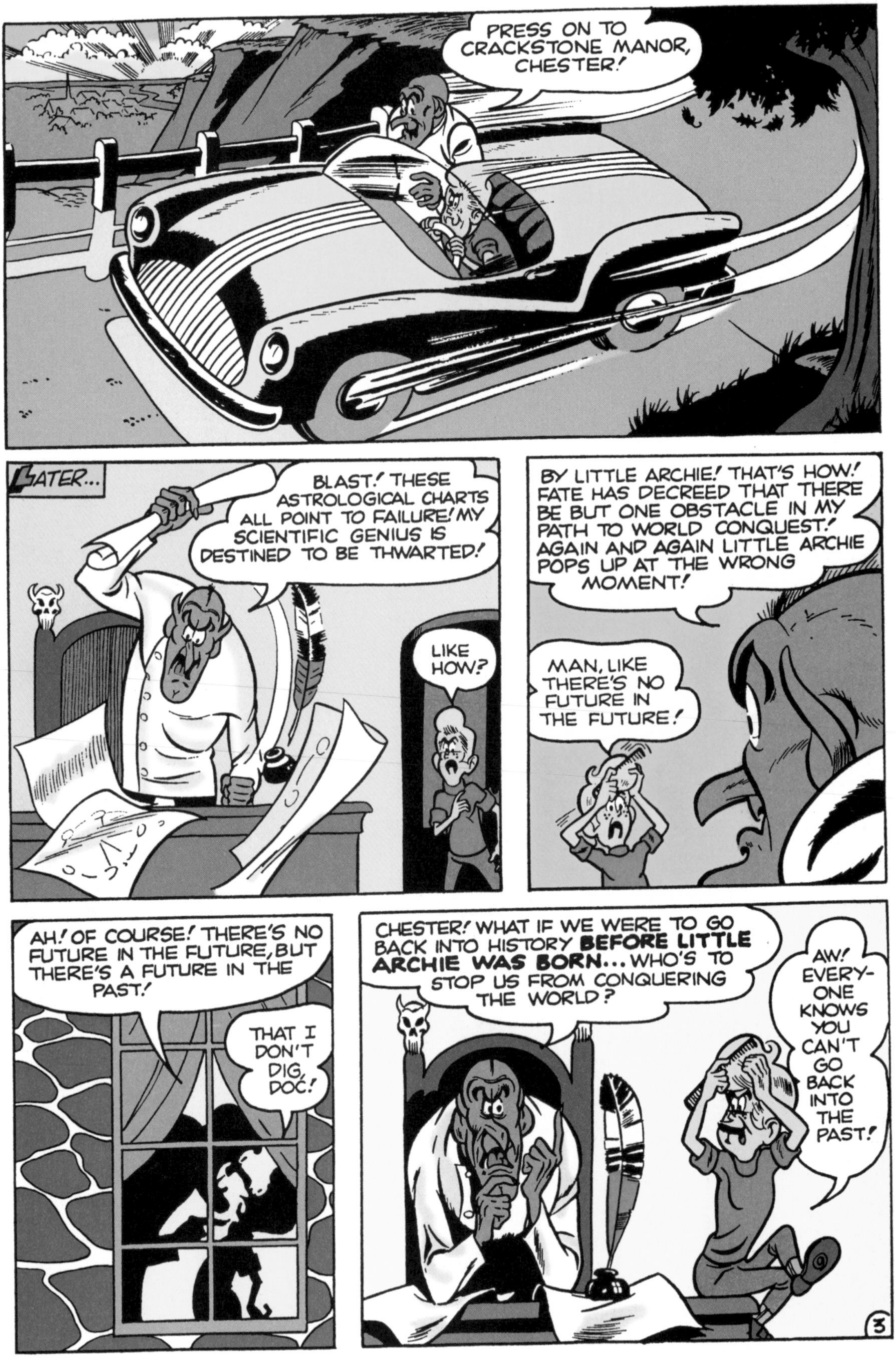
PRESS ON TO CRACKSTONE MANOR, CHESTER!
LATER...
BLAST! THESE ASTROLOGICAL CHARTS ALL POINT TO FAILURE! MY SCIENTIFIC GENIUS IS DESTINED TO BE THWARTED!
LIKE HOW?
BY LITTLE ARCHIE! THAT'S HOW! FATE HAS DECREED THAT THERE BE BUT ONE OBSTACLE IN MY PATH TO WORLD CONQUEST! AGAIN AND AGAIN LITTLE ARCHIE POPS UP AT THE WRONG MOMENT!
MAN, LIKE THERE'S NO FUTURE IN THE FUTURE!
AH! OF COURSE! THERE'S NO FUTURE IN THE FUTURE, BUT THERE'S A FUTURE IN THE PAST!
THAT I DON'T DIG, DOC!
CHESTER! WHAT IF WE WERE TO GO BACK INTO HISTORY **BEFORE LITTLE ARCHIE WAS BORN...** WHO'S TO STOP US FROM CONQUERING THE WORLD?
AW! EVERY-ONE KNOWS YOU CAN'T GO BACK INTO THE PAST!
3

A TIME TAXI?! YOU MEAN THIS THING WILL REALLY TAKE YOU BACK TO B.L.A.*?

HEE! SHE'S NEARLY COMPLETED, CHESTER!

* BEFORE LITTLE ARCHIE

I DON'T WANNA LEAVE THE GANG RUMBLES AND THE DRAG RACES AND—

GET IN! WE SHALL TRAVEL BACK IN TIME, TAKE OVER A LABORATORY AND THEN FASHION A WORLD-CONQUERING DEVICE BEFORE LITTLE ARCHIE ARRIVES ON THE SCENE!

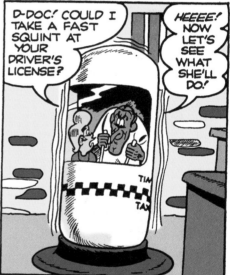

D-DOC! COULD I TAKE A FAST SQUINT AT YOUR DRIVER'S LICENSE?

HEEEE! NOW LET'S SEE WHAT SHE'LL DO!

PWANG

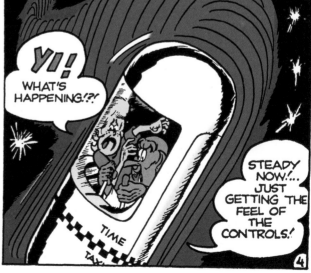

YI! WHAT'S HAPPENING.!?!

STEADY NOW.!... JUST GETTING THE FEEL OF THE CONTROLS!

4

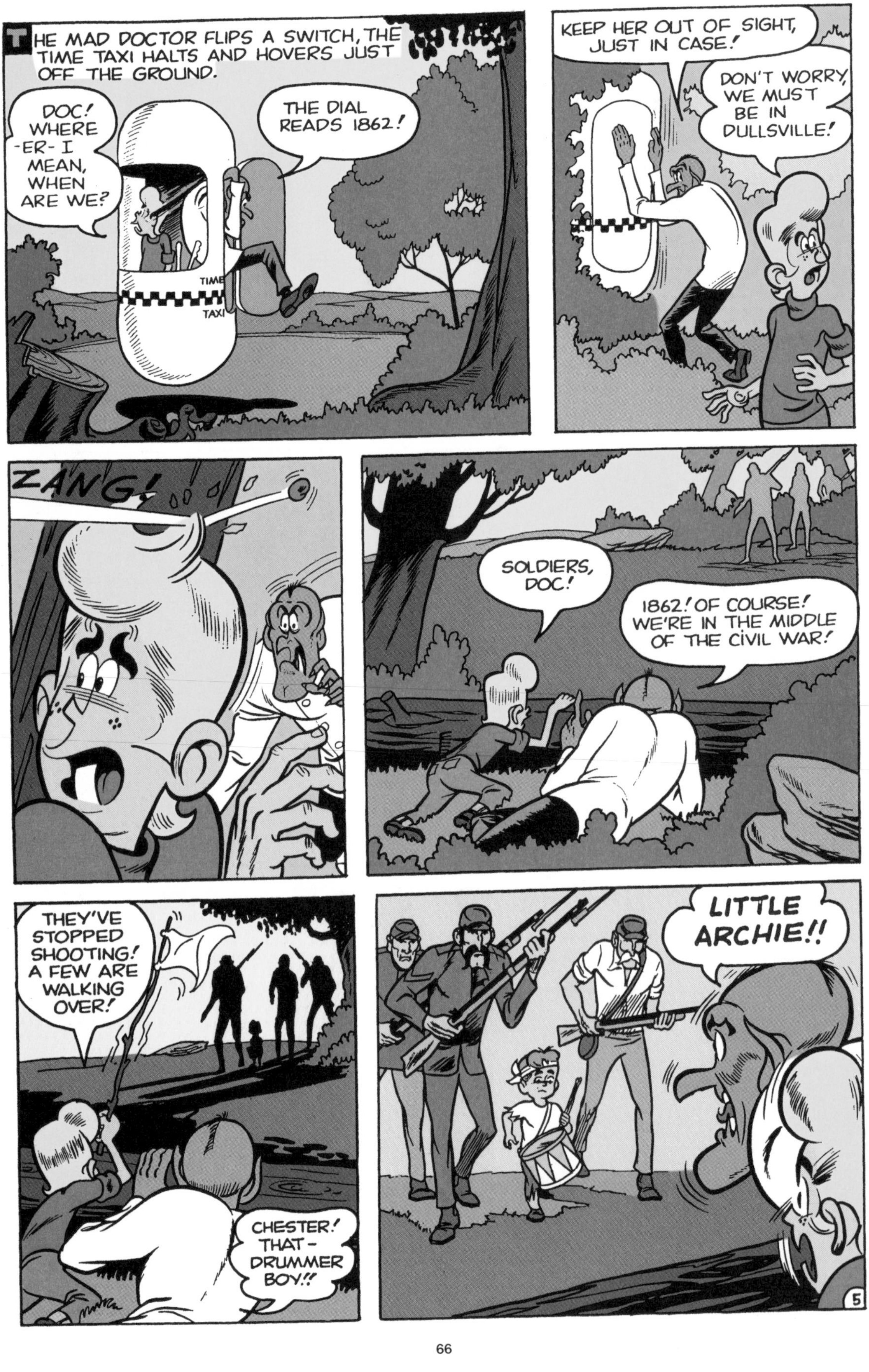
THE MAD DOCTOR FLIPS A SWITCH, THE TIME TAXI HALTS AND HOVERS JUST OFF THE GROUND.
DOC! WHERE -ER- I MEAN, WHEN ARE WE?
THE DIAL READS 1862!
TIME
TAXI
KEEP HER OUT OF SIGHT, JUST IN CASE!
DON'T WORRY, WE MUST BE IN DULLSVILLE!
ZANG!
SOLDIERS, DOC!
1862! OF COURSE! WE'RE IN THE MIDDLE OF THE CIVIL WAR!
THEY'VE STOPPED SHOOTING! A FEW ARE WALKING OVER!
CHESTER! THAT-DRUMMER BOY!!
LITTLE ARCHIE!!
5

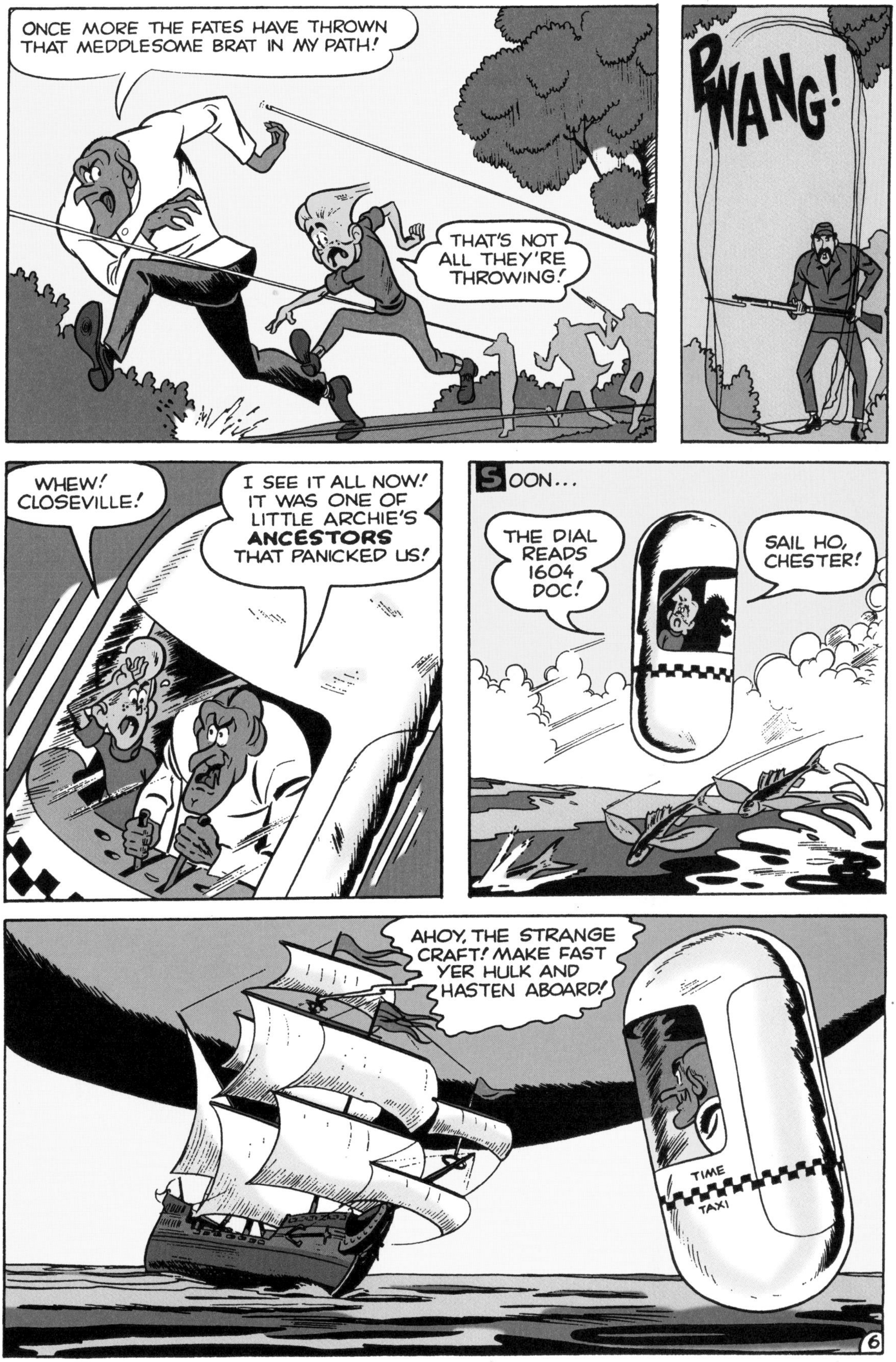
ONCE MORE THE FATES HAVE THROWN THAT MEDDLESOME BRAT IN MY PATH!
THAT'S NOT ALL THEY'RE THROWING!
PWANG!
WHEW! CLOSEVILLE!
I SEE IT ALL NOW! IT WAS ONE OF LITTLE ARCHIE'S **ANCESTORS** THAT PANICKED US!
SOON...
THE DIAL READS 1604 DOC!
SAIL HO, CHESTER!
AHOY, THE STRANGE CRAFT! MAKE FAST YER HULK AND HASTEN ABOARD!
TIME
TAXI
6

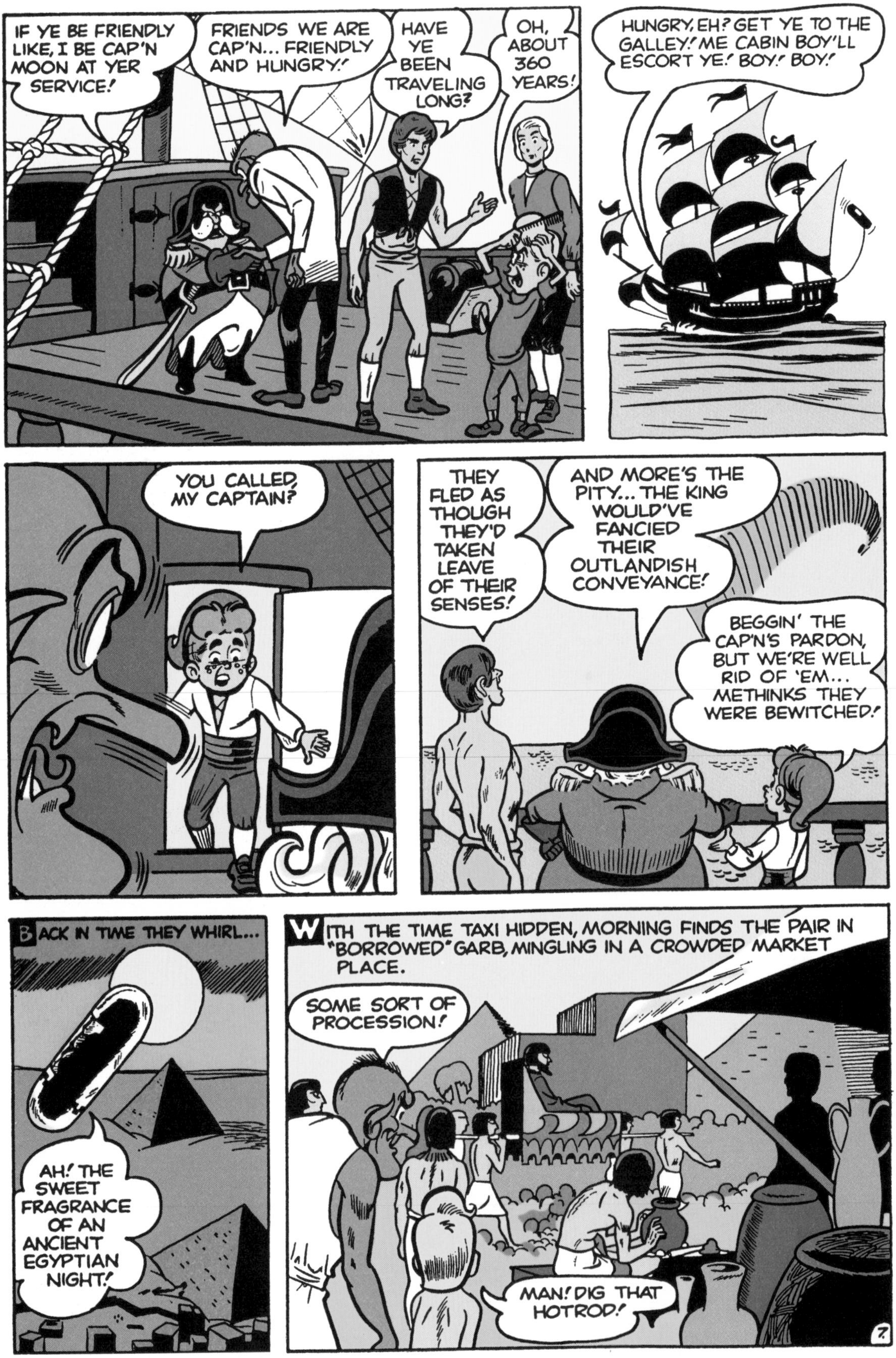
IF YE BE FRIENDLY LIKE, I BE CAP'N MOON AT YER SERVICE!
FRIENDS WE ARE CAP'N... FRIENDLY AND HUNGRY!
HAVE YE BEEN TRAVELING LONG?
OH, ABOUT 360 YEARS!
HUNGRY, EH? GET YE TO THE GALLEY! ME CABIN BOY'LL ESCORT YE! BOY! BOY!
YOU CALLED, MY CAPTAIN?
THEY FLED AS THOUGH THEY'D TAKEN LEAVE OF THEIR SENSES!
AND MORE'S THE PITY... THE KING WOULD'VE FANCIED THEIR OUTLANDISH CONVEYANCE!
BEGGIN' THE CAP'N'S PARDON, BUT WE'RE WELL RID OF 'EM... METHINKS THEY WERE BEWITCHED!
BACK IN TIME THEY WHIRL...
AH! THE SWEET FRAGRANCE OF AN ANCIENT EGYPTIAN NIGHT!
WITH THE TIME TAXI HIDDEN, MORNING FINDS THE PAIR IN "BORROWED" GARB, MINGLING IN A CROWDED MARKET PLACE.
SOME SORT OF PROCESSION!
MAN! DIG THAT HOTROD!
7

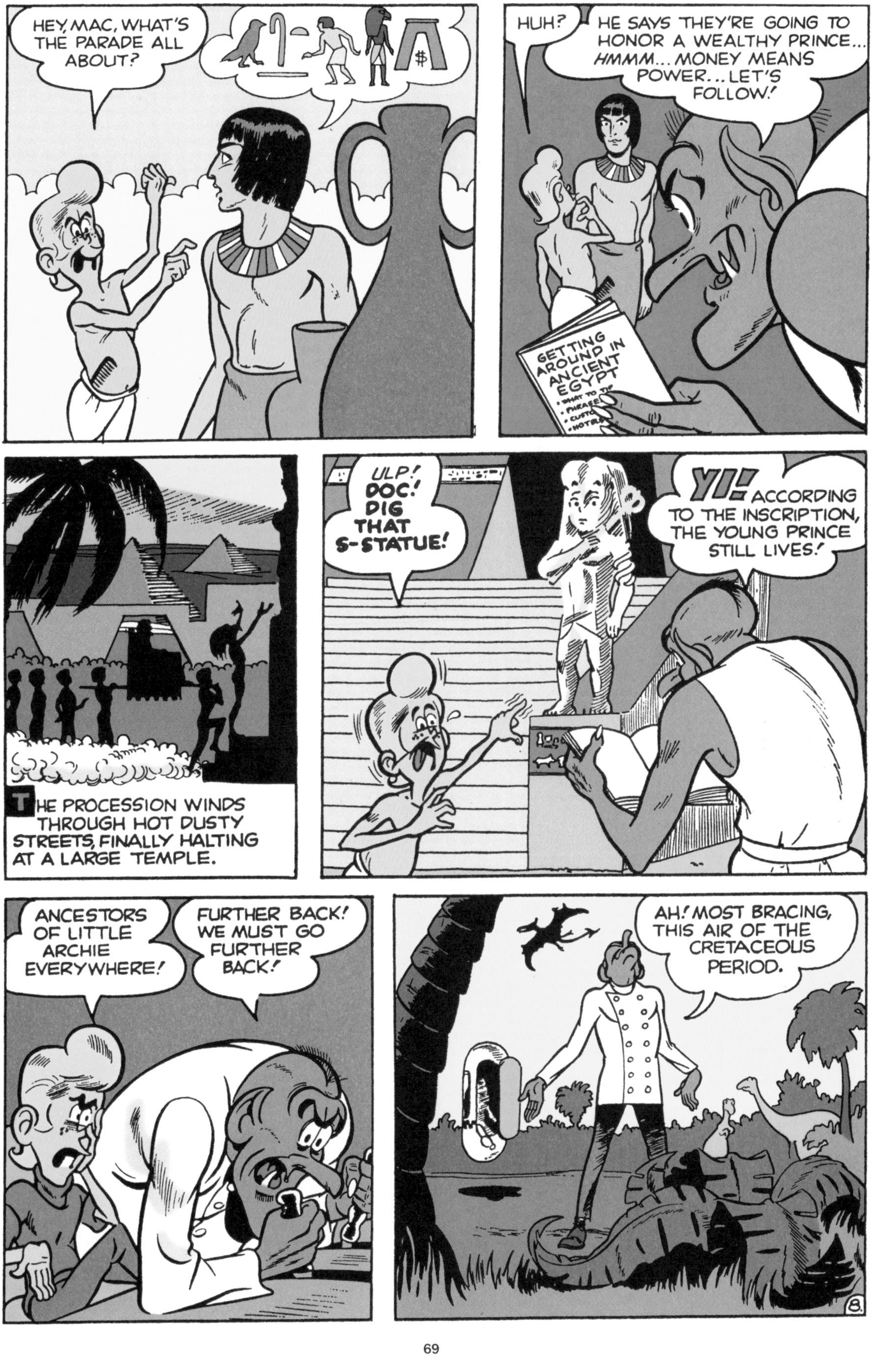
HEY, MAC, WHAT'S THE PARADE ALL ABOUT?
$
HUH?
HE SAYS THEY'RE GOING TO HONOR A WEALTHY PRINCE... HMMM... MONEY MEANS POWER... LET'S FOLLOW!
GETTING AROUND IN ANCIENT EGYPT
THE PROCESSION WINDS THROUGH HOT DUSTY STREETS, FINALLY HALTING AT A LARGE TEMPLE.
ULP! DOC! DIG THAT S-STATUE!
YI! ACCORDING TO THE INSCRIPTION, THE YOUNG PRINCE STILL LIVES!
ANCESTORS OF LITTLE ARCHIE EVERYWHERE!
FURTHER BACK! WE MUST GO FURTHER BACK!
AH! MOST BRACING, THIS AIR OF THE CRETACEOUS PERIOD.
8.

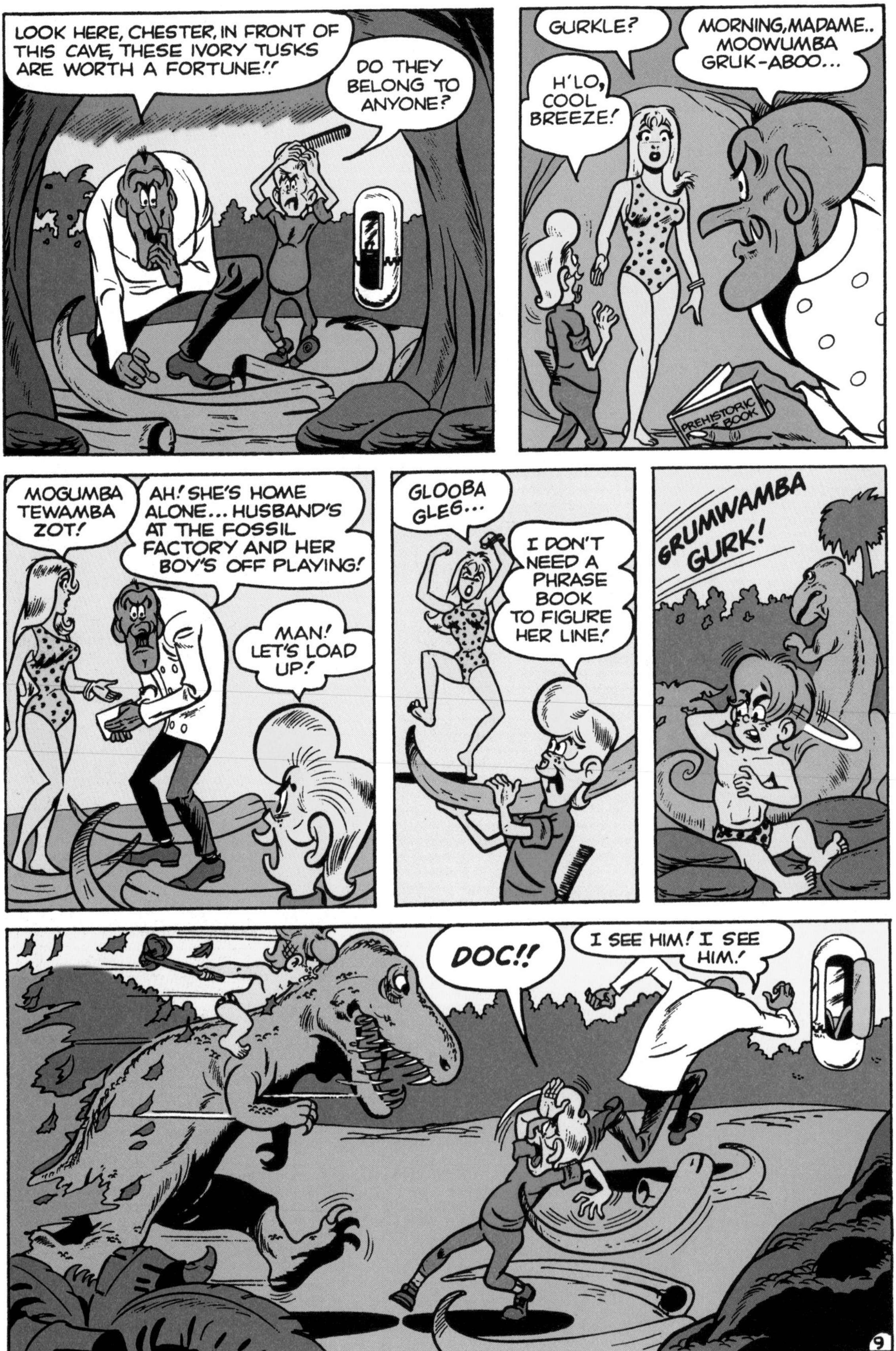
LOOK HERE, CHESTER, IN FRONT OF THIS CAVE, THESE IVORY TUSKS ARE WORTH A FORTUNE!!
DO THEY BELONG TO ANYONE?
GURKLE?
MORNING, MADAME.. MOOWUMBA GRUK-ABOO...
H'LO, COOL BREEZE!
PREHISTORIC PHRASE BOOK
MOGUMBA TEWAMBA ZOT!
AH! SHE'S HOME ALONE... HUSBAND'S AT THE FOSSIL FACTORY AND HER BOY'S OFF PLAYING!
MAN! LET'S LOAD UP!
GLOOBA GLEG...
I DON'T NEED A PHRASE BOOK TO FIGURE HER LINE!
GRUMWAMBA GURK!
DOC!!
I SEE HIM! I SEE HIM!
9

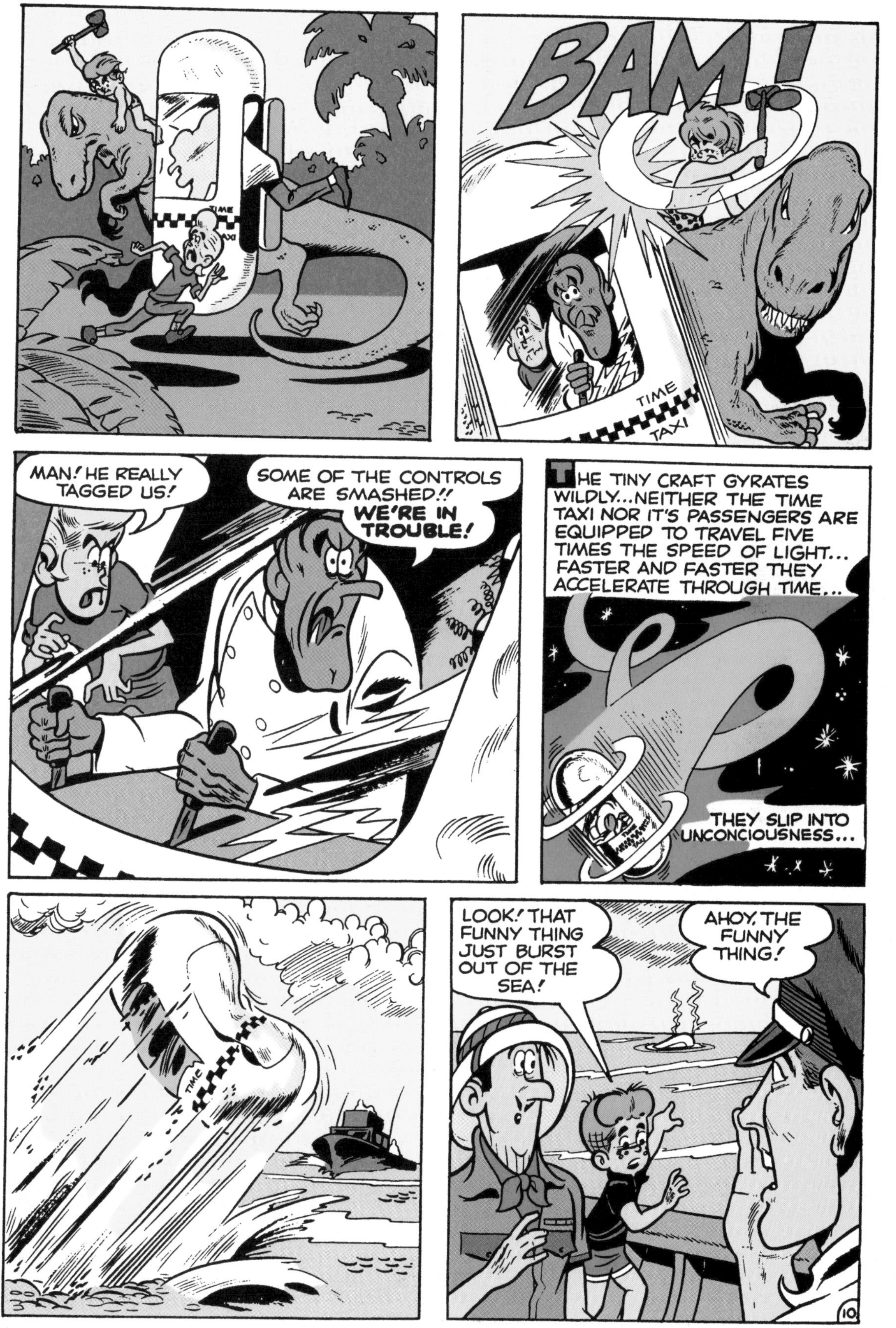
TIME
TAXI
BAM!
TIME
TAXI
MAN! HE REALLY TAGGED US!
SOME OF THE CONTROLS ARE SMASHED!! WE'RE IN TROUBLE!
THE TINY CRAFT GYRATES WILDLY...NEITHER THE TIME TAXI NOR IT'S PASSENGERS ARE EQUIPPED TO TRAVEL FIVE TIMES THE SPEED OF LIGHT... FASTER AND FASTER THEY ACCELERATE THROUGH TIME...
THEY SLIP INTO UNCONCIOUSNESS...
TIME
LOOK! THAT FUNNY THING JUST BURST OUT OF THE SEA!
AHOY, THE FUNNY THING!
10

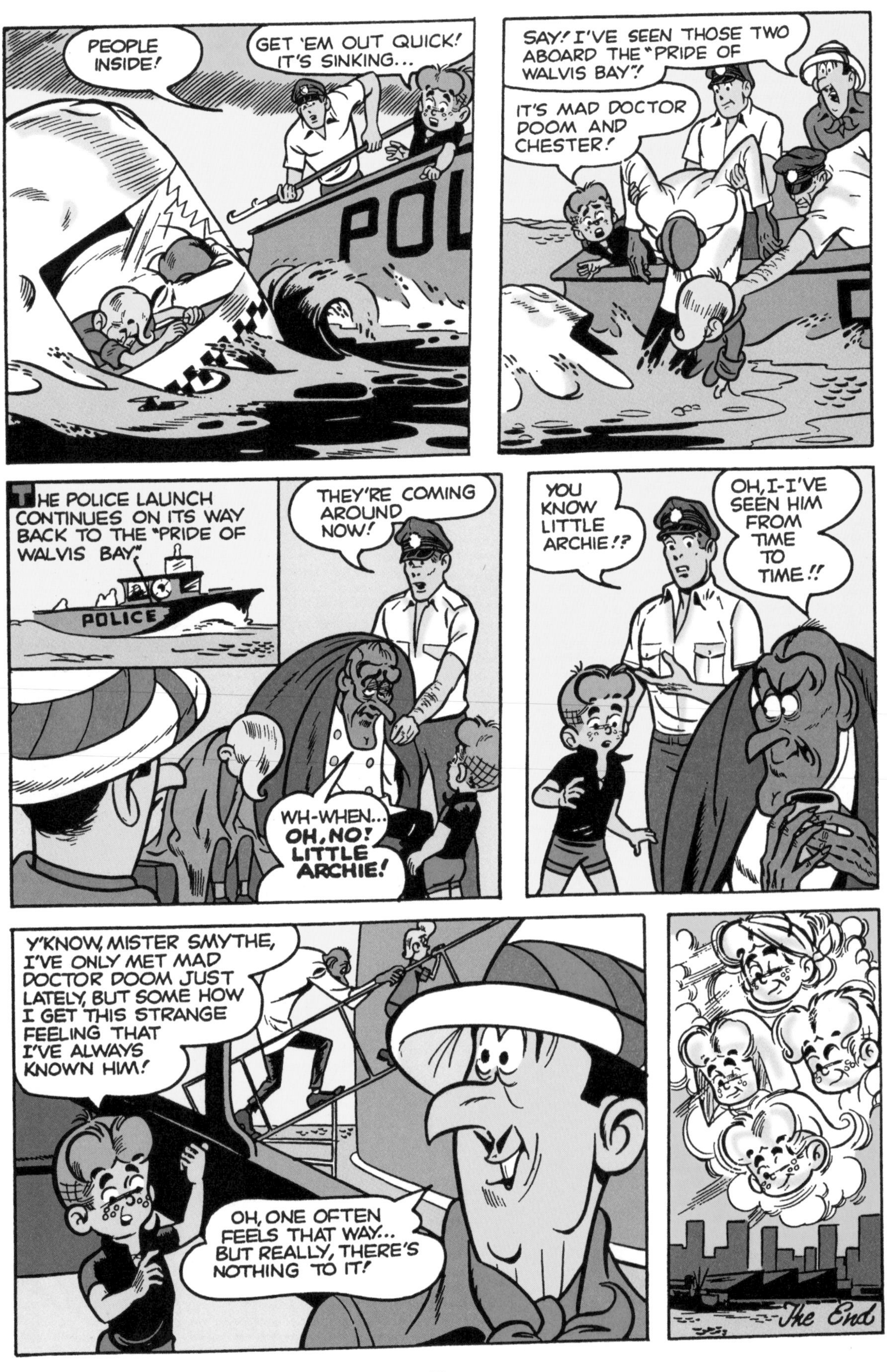
PEOPLE INSIDE!
GET 'EM OUT QUICK! IT'S SINKING...
POL
SAY! I'VE SEEN THOSE TWO ABOARD THE "PRIDE OF WALVIS BAY"!
IT'S MAD DOCTOR DOOM AND CHESTER!
THE POLICE LAUNCH CONTINUES ON ITS WAY BACK TO THE "PRIDE OF WALVIS BAY."
POLICE
THEY'RE COMING AROUND NOW!
WH-WHEN... OH, NO! LITTLE ARCHIE!
YOU KNOW LITTLE ARCHIE!?
OH, I-I'VE SEEN HIM FROM TIME TO TIME!!
Y'KNOW, MISTER SMYTHE, I'VE ONLY MET MAD DOCTOR DOOM JUST LATELY, BUT SOME HOW I GET THIS STRANGE FEELING THAT I'VE ALWAYS KNOWN HIM!
OH, ONE OFTEN FEELS THAT WAY... BUT REALLY, THERE'S NOTHING TO IT!
The End

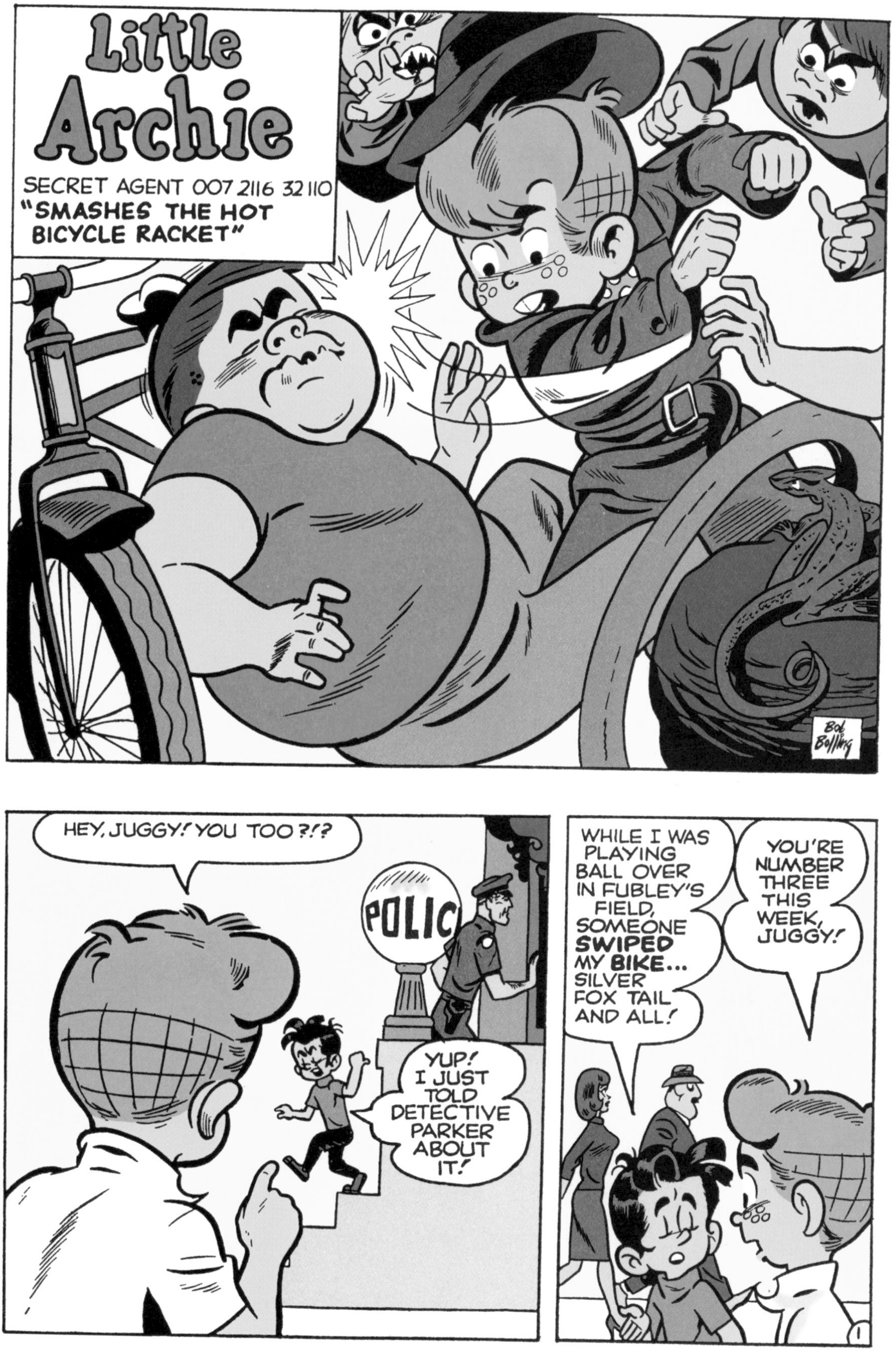
Little Archie
SECRET AGENT 007 2116 32 110
"SMASHES THE HOT BICYCLE RACKET"
Bob Bolling
HEY, JUGGY! YOU TOO?!?
POLIC
YUP! I JUST TOLD DETECTIVE PARKER ABOUT IT!
WHILE I WAS PLAYING BALL OVER IN FUBLEY'S FIELD, SOMEONE **SWIPED** MY **BIKE...** SILVER FOX TAIL AND ALL!
YOU'RE NUMBER THREE THIS WEEK, JUGGY!
1

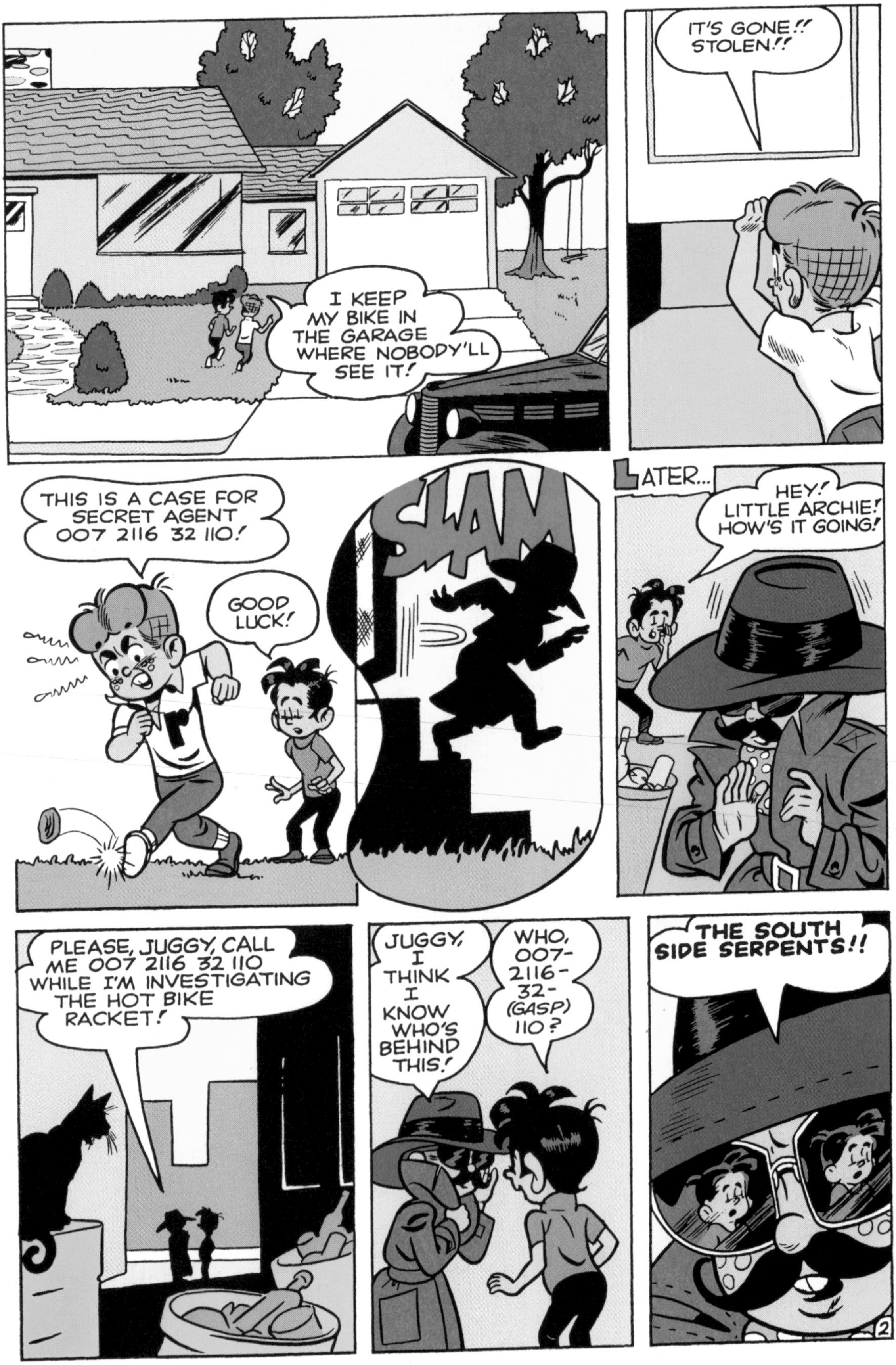
I KEEP MY BIKE IN THE GARAGE WHERE NOBODY'LL SEE IT!
IT'S GONE!! STOLEN!!
THIS IS A CASE FOR SECRET AGENT 007 2116 32 110!
GOOD LUCK!
SLAM
LATER...
HEY! LITTLE ARCHIE! HOW'S IT GOING!
PLEASE, JUGGY, CALL ME 007 2116 32 110 WHILE I'M INVESTIGATING THE HOT BIKE RACKET!
JUGGY, I THINK I KNOW WHO'S BEHIND THIS!
WHO, 007-2116-32-(GASP) 110?
THE SOUTH SIDE SERPENTS!!
2

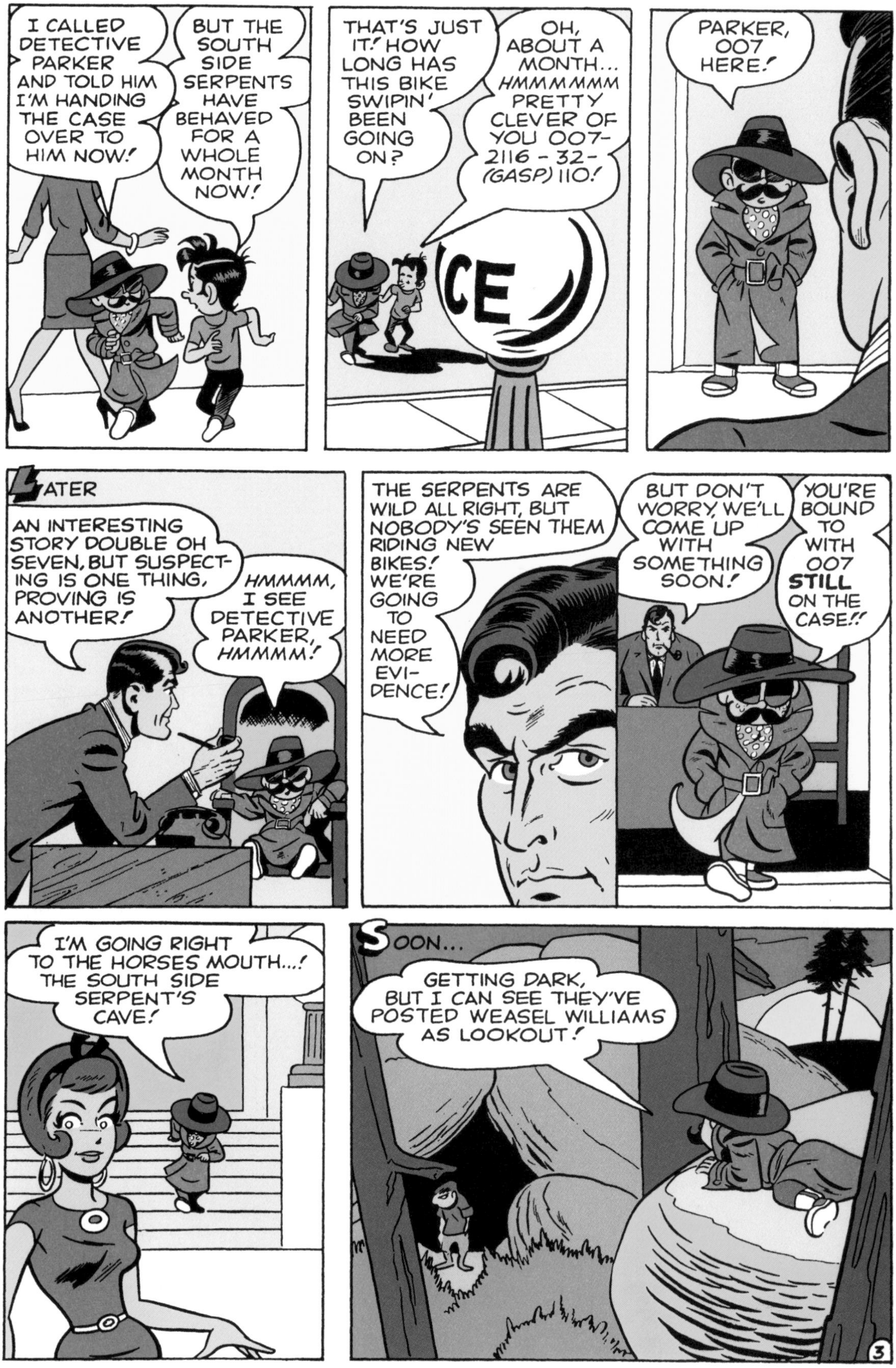
I CALLED DETECTIVE PARKER AND TOLD HIM I'M HANDING THE CASE OVER TO HIM NOW!
BUT THE SOUTH SIDE SERPENTS HAVE BEHAVED FOR A WHOLE MONTH NOW!
THAT'S JUST IT! HOW LONG HAS THIS BIKE SWIPIN' BEEN GOING ON?
OH, ABOUT A MONTH... HMMMMMM PRETTY CLEVER OF YOU 007-2116-32-(GASP) 110!
CE
PARKER, 007 HERE!
LATER
AN INTERESTING STORY DOUBLE OH SEVEN, BUT SUSPECTING IS ONE THING, PROVING IS ANOTHER!
HMMMM, I SEE DETECTIVE PARKER, HMMMM!
THE SERPENTS ARE WILD ALL RIGHT, BUT NOBODY'S SEEN THEM RIDING NEW BIKES! WE'RE GOING TO NEED MORE EVIDENCE!
BUT DON'T WORRY, WE'LL COME UP WITH SOMETHING SOON!
YOU'RE BOUND TO WITH 007 STILL ON THE CASE!!
I'M GOING RIGHT TO THE HORSES MOUTH...! THE SOUTH SIDE SERPENT'S CAVE!
SOON...
GETTING DARK, BUT I CAN SEE THEY'VE POSTED WEASEL WILLIAMS AS LOOKOUT!
3

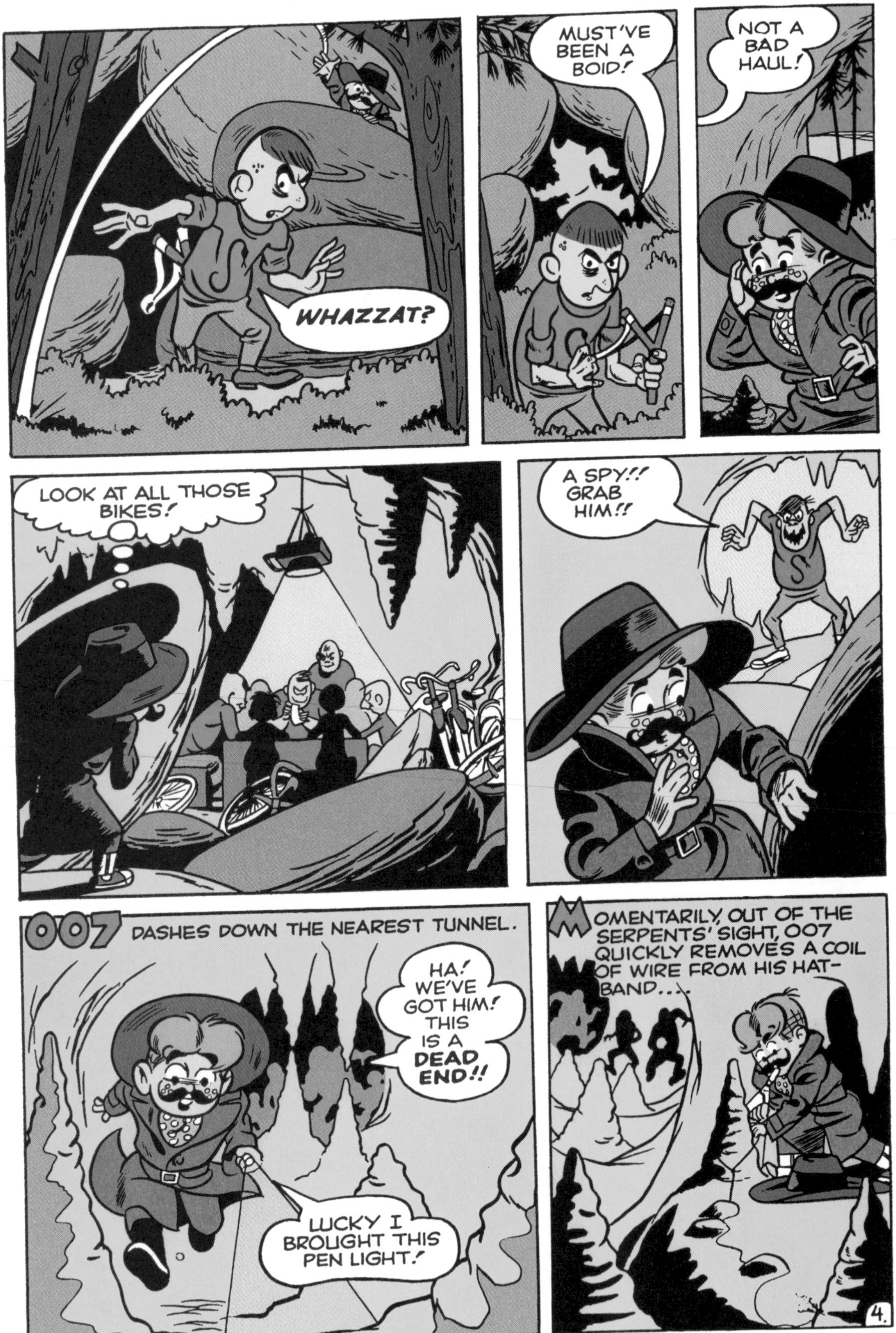
WHAZZAT?
MUST'VE BEEN A BOID!
NOT A BAD HAUL!
LOOK AT ALL THOSE BIKES!
A SPY!!! GRAB HIM!!
007 DASHES DOWN THE NEAREST TUNNEL.
HA! WE'VE GOT HIM! THIS IS A DEAD END!!
LUCKY I BROUGHT THIS PEN LIGHT!
MOMENTARILY, OUT OF THE SERPENTS' SIGHT, 007 QUICKLY REMOVES A COIL OF WIRE FROM HIS HAT-BAND....
4.

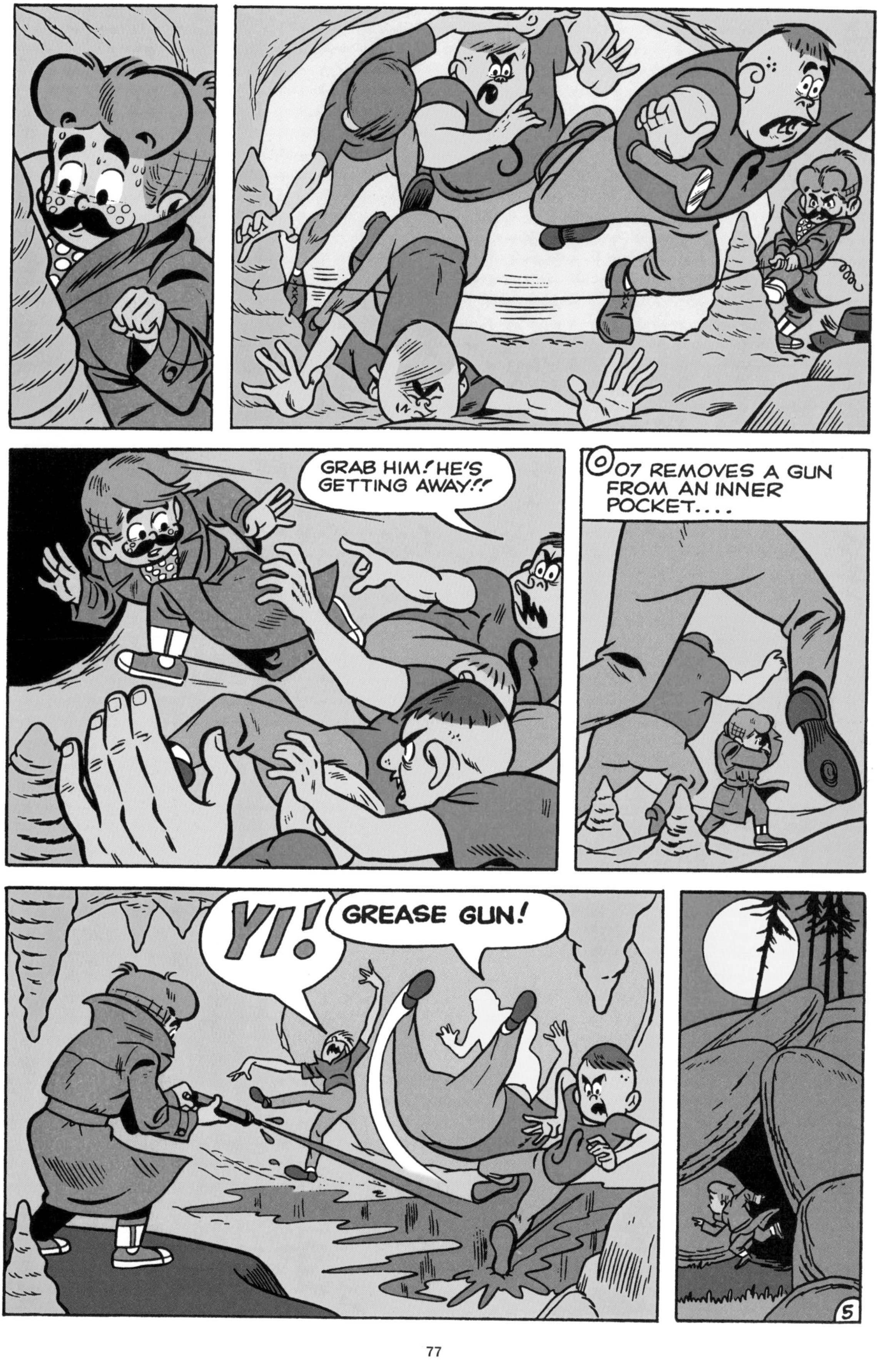
GRAB HIM! HE'S GETTING AWAY!!
007 REMOVES A GUN FROM AN INNER POCKET....
YI!
GREASE GUN!
5

LET HIM GO! IT'S DARK ENOUGH TO MAKE A DELIVERY!

ANYTHING YOU SAY, FANGS!

THAT'S RIGHT DETECTIVE (PUFF) PARKER! STOLEN BIKES IN THE (PUFF) SERPENTS' CAVE!

HMMMM, THE SERPENTS' CAVE YOU SAY!

SHORTLY...

NOTHING HERE! SURE YOU WEREN'T IMAGINING—

007 NEVER MAKES A MISTAKE!

NEXT DAY...

GOSH! DETECTIVE PARKER TREATS ME LIKE A KID... HE DOESN'T BELIEVE—

BOY, OH BOY, OH BOY!

WHERE YOU GOIN', JUGGY?

POLICE STATION, THAT'S WHERE!!

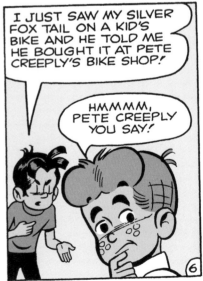

I JUST SAW MY SILVER FOX TAIL ON A KID'S BIKE AND HE TOLD ME HE BOUGHT IT AT PETE CREEPLY'S BIKE SHOP!

HMMMM, PETE CREEPLY YOU SAY!

6

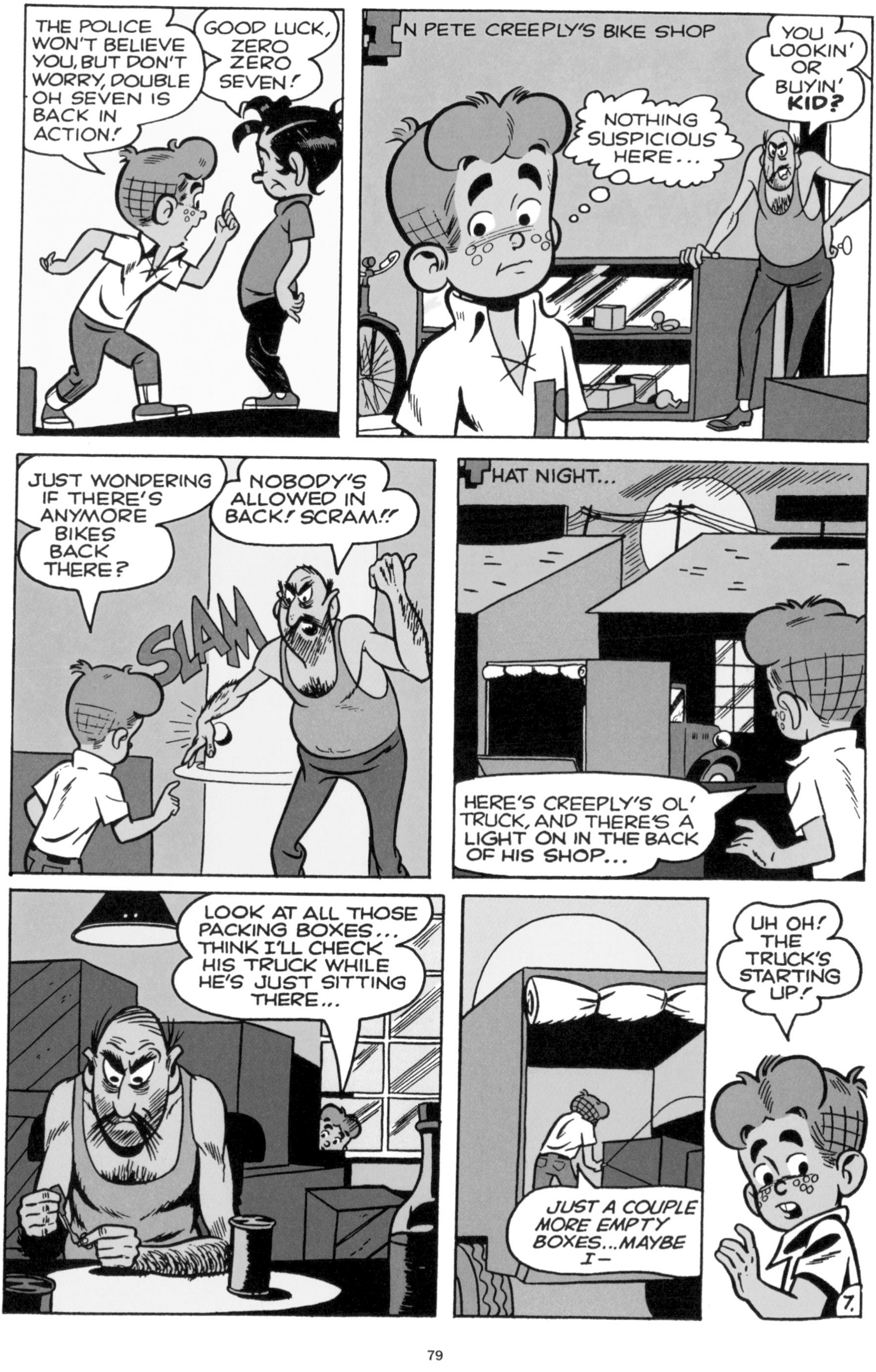
THE POLICE WON'T BELIEVE YOU, BUT DON'T WORRY, DOUBLE OH SEVEN IS BACK IN ACTION!
GOOD LUCK, ZERO ZERO SEVEN!
IN PETE CREEPLY'S BIKE SHOP
NOTHING SUSPICIOUS HERE...
YOU LOOKIN' OR BUYIN' KID?
JUST WONDERING IF THERE'S ANYMORE BIKES BACK THERE?
NOBODY'S ALLOWED IN BACK! SCRAM!!
SLAM
THAT NIGHT...
HERE'S CREEPLY'S OL' TRUCK, AND THERE'S A LIGHT ON IN THE BACK OF HIS SHOP...
LOOK AT ALL THOSE PACKING BOXES... THINK I'LL CHECK HIS TRUCK WHILE HE'S JUST SITTING THERE...
JUST A COUPLE MORE EMPTY BOXES...MAYBE I—
UH OH! THE TRUCK'S STARTING UP!
7.

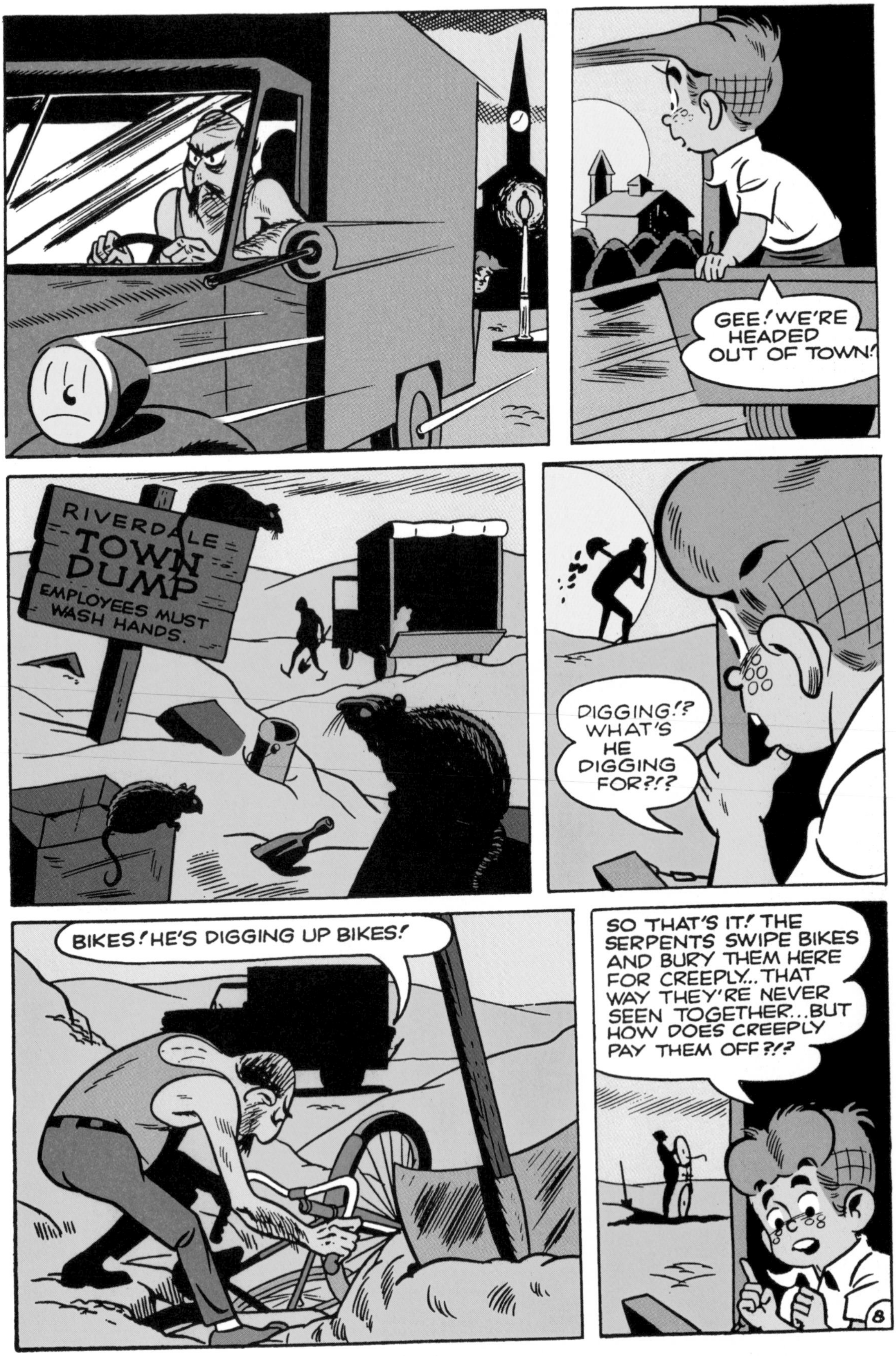
GEE! WE'RE HEADED OUT OF TOWN!
RIVERDALE TOWN DUMP
EMPLOYEES MUST WASH HANDS.
DIGGING!? WHAT'S HE DIGGING FOR?!?
BIKES! HE'S DIGGING UP BIKES!
SO THAT'S IT! THE SERPENTS SWIPE BIKES AND BURY THEM HERE FOR CREEPLY...THAT WAY THEY'RE NEVER SEEN TOGETHER...BUT HOW DOES CREEPLY PAY THEM OFF?!?
8

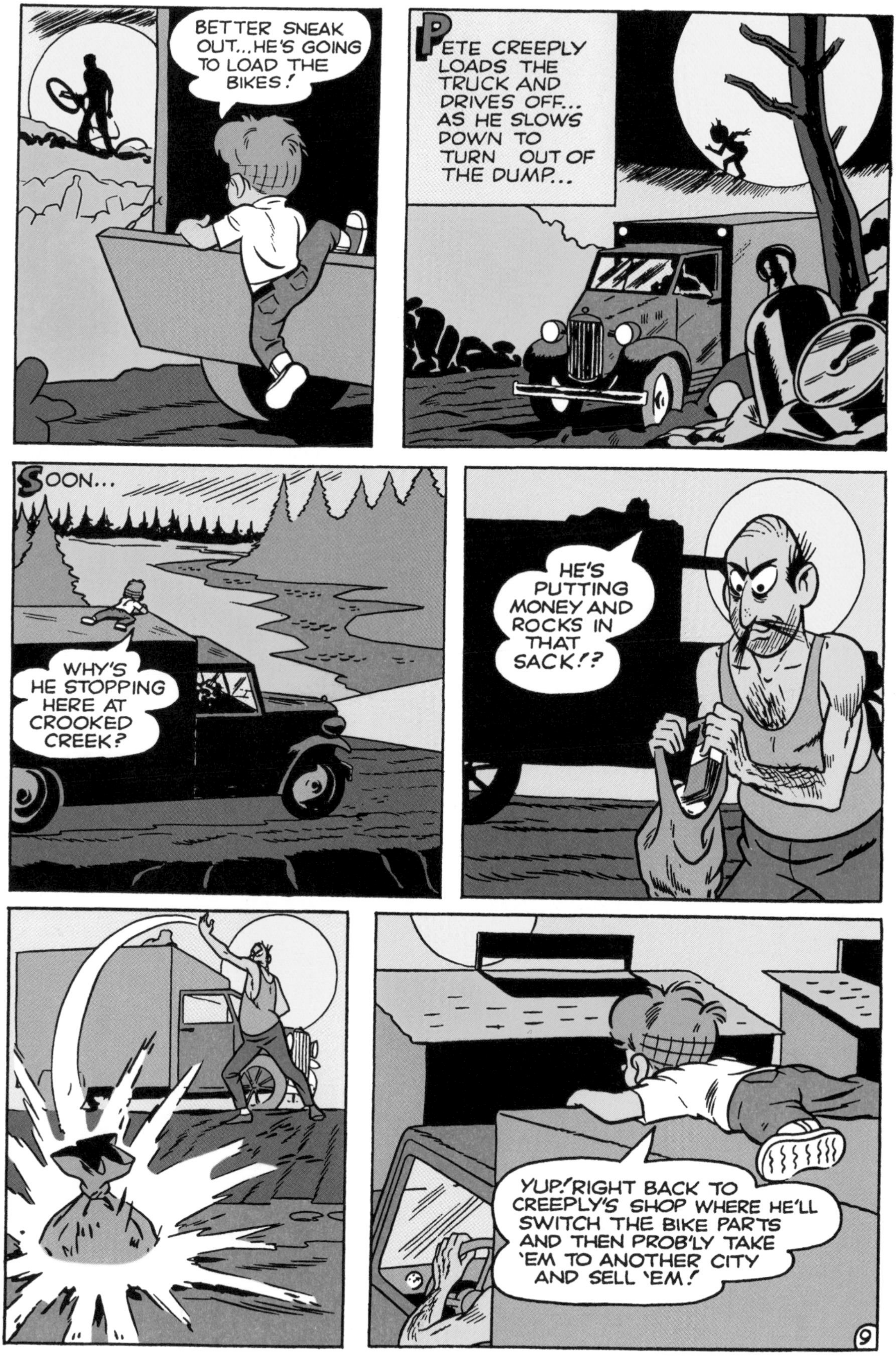
BETTER SNEAK OUT...HE'S GOING TO LOAD THE BIKES!
PETE CREEPLY LOADS THE TRUCK AND DRIVES OFF... AS HE SLOWS DOWN TO TURN OUT OF THE DUMP...
SOON...
WHY'S HE STOPPING HERE AT CROOKED CREEK?
HE'S PUTTING MONEY AND ROCKS IN THAT SACK!?
YUP! RIGHT BACK TO CREEPLY'S SHOP WHERE HE'LL SWITCH THE BIKE PARTS AND THEN PROB'LY TAKE 'EM TO ANOTHER CITY AND SELL 'EM!
9

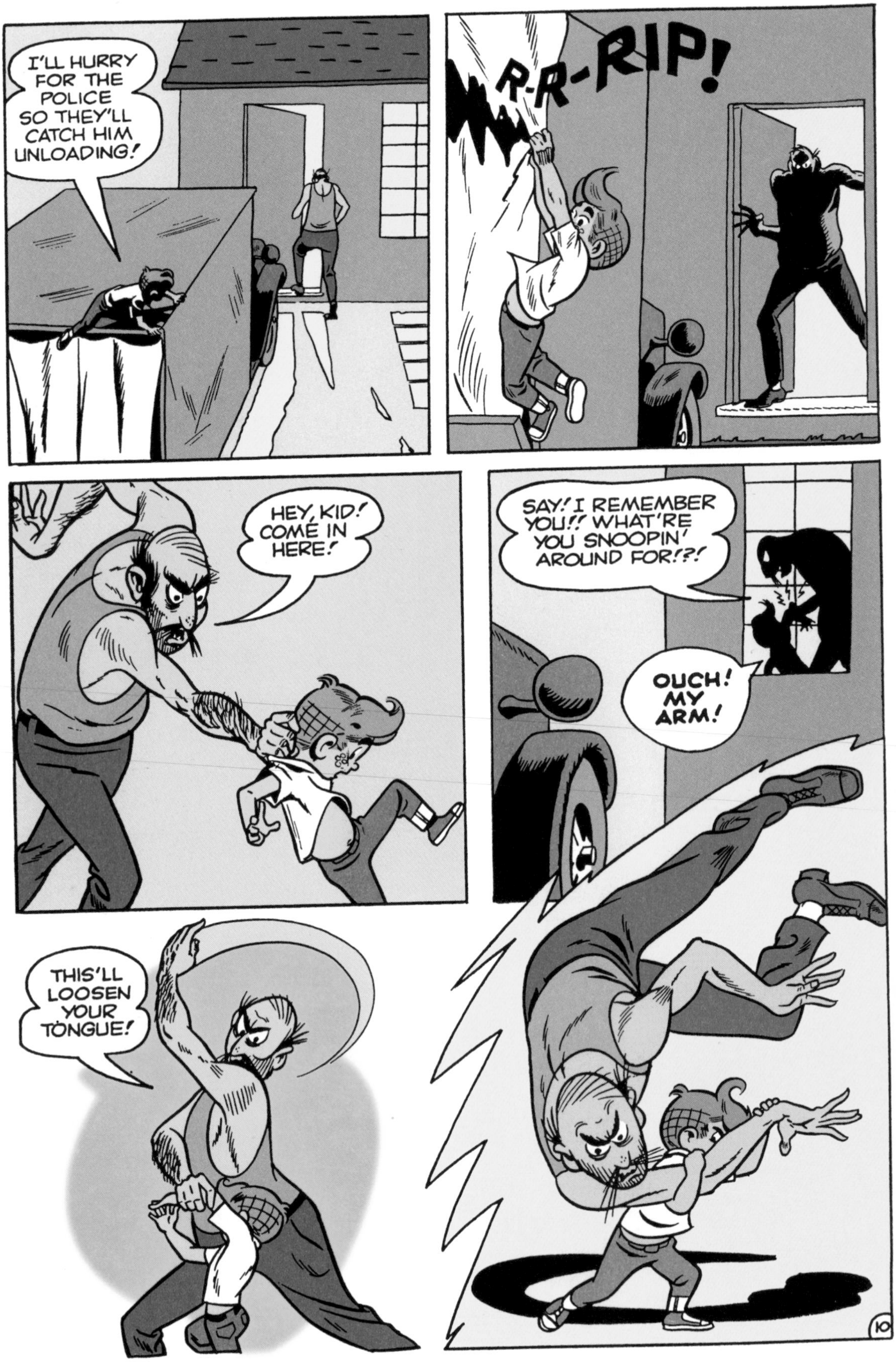
I'LL HURRY FOR THE POLICE SO THEY'LL CATCH HIM UNLOADING!
R-R-RIP!
HEY, KID! COME IN HERE!
SAY! I REMEMBER YOU!! WHAT'RE YOU SNOOPIN' AROUND FOR!?!
OUCH! MY ARM!
THIS'LL LOOSEN YOUR TONGUE!
10

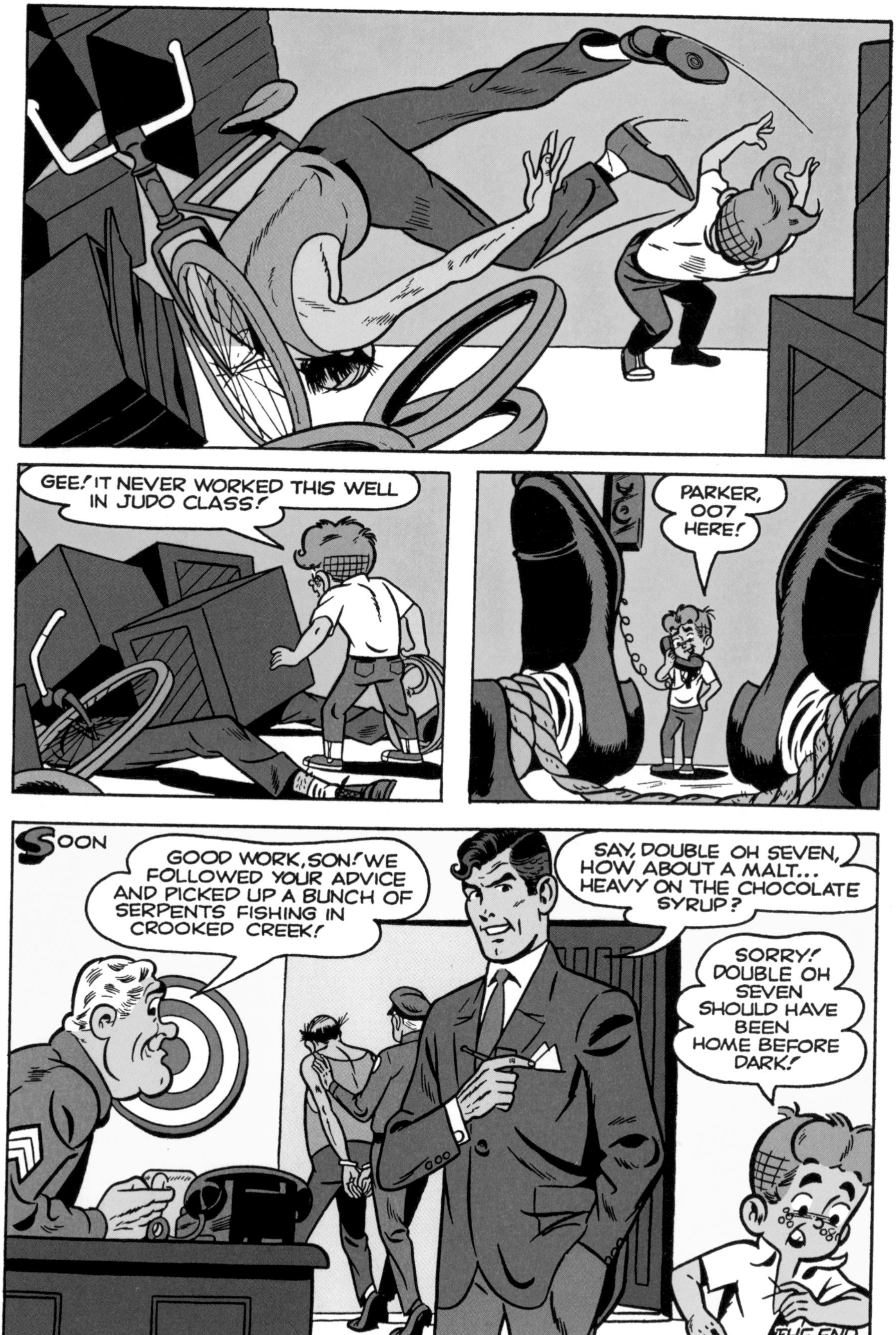
GEE! IT NEVER WORKED THIS WELL IN JUDO CLASS!
PARKER, 007 HERE!
SOON
GOOD WORK, SON! WE FOLLOWED YOUR ADVICE AND PICKED UP A BUNCH OF SERPENTS FISHING IN CROOKED CREEK!
SAY, DOUBLE OH SEVEN, HOW ABOUT A MALT... HEAVY ON THE CHOCOLATE SYRUP?
SORRY! DOUBLE OH SEVEN SHOULD HAVE BEEN HOME BEFORE DARK!
THE END

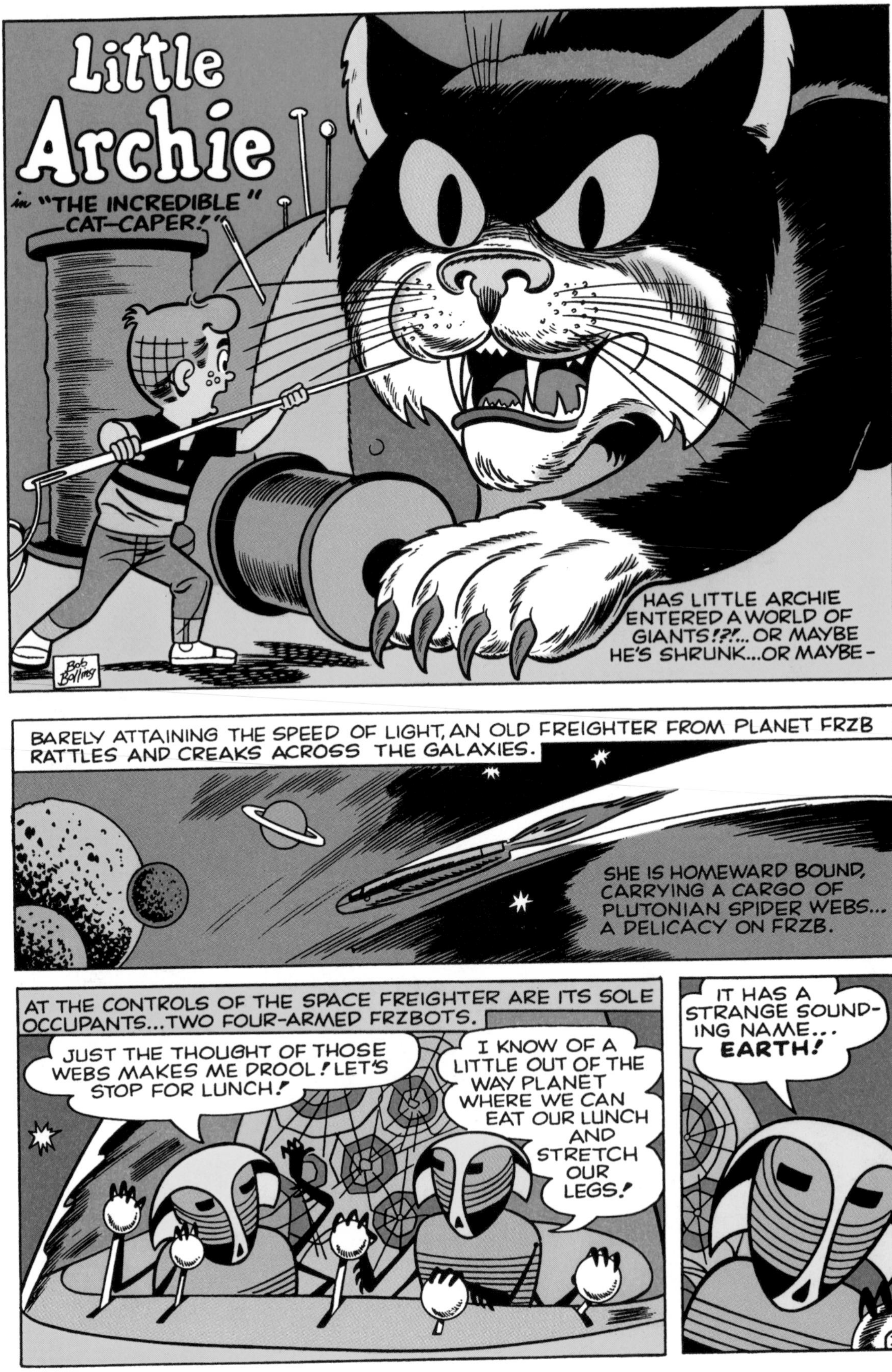
Little Archie
in "THE INCREDIBLE" CAT-CAPER!"
HAS LITTLE ARCHIE ENTERED A WORLD OF GIANTS!?!... OR MAYBE HE'S SHRUNK...OR MAYBE -
Bob Bolling
BARELY ATTAINING THE SPEED OF LIGHT, AN OLD FREIGHTER FROM PLANET FRZB RATTLES AND CREAKS ACROSS THE GALAXIES.
SHE IS HOMEWARD BOUND, CARRYING A CARGO OF PLUTONIAN SPIDER WEBS... A DELICACY ON FRZB.
AT THE CONTROLS OF THE SPACE FREIGHTER ARE ITS SOLE OCCUPANTS...TWO FOUR-ARMED FRZBOTS.
JUST THE THOUGHT OF THOSE WEBS MAKES ME DROOL! LET'S STOP FOR LUNCH!
I KNOW OF A LITTLE OUT OF THE WAY PLANET WHERE WE CAN EAT OUR LUNCH AND STRETCH OUR LEGS!
IT HAS A STRANGE SOUNDING NAME... EARTH!
I

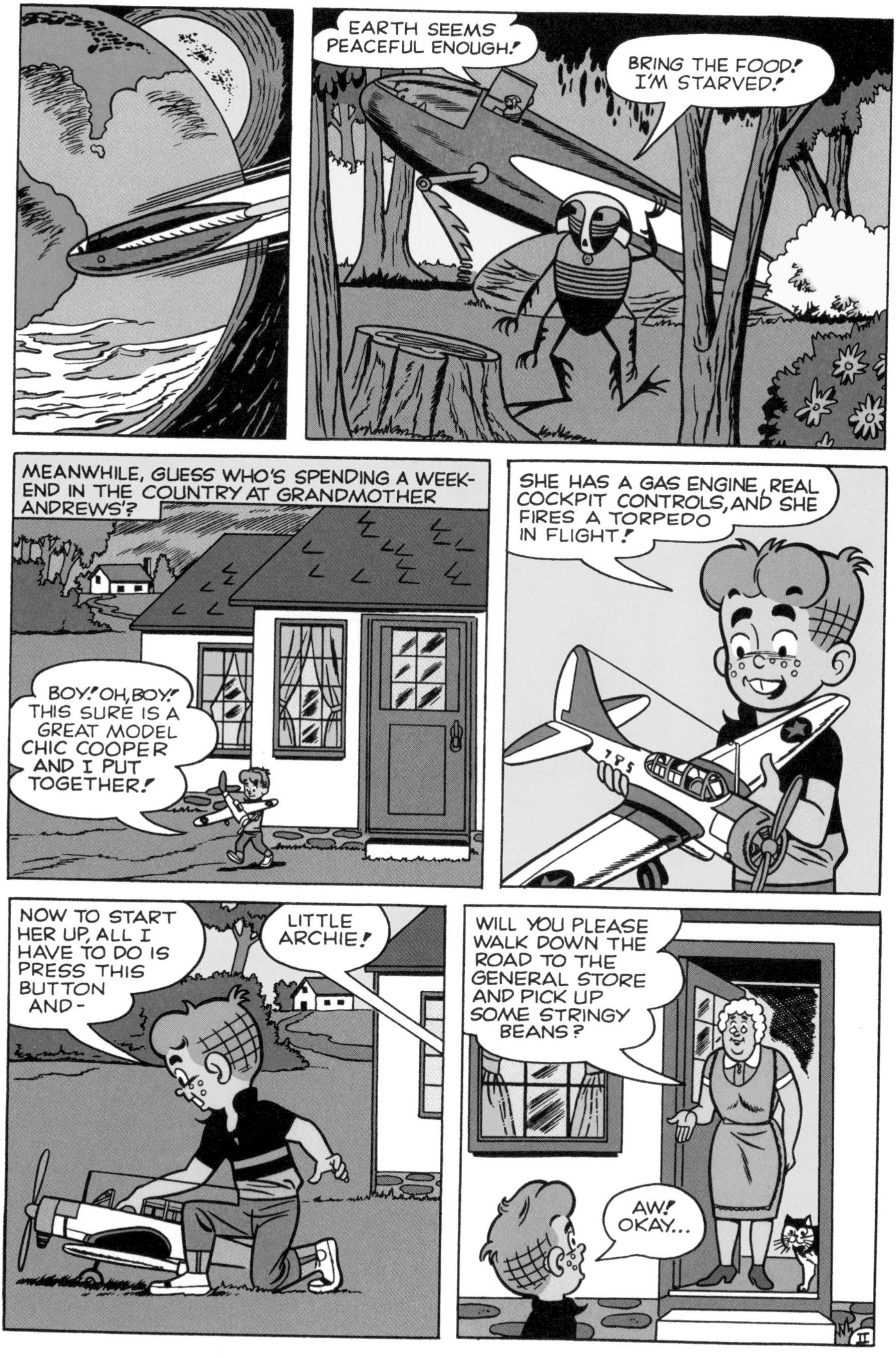
EARTH SEEMS PEACEFUL ENOUGH!
BRING THE FOOD! I'M STARVED!
MEANWHILE, GUESS WHO'S SPENDING A WEEK-END IN THE COUNTRY AT GRANDMOTHER ANDREWS'?
BOY! OH, BOY! THIS SURE IS A GREAT MODEL CHIC COOPER AND I PUT TOGETHER!
SHE HAS A GAS ENGINE, REAL COCKPIT CONTROLS, AND SHE FIRES A TORPEDO IN FLIGHT!
NOW TO START HER UP, ALL I HAVE TO DO IS PRESS THIS BUTTON AND-
LITTLE ARCHIE!
WILL YOU PLEASE WALK DOWN THE ROAD TO THE GENERAL STORE AND PICK UP SOME STRINGY BEANS?
AW! OKAY...

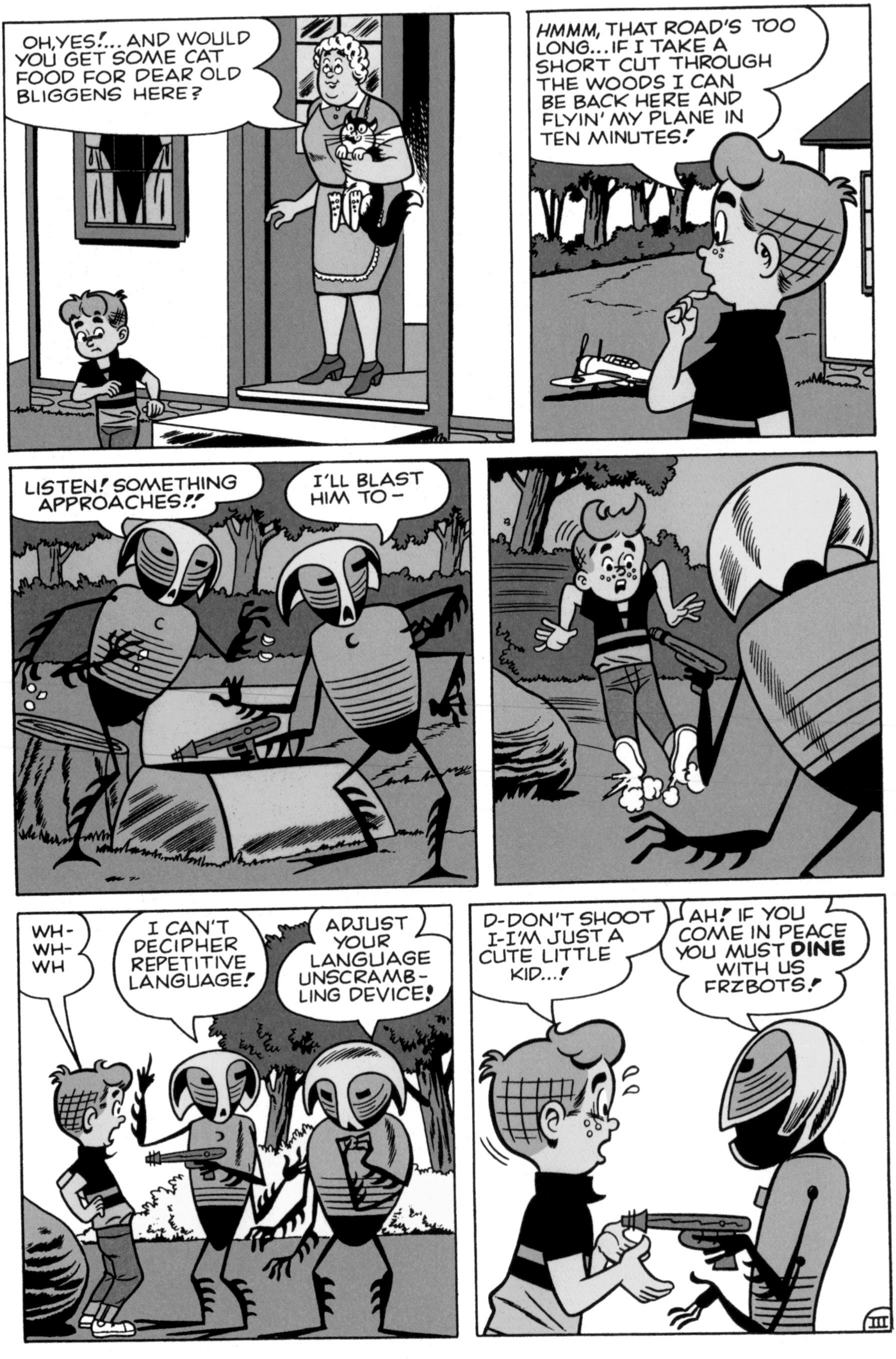
OH, YES!... AND WOULD YOU GET SOME CAT FOOD FOR DEAR OLD BLIGGENS HERE?
HMMM, THAT ROAD'S TOO LONG... IF I TAKE A SHORT CUT THROUGH THE WOODS I CAN BE BACK HERE AND FLYIN' MY PLANE IN TEN MINUTES!
LISTEN! SOMETHING APPROACHES!!
I'LL BLAST HIM TO—
WH-WH-WH
I CAN'T DECIPHER REPETITIVE LANGUAGE!
ADJUST YOUR LANGUAGE UNSCRAMB-LING DEVICE!
D-DON'T SHOOT I-I'M JUST A CUTE LITTLE KID...!
AH! IF YOU COME IN PEACE YOU MUST **DINE** WITH US FRZBOTS!
III

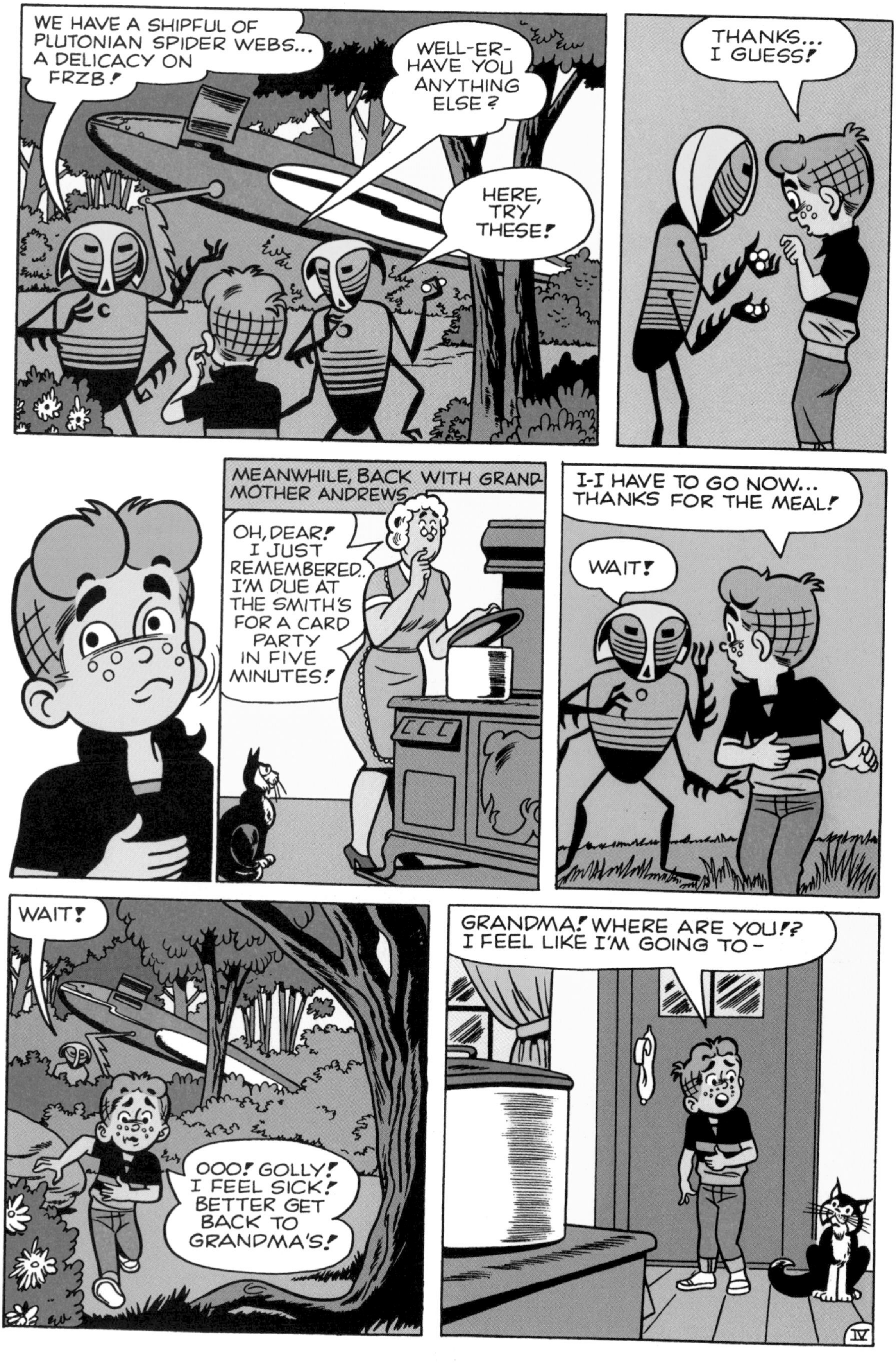
WE HAVE A SHIPFUL OF PLUTONIAN SPIDER WEBS... A DELICACY ON FRZB!
WELL-ER- HAVE YOU ANYTHING ELSE?
HERE, TRY THESE!
THANKS... I GUESS!
MEANWHILE, BACK WITH GRAND-MOTHER ANDREWS
OH, DEAR! I JUST REMEMBERED.. I'M DUE AT THE SMITH'S FOR A CARD PARTY IN FIVE MINUTES!
I-I HAVE TO GO NOW... THANKS FOR THE MEAL!
WAIT!
WAIT!
OOO! GOLLY! I FEEL SICK! BETTER GET BACK TO GRANDMA'S!
GRANDMA! WHERE ARE YOU!? I FEEL LIKE I'M GOING TO -
IV

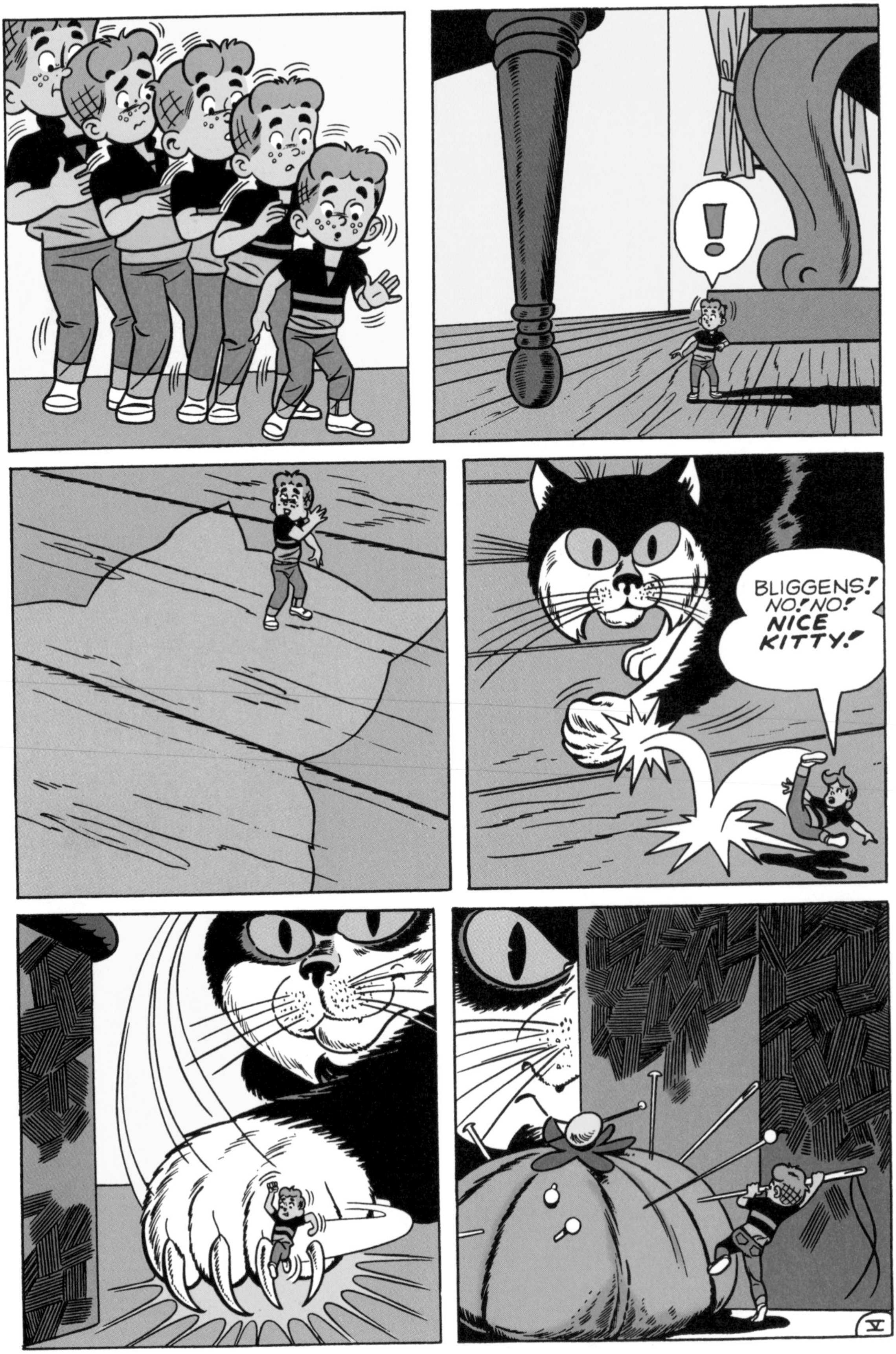
!
BLIGGENS! NO! NO! NICE KITTY!

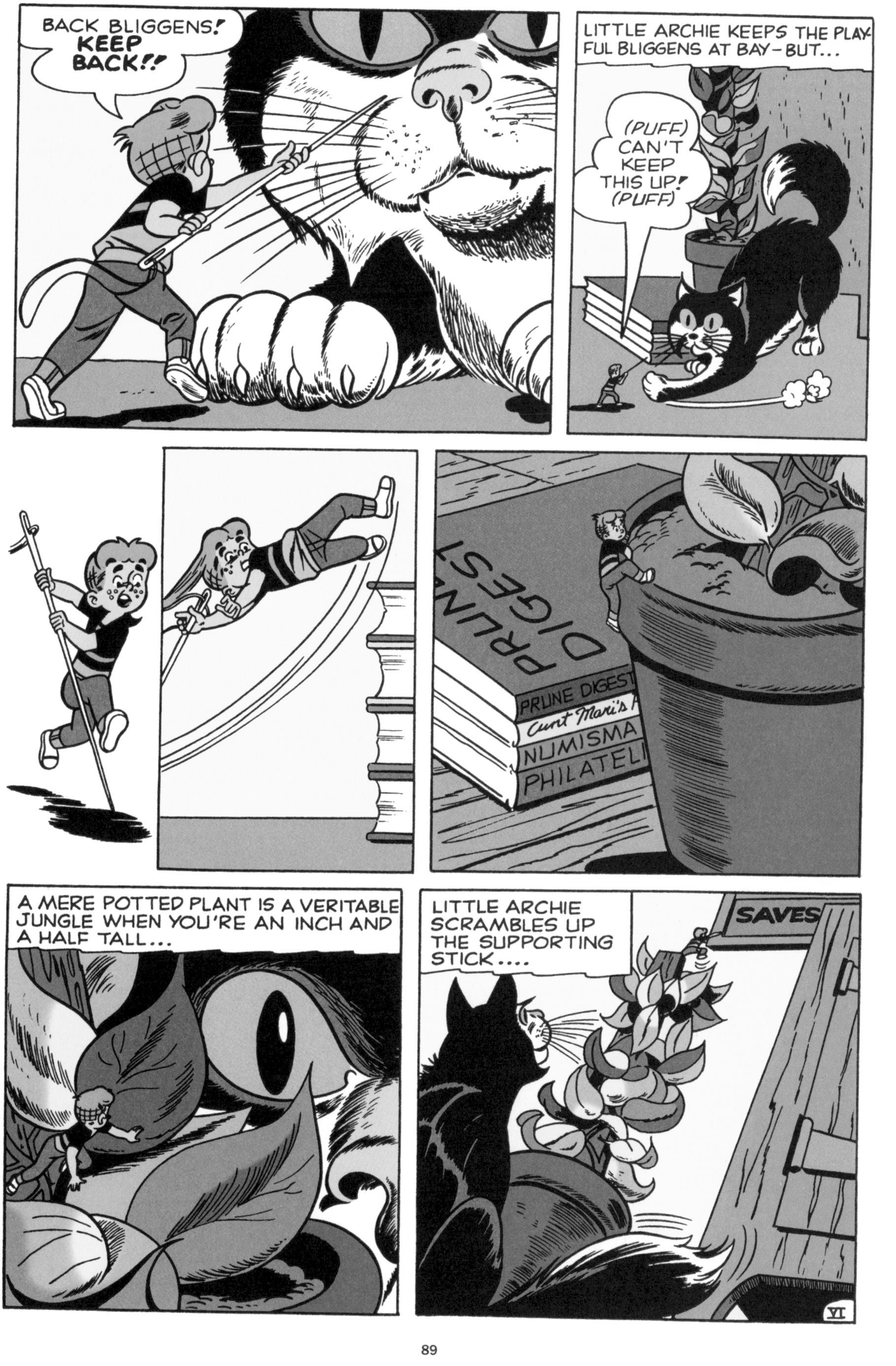
BACK BLIGGENS! KEEP BACK!!
LITTLE ARCHIE KEEPS THE PLAYFUL BLIGGENS AT BAY—BUT...
(PUFF) CAN'T KEEP THIS UP! (PUFF)
PRUNE DIGEST
PRUNE DIGEST
Aunt Mari's
NUMISMA
PHILATELI
A MERE POTTED PLANT IS A VERITABLE JUNGLE WHEN YOU'RE AN INCH AND A HALF TALL...
LITTLE ARCHIE SCRAMBLES UP THE SUPPORTING STICK....
SAVES
VI

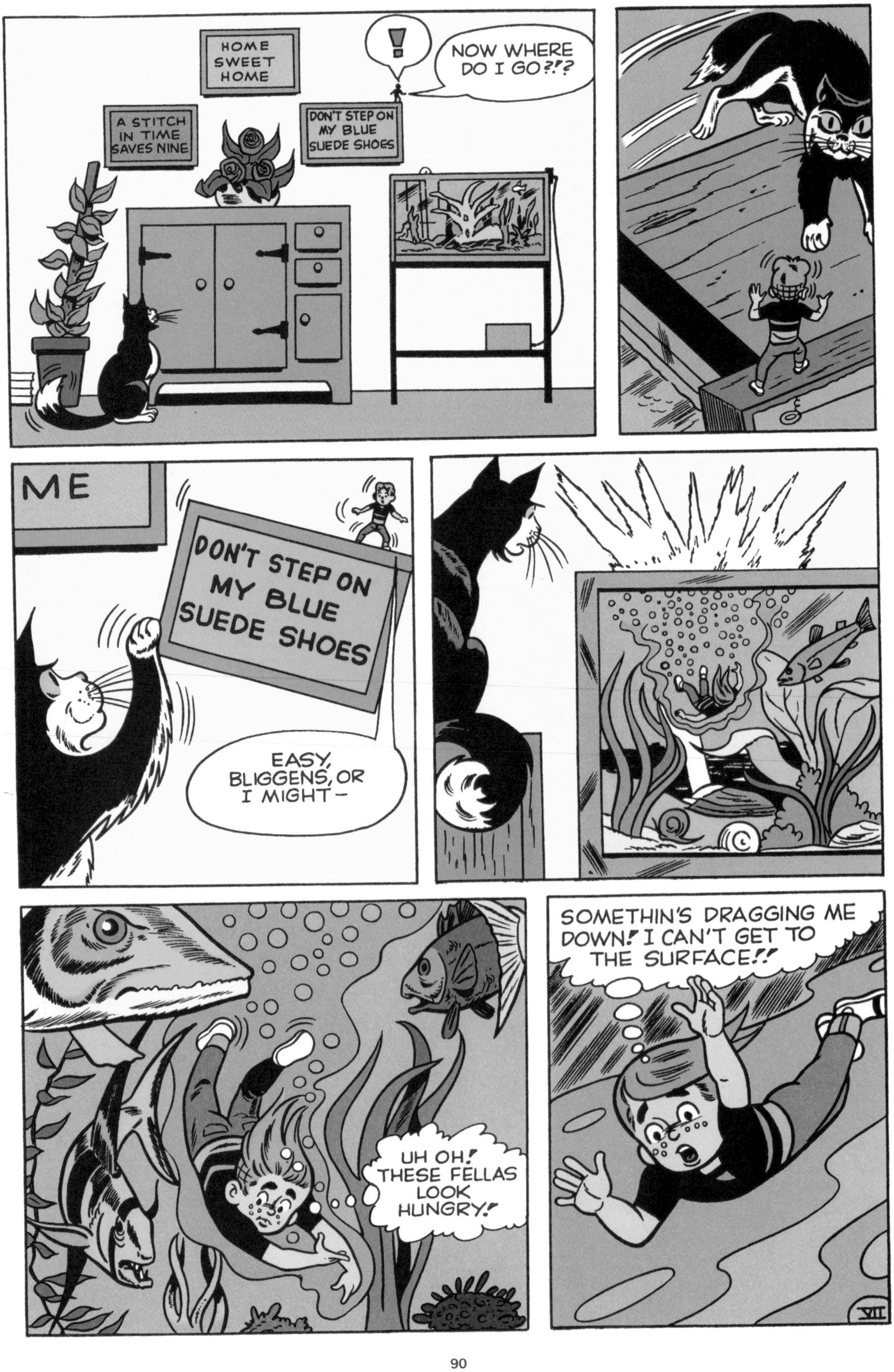
HOME SWEET HOME
A STITCH IN TIME SAVES NINE
DON'T STEP ON MY BLUE SUEDE SHOES
!
NOW WHERE DO I GO?!?
ME
DON'T STEP ON MY BLUE SUEDE SHOES
EASY, BLIGGENS, OR I MIGHT–
UH OH! THESE FELLAS LOOK HUNGRY!
SOMETHIN'S DRAGGING ME DOWN! I CAN'T GET TO THE SURFACE!!
VII

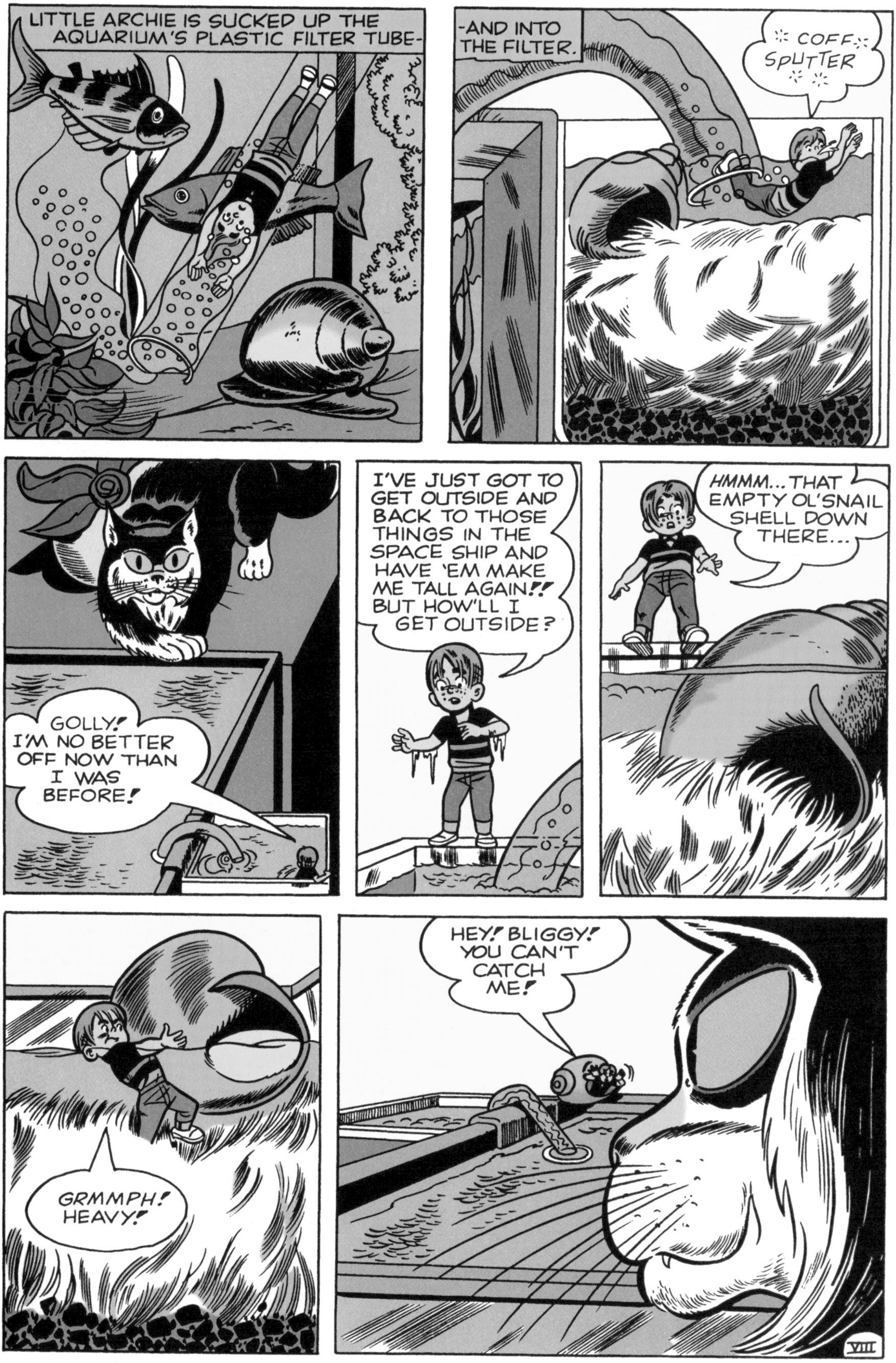
LITTLE ARCHIE IS SUCKED UP THE AQUARIUM'S PLASTIC FILTER TUBE-
-AND INTO THE FILTER.
COFF SPUTTER
GOLLY! I'M NO BETTER OFF NOW THAN I WAS BEFORE!
I'VE JUST GOT TO GET OUTSIDE AND BACK TO THOSE THINGS IN THE SPACE SHIP AND HAVE 'EM MAKE ME TALL AGAIN!! BUT HOW'LL I GET OUTSIDE?
HMMM... THAT EMPTY OL'SNAIL SHELL DOWN THERE...
GRMMPH! HEAVY!
HEY! BLIGGY! YOU CAN'T CATCH ME!
VIII

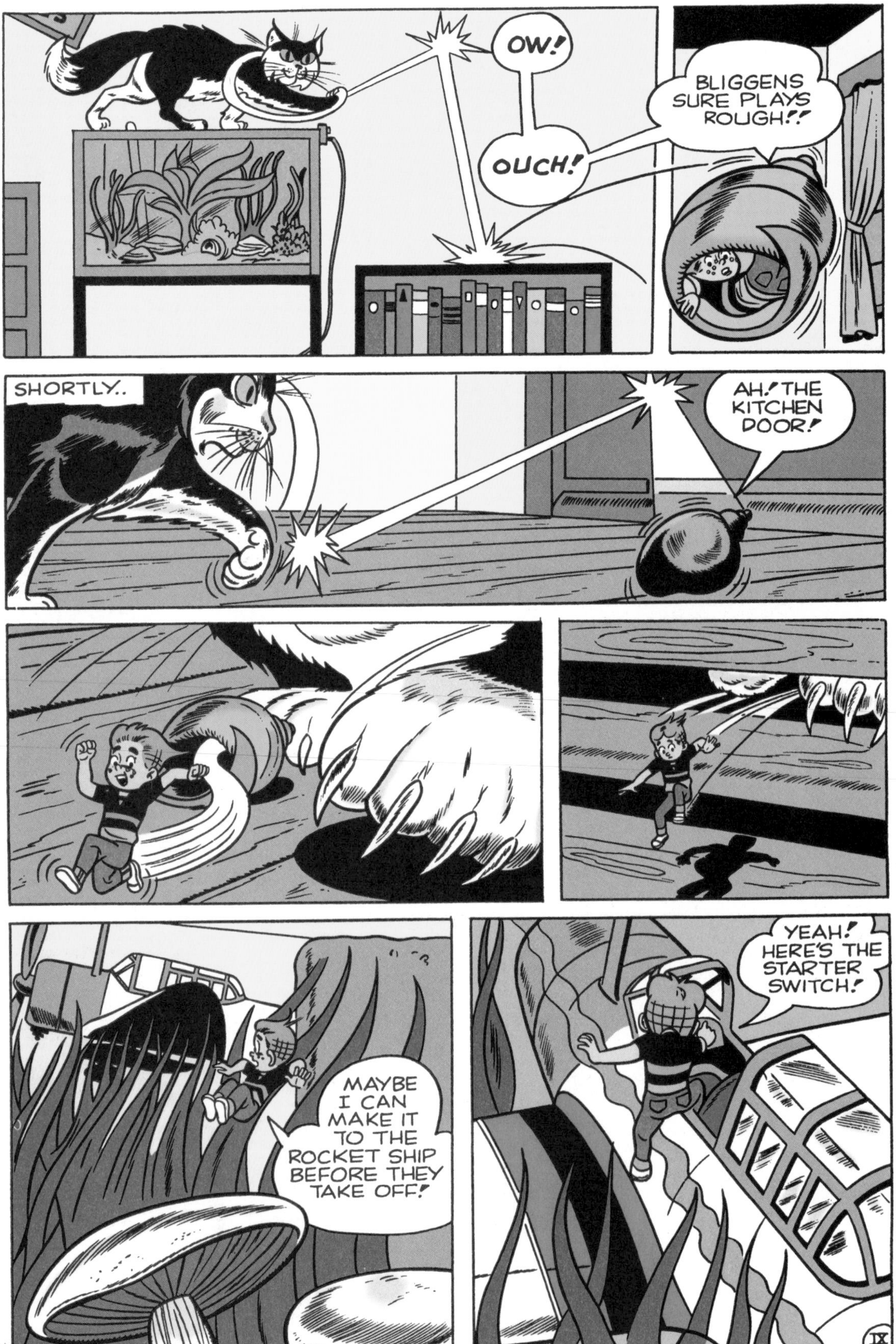
OW!
OUCH!
BLIGGENS SURE PLAYS ROUGH!!
SHORTLY..
AH! THE KITCHEN DOOR!
MAYBE I CAN MAKE IT TO THE ROCKET SHIP BEFORE THEY TAKE OFF!
YEAH! HERE'S THE STARTER SWITCH!
IX

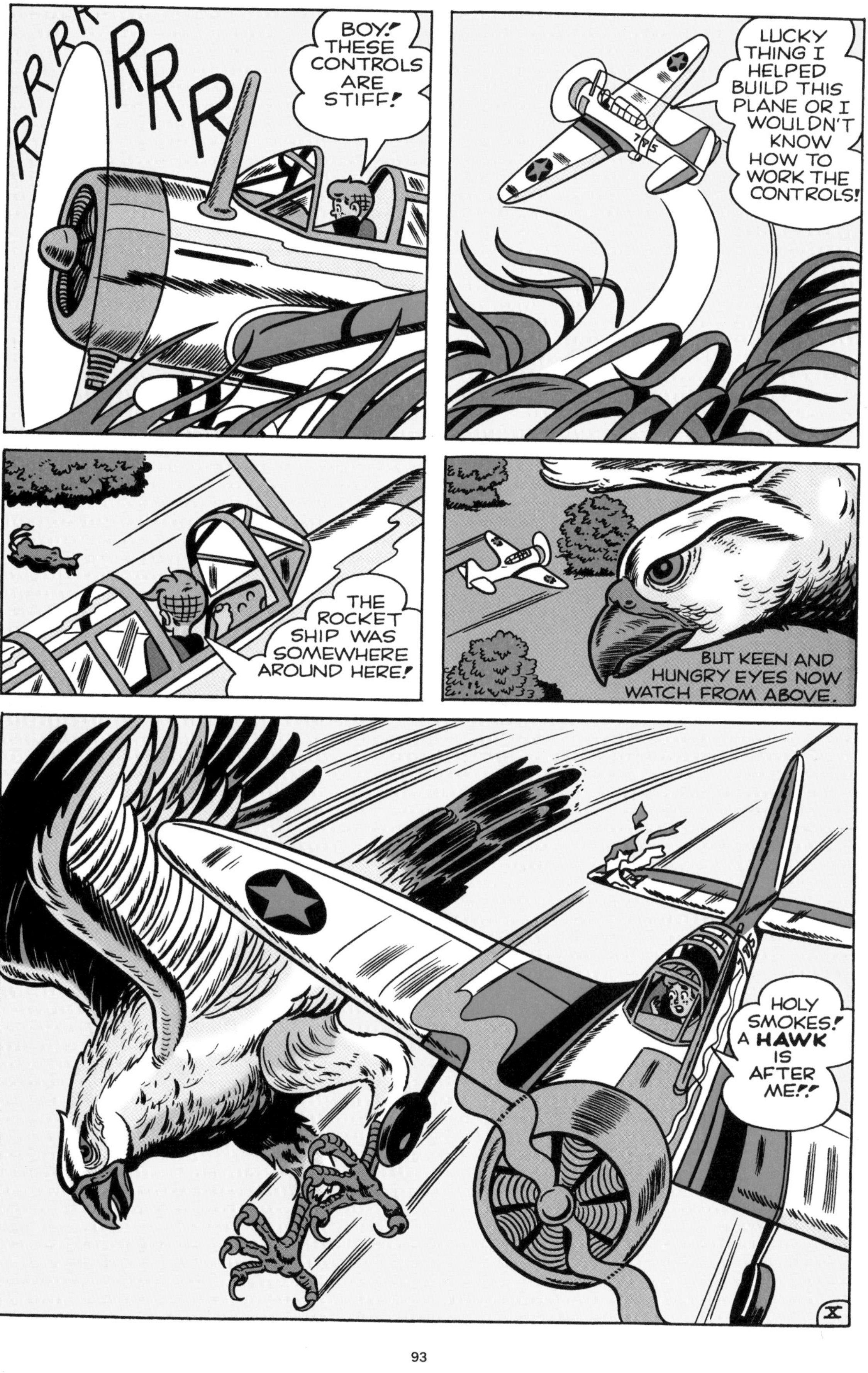
RRRRRRR
BOY! THESE CONTROLS ARE STIFF!
LUCKY THING I HELPED BUILD THIS PLANE OR I WOULDN'T KNOW HOW TO WORK THE CONTROLS!
THE ROCKET SHIP WAS SOMEWHERE AROUND HERE!
BUT KEEN AND HUNGRY EYES NOW WATCH FROM ABOVE.
HOLY SMOKES! A **HAWK** IS AFTER ME!!

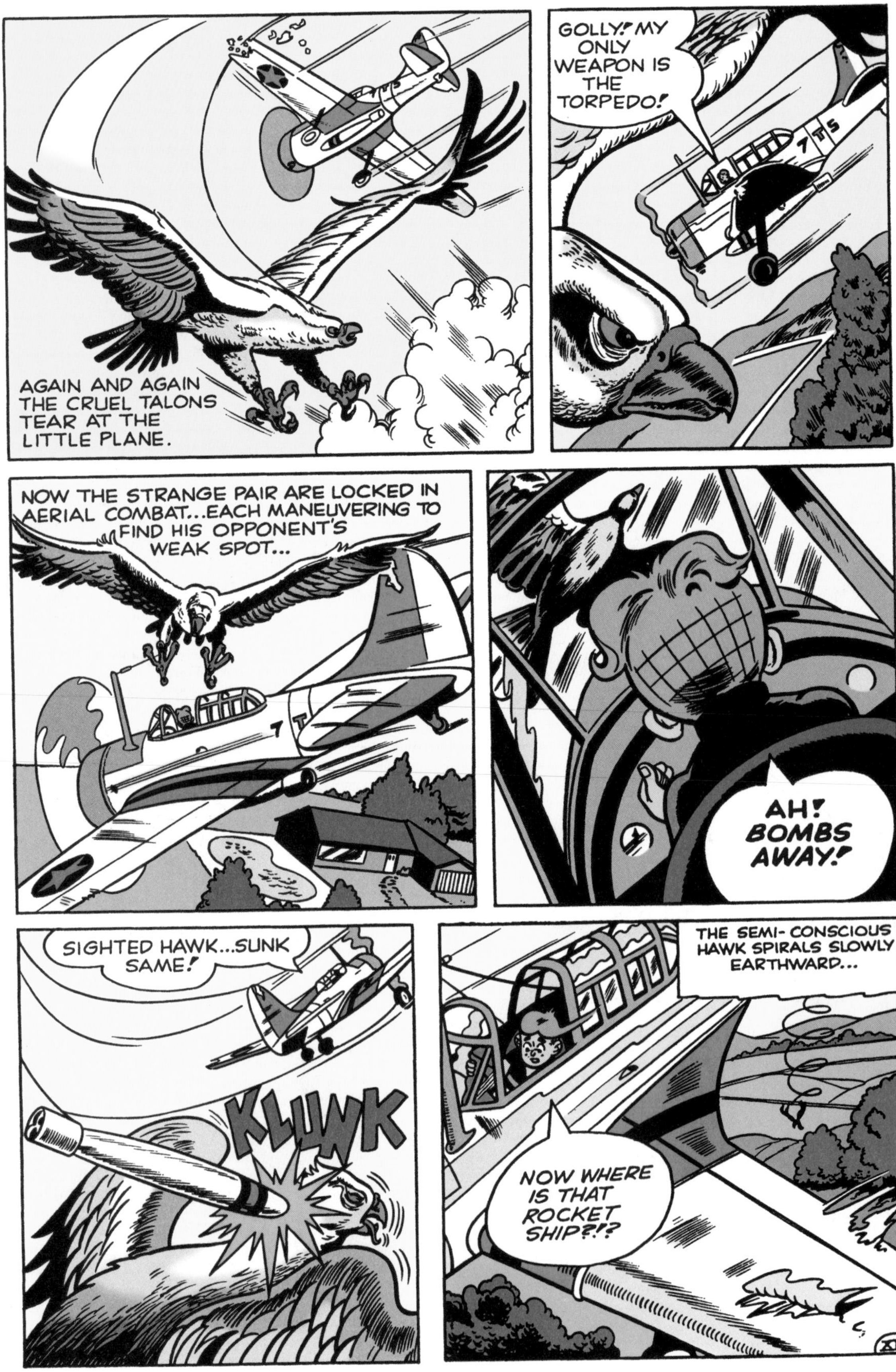
AGAIN AND AGAIN THE CRUEL TALONS TEAR AT THE LITTLE PLANE.
GOLLY! MY ONLY WEAPON IS THE TORPEDO!
7 TS
NOW THE STRANGE PAIR ARE LOCKED IN AERIAL COMBAT...EACH MANEUVERING TO FIND HIS OPPONENT'S WEAK SPOT...
AH! BOMBS AWAY!
SIGHTED HAWK...SUNK SAME!
KLUNK
THE SEMI-CONSCIOUS HAWK SPIRALS SLOWLY EARTHWARD...
NOW WHERE IS THAT ROCKET SHIP?!?
XI

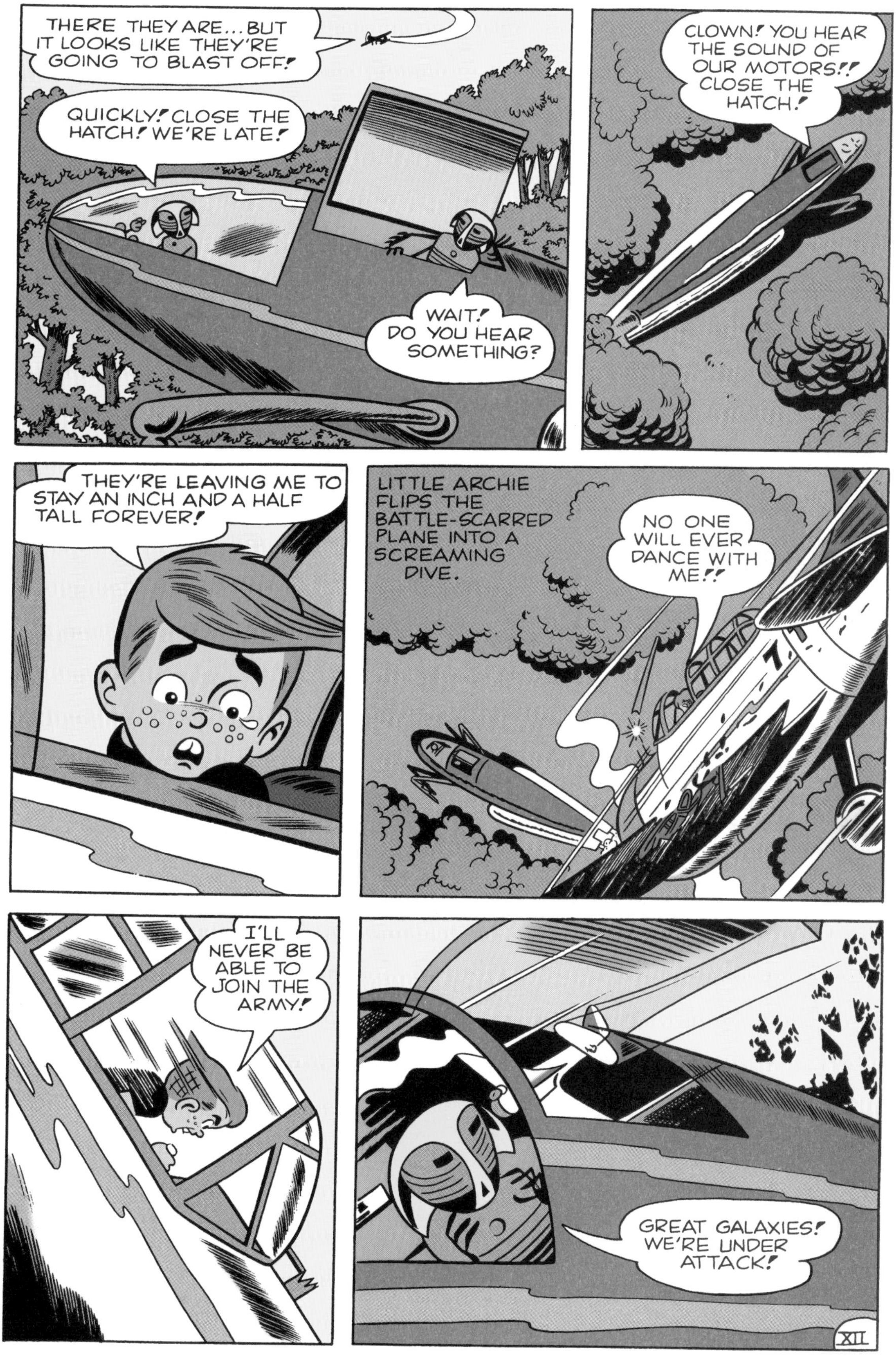
THERE THEY ARE... BUT IT LOOKS LIKE THEY'RE GOING TO BLAST OFF!
QUICKLY! CLOSE THE HATCH! WE'RE LATE!
WAIT! DO YOU HEAR SOMETHING?
CLOWN! YOU HEAR THE SOUND OF OUR MOTORS!! CLOSE THE HATCH!
THEY'RE LEAVING ME TO STAY AN INCH AND A HALF TALL FOREVER!
LITTLE ARCHIE FLIPS THE BATTLE-SCARRED PLANE INTO A SCREAMING DIVE.
NO ONE WILL EVER DANCE WITH ME!!
I'LL NEVER BE ABLE TO JOIN THE ARMY!
GREAT GALAXIES! WE'RE UNDER ATTACK!
XII

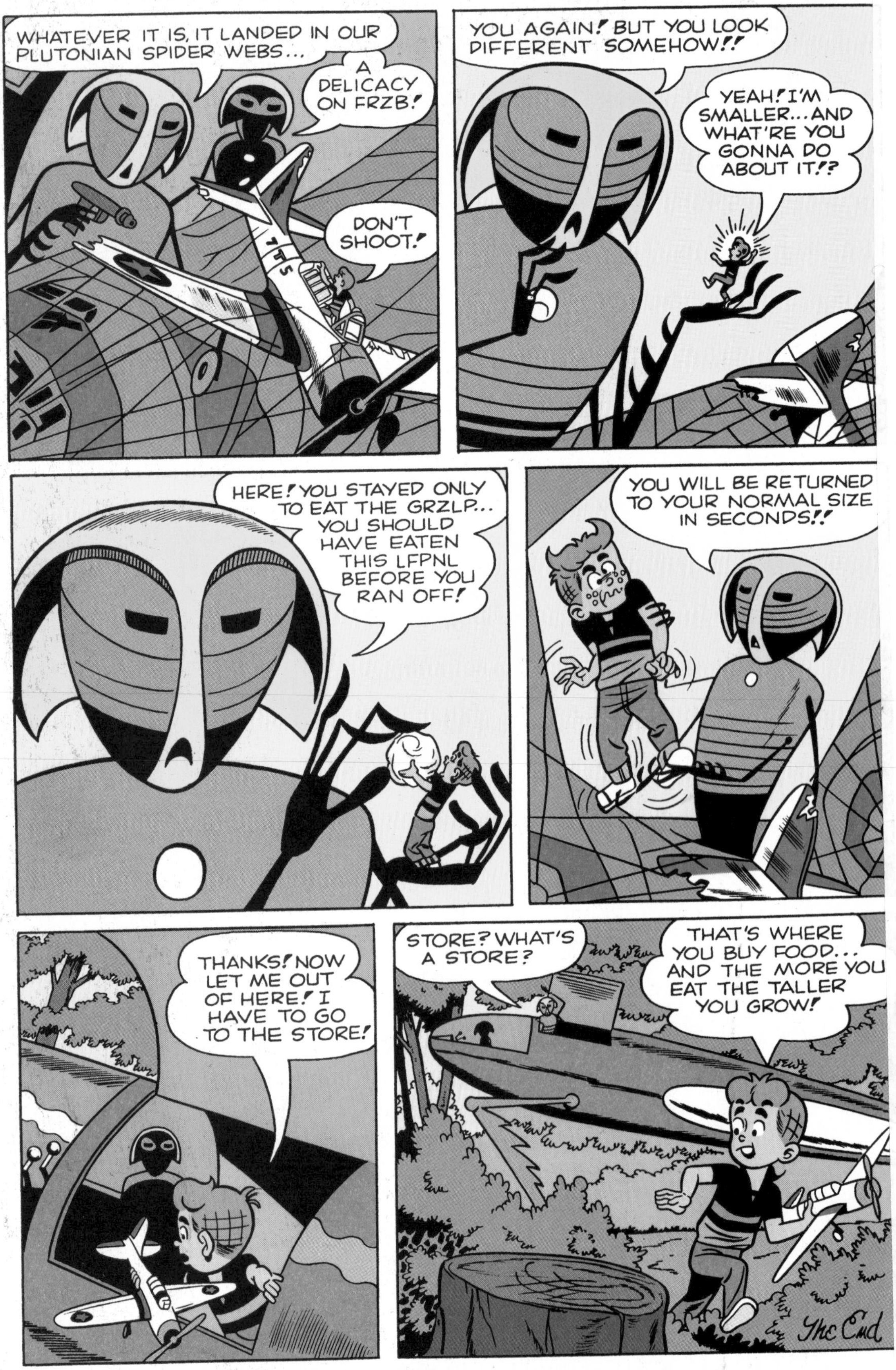
WHATEVER IT IS, IT LANDED IN OUR PLUTONIAN SPIDER WEBS...
A DELICACY ON FRZB!
DON'T SHOOT!
YOU AGAIN! BUT YOU LOOK DIFFERENT SOMEHOW!!
YEAH! I'M SMALLER...AND WHAT'RE YOU GONNA DO ABOUT IT!?
HERE! YOU STAYED ONLY TO EAT THE GRZLP... YOU SHOULD HAVE EATEN THIS LFPNL BEFORE YOU RAN OFF!
YOU WILL BE RETURNED TO YOUR NORMAL SIZE IN SECONDS!!
THANKS! NOW LET ME OUT OF HERE! I HAVE TO GO TO THE STORE!
STORE? WHAT'S A STORE?
THAT'S WHERE YOU BUY FOOD... AND THE MORE YOU EAT THE TALLER YOU GROW!
The End